Gossip

Katy Hayes

PHŒNIX

A PHOENIX PAPERBACK

First published in Great Britain in 2000
by Phoenix House
This paperback edition published in 2001
by Phoenix,
an imprint of Orion Books Ltd,
Orion House, 5 Upper St Martin's Lane,
London WC2H 9EA

Copyright © Katy Hayes 2000

The right of Katy Hayes to be identified as the
author of this work has been asserted by her in accordance
with the Copyright, Designs and Patents Act 1988.

All rights reserved. No part of this publication may be
reproduced, stored in a retrieval system, or transmitted,
in any form or by any means, electronic, mechanical,
photocopying, recording or otherwise, without the prior
permission of the copyright owner.

A CIP catalogue record for this book
is available from the British Library.

ISBN 0 75381 081 6

Printed and bound in Great Britain by
Clays Ltd, St Ives plc

TO MY PARENTS

Tom Hayes,
who ran away with the circus
and
Anna Hayes,
who fed us stories like bread

What's up, Doc?

'The problem is,' he said, 'that you are simply reaping the rewards of the years of abuse your body has experienced. You are fat. You are nearing the end of your fourth decade. You are aerobically unfit, thanks to a complete lack of exercise in your daily routine and your (*disgusting, revolting*) habit of smoking forty cigarettes a day. You have underdeveloped stomach muscles, abdominal muscles, pectorals. You sit at a desk that was flung together in a pre-ergonomic age. Of course your back is going to ache. It has the unenviable task of hauling your bulk around the place. Oh, and you drink too much. All these things are related.'

You lack moral fibre. And when the rot sets in to one area, it corrupts all.

It could be argued that Dr James Coogan was rather frank and antagonistic, hadn't quite got the bedside manner, but Colm Cantwell liked them like that. When it came to the medical profession, he was a masochist. He liked abuse. Catholic upbringing. Confession; abuse; repentance; contrition: followed by absolution and sanctity.

'You are thirty-eight years old. I see men your age in better shape than you, who are experiencing their first cardiac events. Your back is simply an advance warning to you to get your proverbial act together.'

Colm hung his head and contemplated Dr Coogan's thighs. Great bulging thirty-five-year-old trunks, barely contained by the layer of pressed linen. One thigh was so large it had a little twitch, and the top layer of flesh was exercising itself independently of its owner. The sheer bulk was fascinating, obscene. Colm's eye went to his own leg. Trifle. His thighs had the wobbly consistency of trifle. Depressing. He wanted to go to the pub.

'So, here's a prescription to get you over the current problem, it will bring down the inflammation in your back. It is, however, only a short-term remedy.'

Colm liked short-term remedies.

'Pay particular attention to anything you sit on, make sure it has back support.'

'Fine.'

'Avoid, for example, barstools.'

'Okey-doke.'

'Here's the card for the physiotherapist, tell him your case is urgent.'

Colm looked at the card. 'Frank Ingoldsby. Fitness Instructor.'

'And phone me if you need a repeat prescription.'

Now, get the fuck out of my surgery, you miserable unfit slob who doesn't deserve to breathe.

He didn't actually say this last bit. It was communicated by a particularly articulate look.

'Thank you very much, Dr Coogan,' said Colm, as he grovelled out the door, supporting himself with the furniture, as he couldn't stand up straight. Pain had rendered him particularly contrite. He made his way out of the surgery and, holding on to the railing, surveyed the surrounding landscape. To his right, about forty yards off, was a pub. To his left, at a distance of about a hundred yards, was a pub. It was a great country. Pubs everywhere. The establishment on his right, with a rather attractive lit-up blinky Guinness pelican sign, had the disadvantage of being across the street. He wasn't entirely confident that he could make it over unaided. He set off to the left at a slow pace, using the railing for support. Dr Coogan had squeezed him in to his night surgery at short notice as his final appointment, and it was now nine o'clock. A good drinking time. Colm braced himself with the railing and eased himself into a comfortable vertical. The surgery door opened and the doctor emerged, bounding on his great thighs, and hopped into a sporty car parked at the kerb. Even his car looked fit. He was probably going off to have great sex with ... some gorgeous nurse ... in a nurse's uniform ...

See what bad shape my mind is in. See how unoriginal *it is. See what trouble I am in.*

Colm shuffled along, soon got the hang of it and began to pick up a bit of speed. If he tilted a little to his left, and stuck his chin forward and his elbow out, he could get along with a certain degree of comfort. It took him what seemed like fifteen minutes to get to the pub, and he happily entered its smoky atmosphere. He'd been in here before; it was at the outer limits of the circumference which he judged a reasonable distance to walk from his home for a pint. It was a big place that had recently been done up. Colm worked his way over to the bar and climbed up on one of the forbidden un-ergonomic bar-stools, and slumped himself over the bar, supported by his elbows. He ordered a forbidden pint, and took out a crumpled pack of forbidden fags. His pint arrived, he puffed a fag, and as he lowered the drink slowly, he relished the taste by rolling the stuff back and forth over his tongue.

The barman was chatty. So was Colm. Colm's gift was the ability to hold conversations. It was often remarked of him that he could talk to anyone. Lord Mayors, five-year-olds, painter-decorators, inanimate objects. It was true. He had that knack. He was also immediately endearing to people. People wanted to help him. He told his sorry tale about his back to the barman, who offered to send the lounge boy out to the late-night pharmacy to get the prescription. Colm had thought he might just do that if he played his cards right. Great. A fine establishment.

'And how'll you get home, since you're so crippled?' asked the barman.

'I'll phone the wife, she'll come and get me, but not until I've had a few.' *Wink wink.*

'You're lucky she lets you out. Nowadays the women do be the bosses everywhere.'

'My wife *is* the boss. She's a schoolteacher.'

The lounge boy, a gawky youth with a bad haircut and a nervous twitch, returned with the prescription, a plastic jar of interesting pink-and-white tablets. Colm had always wondered why he hadn't got more into drugs. He was an absolute candidate for it. It had just sort of passed him by, in the same way that regular employment had passed him by. He hadn't hung out with the right crowd for employment, or for drugs.

'Take one four times daily,' read the label. Colm threw in two, and washed them down with a huge slug of Guinness. Just to get the show on the road. Whether it was the pink-and-white, or the black, soon he began to feel no pain.

The television was on in the far corner of the bar and the screen was filled by a bunch of incredibly young boys cavorting in a band. Colm had wanted to be a rock star. How had that not happened to him? All these other tossers were rock stars. How come he wasn't? He confidently leapt off the bar stool to go for a slash. Whoops. Pain. Excruciating bolts of agony. He made his way across to the gents, supported by a dado rail. He had always wondered what those stupid rails were for. Now he knew. He positioned himself at the furthest urinal, in order to use the wall for support if necessary.

He grinned as he remembered a dream, a nightmare, he often had. In the dream he goes into a urinal like this one to have a piss, and when he opens his flies to take out his

4

penis, there is nothing there. No penis. Sometimes there are other men in the urinal, and when he discovers the absence, he gives a terrible yelp of fright. The other men all come to inspect him, and they tut-tut in a doctorly fashion before straightening their hats and ties and leaving him alone. It's a terrible dream, and he always wakes in a panic and puts his hand down to make sure it is still there. And it is always still there. Curled up and sleeping, untroubled, unlike him. *It* didn't get much exercise any more either.

He fished out his penis, which happily was indeed there, and had a nice long beery piss, which seemed to go on for ever. He went over to the mirror, and combed his hair. It had gone a bit wild-looking in the wind outside. He scrutinised himself in the glass. He was attractive in a John-Belushi-just-before-he-dropped kind of way. Pudgy face, lank oily hair, but he had nice eyes. People always said he had nice eyes. He looked a bit closer. They were totally bloodshot. They weren't nice at all now.

After tomorrow I'll get my act together.

At eleven o'clock he phoned Janet.

'Where?'

'Corcorans.'

'I'll be down in a minute,' she said with no emotion. She wasn't mad. She didn't feel abused by being treated like a taxi service. She would simply come and get him in a civil and pleasant fashion, perhaps even crack a joke. Then take him home to the cool bed they shared, where his fat flesh no longer felt the touch of love.

A New Leaf

Colm presented himself at the clinic of Frank Ingoldsby, Fitness Instructor, with a firm purpose of amendment. Frank was a kindly creature with long hair in a ponytail and a sympathetic aspect. A lanky, rangy figure, with long arms and very large hands which seemed to trail the floor. Colm lay on his stomach on the bench, very gingerly, looking suspiciously over his shoulder.

'Does this hurt?'

'Jaysus!' and Colm nearly leapt up off the bench with a screech. He wasn't a one for suffering in silence. He tended to suffer at a very high decibel level.

'Part of your problem is tension,' said Frank. 'Relax. Trust in me, as the fella said.'

Frank continued to work up and down Colm's vertebrae, gently easing out the tension.

'Apart from the weakness in the lower back, you have knots of tension in the shoulder area, and your right shoulder is in a mild spasm. You're in shocking shape.'

Colm was nearly crying with the pain of it, and the ecstasy of the relief.

'Fitness,' said Frank, 'is all in the mind. You have to think healthy, and you'll be healthy. You are what you eat. Get your diet in order. Love your body, so don't abuse it with junk.'

'OK.'

'Have you got kids?'

'Yes. Two. I mean three.'

'You wouldn't feed your kids junk, why do you feed

your own body junk? Hey. How many kids do you have? Two or three?'

'I have two kids and a stepkid. Only the stepkid isn't a kid any more, she's a young adult, or so she insists.'

'And exercise. You've got to get a programme going. Just a couple of hours a week. Take the kids out for walks. Go jogging with the stepkid. If you get into the swing of it, you'll be amazed how easy it is.'

'I've got to think positive.'

'It'll improve every area of your life. And I mean *every* area of your life,' said Frank, holding Colm's gaze with his bright blue eyes.

He didn't mean every area of my life. He meant sex. That was what he meant. Is it obvious by the look of me that I haven't had sex in years? Can it be smelt off me?

Colm was determined to lick the rot. He was going to get his shit together. It wasn't too late to correct a seriously misspent life at thirty-eight. He would have to get to the root of the problem. He would have to figure out why all this bad stuff had happened. He had seen photographs of himself as a baby, in his mother's arms, innocent and delightful. How had that lovely baby grown up to be this wreck? Even ten years ago he had a bit of go in him.

Tell me what I have to do.

Frank laid Colm down again on the bench and applied a cool jelly to his back, then massaged him with a buzzing machine.

'This is ultrasound. It reaches the parts that I can't.'

Colm must have passed out, or fallen asleep, because the next thing he knew Frank was shaking his shoulder gently. He had this trick of falling asleep very easily and dozing for a while. Narcolepsy. He liked the sound of that. It sounded like something vampires got up to, having sex with narcotic addicts or something. His little cat-naps were wonderfully refreshing, though the condition could have its disadvantages.

'You fell asleep,' said Frank. 'I let you sleep for a half an hour, because I had a window in my appointment book, but I've somebody due in five minutes.'

'I've been asleep?' said Colm, startled. It usually only happened when he was alone. Or in the theatre. He had snoozed his way through countless productions. Something about the warmth and immobility. Something about the theatre.

Frank smiled at him, and rubbed his hands together in front of Colm's face. 'I think we must have banished some of that tension.'

Colm did feel a lot better. He put his clothes back on, and shook hands with Frank.

'Same time next week.'

Colm felt profoundly grateful. As he took out the cash to pay for the visit, he realised he was on the verge of tears. This was the problem with releasing tension. He liked tension. He needed tension. It was the tension that kept the organism functioning, provided the steel pin which kept the mushy fleshy bits together. He grunted a 'thanks mate,' and escaped.

Going to a shrink would be less of a mind-fuck.

Outside in the waiting room, he saw a fizzy drinks dispenser. He had been at a few functions the night before and the dodgy wine had left him with a raging thirst. He rooted in his pockets and found a 50p and was going to get himself a coke, but changed his mind. Coke bad. Mineral water good. He pressed the selector button for fizzy mineral water. At least it had a little fizz in it. Fizz wasn't bad for you.

See how easy that was? See how easy it was to take the healthy option? See?

The money window flashed 20p. Colm then realised that the water cost 70p, as opposed to the more reasonable 50p for coke. A bloody disgrace. 20p extra for fizzy water. Water which was produced by nature. Didn't have to be

8

manufactured. Under no circumstances. He pressed the coke button, and out came an ice-cool can of coke. He pressed the can against his temple to cool down his brain. Very versatile, very *utile*, these cans. And then he opened it and relished the sugary cool liquid going down his throat and liquefying his insides.

He walked home. The clinic was in Ballsbridge, and it was a nice trot up to Rathmines. Colm was very happy not to be able to drive. He had early on decided to refrain from driving. It put you immediately into the driven class, rather than the driving class. Janet was able to drive, therefore she could cover all the tasks that involved automobiles: supermarket shopping; collecting drunk husband from pub; taking children to swimming/ballet/Irish dancing/guitar/pogo-stick lessons. Also, one could booze to one's heart's content and never be in danger of drunk driving, if one didn't know how to drive. If one used the pins to get around, one inadvertently got quite a lot of exercise – by accident, free gratis and for nothing. Also, Colm was mad for public transport. He loved the idea of it and lamented its paucity in the city. At election time, when canvassers called to his home, he always quizzed them on their party's policy regarding public transport, and whoever told the most magnificent lies on the subject always got his vote. Whosoever's vision of a bus lane utopia was the most convincing got his number one. No matter who was elected, nothing ever improved. Bus users weren't the most effective lobby group. They were usually too busy staying alive to get militant. The government were promising a tram system, but years went by as they argued whether it should be overground, underground or airborne.

Colm walked happily home, full of determined resolution. Candlewick Avenue was a leafy road with a traffic island and ramp in the middle as a traffic-calming measure to stop drivers from killing tiny tots. The Cantwell family lived in number thirty, which was halfway down on the right.

Colm and Janet bought the house ten years earlier just after their marriage, with finances very kindly provided by a recently deceased unknown relative of Colm's in Australia. Colm and Janet had made all their wedding plans (*Janet had made them*) and had been looking about for a little flat. They had a small sum saved, and both their jobs were insecure, so only a small mortgage could be got. Janet was teaching, but on nine-monthly contracts. Colm had a job copy-editing with a magazine, but every week there were changes in personnel because the owner of the magazine appeared deranged, and every day one wondered for whom the bell would be tolling. They were about to put their few bob down on a dingy tiny apartment in Terenure, when a stranger came to the front door and identified himself as a lawyer engaged by an Australian firm to see that Colm Cantwell, nephew of estranged Great Aunt Julia Cantwell from Sydney, got what was coming to him. An inheritance in that nineteenth-century novel kind of way, a fortune made from sheep farming in the colonies. And he wasn't even a plain and lowly governess in love with his betters. Colm felt his life was charmed. He needed money to buy a house and magic, money came and provided.

No sweat. No hassle. Cool.

So, thanks to dead Aunt Julia, Colm and Janet started off their married life in this beautiful old redbrick Rathmines house, entirely paid for, with enough money left over to do it up to their tastes. Janet put in a lot of bathrooms. After her redesign of the house there were five comfortable locations in which a person could pee: two en suites, a family bathroom, a downstairs visitors' bathroom, and another bathroom of uncertain purposes. When people came to visit them in the early days, and they were showing off the house, Colm took them on the loo tour.

10

Colm soon gave up his copy-editing job. Suspecting that he was next in line for the chop, he delighted in his pre-emptive strike. He went freelance.

Was that the beginning of the problem?

At the time, most of the other houses on the road had been divided up into flats. Slowly over the ten years since, they had been reclaimed for private ownership as fashions changed and people wanted to live closer to the city once more. One by one the multiple doorbells and bicycles chained to the front railings were replaced by lilting chimes and BMWs. The people who came with their money didn't look to left or right, just nested aloof from each other in their gracious drawing rooms, as they ferried their chickies to private crèches. They never greeted you on the street. At least they never greeted Colm. He looked poor and dodgy.

There was one house which was still in flats, one last bastion of slum landlordism. Number five. Loud music emanated from this house, and the spuriously curtained windows were constantly open in the summer months. Various characters moved in and out. The rent was cheap, and the inhabitants colourful. A single mother with a little boy. A Bosnian refugee. A very tall man called Brian who had a magazine stall down in the centre of Rathmines. He always greeted Colm as 'brother', and was very friendly. Colm often stopped to chat, and a few times went in for coffee. Brian lived in a sunny room at the back. The house was identical in layout to number thirty and Brian's den was the equivalent room to the Cantwell family kitchen. Brian was the chief of the house, had been there longest and was charged with maintaining the place, collecting rent and vetting new tenants. The landlord lived in a fancy place in County Cork. Colm felt an affinity with Brian, with these people, the flotsam. From time to time a battered sign appeared in the front window of the house,

11

'room to let'. Somebody would be gone, somebody new would arrive. Once they had a wedding.

Next door to Colm's house was a mad lady, who lived alone and had old money. She was about fifty now, her hair long and grey and tied neatly in girlish bunches. She wore knee-length schoolgirl skirts and knee-high socks and at night she talked to herself in voices. Often it was very loud. When Colm and Janet had first moved in they thought there was an entire family next door, including a dog, but it soon became clear that it was just the mad lady. With a different education she could have made a living as a ventriloquist – a licensed speaker of voices. She always greeted Colm with an elaborate girlishly flirtatious look, and a little winsome smile. It mortified him. But she had a kind face. There was no badness in her. Colm liked her, but every time he saw her he couldn't help picturing her flopping her pigtails and barking like a dog.

He walked up his garden path and let himself in the front door, happily making his way through the strands of light which bounced off the old stained glass. He loved this house, with its colours and its corners and its spiders.

He made himself a strong cup of coffee and sat down at the kitchen table. He got out a piece of paper from the paper-and-string drawer, and made a list. A list of how to remedy the things in life that were oppressing him.

1: See physiotherapist regularly.
2: Improve diet.
3: Booze less.
4: Institute programme for phasing out fags.
5: Join fitness programme of some sort.
6: Attend to professional difficulties; see why you are unable to write; if necessary see psychiatrist.
7: Attend to parental responsibilities with more diligence.
8: Examine problem relating to Cordelia.

9: Attend to marital difficulties; if necessary, see psychiatrist.
10: Try and introduce some sexual activity into your life with a view to improving physical and mental fitness, ideally with wife, but if not, elsewhere.

If he could lick even half of these subjects, he'd at least have some chance of a decent and fulfilling existence. However, he was aware there wasn't a single area of his life that he was satisfied with. In fact, this list was a very damning indictment of where he was at. The *list* was oppressing him.

He heard the front door open. The sound of jingle bells announced the arrival of Cordelia. She had developed this new fad of sewing little bells into the linings of her long skirts. Some fashion trend or other that was a big deal in the transition year at the convent she attended. She could be heard a mile off. She appeared, her fair head first, around the kitchen door.

'Oh, you're here,' she said as she jingled into the room. Colm was aware that he found the jingling unreasonably irritating, so he fought against it, this feeling. Cordelia's words could be construed as a friendly greeting, considering their source, and that source's liking for the grunt as a means of expression. Colm folded up his ten commandments, and put them in his pocket.

'Would you like some coffee?' he offered.

'Sure,' answered Cordelia.

Colm in private referred to Cordelia as the Chopper. Child Of a Previous Relationship. She was the living spit of her mother, her absent and absconded father's genetic material having failed to make much of an imprint. It had continued to strike Colm as bizarre for Janet to have called her fatherless child Cordelia. To call any child Cordelia. Her friends had shortened the name to Cordy.

Cordelia's father had shown up for the first time ever a

13

month previously. He had been let out of his drug rehab unit in the United States and been deported back to Ireland. He decided belatedly to get in touch. The event had been a big drama in the household. He was a wreck of a man, a shell. Tall, gangly, orangey hair, bad teeth. Had spent the past fifteen years being a Californian beach bum – 'The oranges are as big as melons. You can live off the streets, man' – and taking too many drugs. Cordelia had been horrified by him, and afterwards refused to discuss the event.

Janet's taste in men has obviously always been fierce bad. It's not just me.

Colm poured the coffee and put it down in front of the teenager, who slung her schoolbag on the bench and sat opposite him and said nothing, just stared at him with her angelic impassive features. The older she got the more she resembled her mother, not just visually but in temperament also. Earnest, truthful, hardworking, principled and curiously lacking in joy. Now fifteen, she was becoming a young woman. She was a very active kid – on every committee in the school, helped out with all the charities at the weekend, ran an ecological programme for her whole class, collected bottle tops and melted them down for the starving. (*Could they eat them?*) Collected old clothes and blankets for the poor. Really, she was a walking mission station. Colm knew that she looked on him as a kind of human ecological disaster zone.

'Want a cigarette?' he asked her with a smirk as he lit up. She didn't answer, just added a shade of contempt to her expression.

'What are you doing home so early?' he asked.

'We were sent home to work on our projects,' she said. 'My ecological project needs to be written up.' She coughed a little in an eighteenth-century comedy of manners type of way, took up her coffee and jingled out of the room. Colm stood up to wash his cup and had his back

14

to her as she was leaving. He could have sworn he heard a sharp hiss, but when he looked around at her face the features were composed and impassive as always.

If she had taken to hissing at him, things had reached a new low. Those bells were cat bells.

Somehow, things had been allowed to go very wrong with Cordelia. She came home from school each day with new and more splendid terms with which to describe Colm. 'Dork' was a favourite for a while. 'Slob thing' had had quite an innings. 'The Toad in the Hole' was how she described him when he was in his study. 'Space Hog' was another *bon mot* which enjoyed prominence for a while. Janet had used to chastise her for this but lately the family policy was to ignore it. She'd grow out of it. She was a teenager. Colm put up with it because he didn't know what else to do. Also, Cordelia was Janet's child, and disciplining her had always been Janet's arena.

It had been grand in the early days. Colm and Cordelia had got on great when she was a child: played hide and seek together; he sneaked her sweets and biscuits behind her mother's back. He and she went on illicit forays to McDonald's where they gorged on grease and ketchup and too much salt, and had a right laugh. Things started to go badly once she reached the age of reason.

I get on better with the pre-reasonable.

Things started to go badly once she began to turn into her mother.

The Office

Colm went out the front door and ambled down the street towards the main road. It was a chill afternoon, the world was beginning to emerge from the stagnation of winter. Brian was sitting on the wall of number five.

'I'm waiting for a new tenant,' he said. 'A young girl from Galway. I told her "no students" and she insisted that she wasn't a student, she was a waitress, but after I agreed to let her have the place and she left, once she no longer was pointing her little bright eyes at me, I gained the impression she was spinning tales.'

Brian ran a no students policy in his domain. He didn't like students. He wanted his co-habitants to inhabit the real world. Didn't want any softies sponsored by parents.

'I hate students, you know. Too cock-sure of themselves. You never saw anything like students for ignorance. And it's taxpayers' money is paying for them and they act like it's no less than their due. Your and my taxes.'

Colm, a scant taxpayer himself, considered Brian, his long browny-grey hair and nicotine-stained hands. He reckoned that they were neither of them in the major league as far as taxpaying was concerned.

Just then, the Galway girl appeared at the end of the road. Brian stood up straight and mentally dusted himself down. Colm set off, passing the girl who gave him a huge smile, obviously taking him for a resident of number five and therefore a future housemate. Colm smiled back.

He liked his bus. The 15B. It was a fine, frequent bus

that chugged along into town at its own pace, unhurried, unstressed. He liked looking at the people who got on, examining their faces, smelling them. Often the mad lady got this bus and made sheep's eyes at him all the way to town. On these occasions he dived into his newspaper and tried not to think of her on all fours and barking like a dog. He knew most of the bus regulars, the happy driver, the miserable one. The women struggling with babies and buggies. The drunks. The old people. The schoolchildren. People who had no dough.

He got off the bus at its terminus, and strolled on down to Castle Grub Street. Colm had worked for the *Grub Street Gazette* in various capacities over the years: night desk editor, feature writer, freelance journalist. He had now slimmed his job down to writing the weekly gossip column. Colm had been into downsizing long before the term was invented. He delivered his copy every Friday afternoon. The income from this, coupled with Janet's salary and the fact that they didn't have a mortgage, meant that they could survive quite well. They weren't wealthy, but they were comfortable. Who needs foreign holidays anyway? Foreign sunshine doesn't suit Irish skin. Colm had no interest in money. He wore old clothes that were the antithesis of fashion. He took no interest in the matter, and Janet managed the whole thing, making a biannual seasonal foray into Marks and Spencer, and returning home with the usual greys and browns. He wasn't visually offensive, but was a long way off stylish.

Colm smiled at Dan the Doorman, who was sitting in his little cubby-hole smoking a fag. Smoking restrictions had been brought in all over the building, but Dan simply paid no attention and smoked away in his cubicle, which was small and snug, like a coffin. Dan was seventy-five at least, but he managed to evade compulsory retirement by passing himself off as one of his younger brothers who had emigrated to the USA in the fifties. When challenged by an investigatory committee on retirement, he produced a birth certificate for one Declan Reardan and insisted Dan was short for Declan, not Daniel. Records showed that D. Reardan had been there since 1940, which meant Dan was eight years old when first appointed as assistant doorman, but Dan pointed out that there had been a D. Reardan on the books since 1890 – his father before him. Not Daniel, not Declan, but Donal. The Ds ran in the family. The high hats had no legal choice but to retain him. They couldn't prove he wasn't who he said he was. They tried to bribe him with early-retirement packages but there was no shifting Dan. He was Dan the Doorman. That was his identity. He said that if he couldn't work any more, they might as well put him in a box.

Colm gave Dan a warm greeting. He thought he was a great old codger, and was very impressed with the wily birth certificate trick. Dan was about as impressed with Colm as he was with any of the other journos. Sometimes he acknowledged greetings, sometimes not. Colm made his way up the stairs to the top of the building where his copy was awaited.

He had a new editor to deal with. She had been appointed a month previously, and Colm wasn't thrilled with her. She was a new-fangled young one, about thirty, and a complete bossyboots, all haircuts and lipstick and teeth. In the gym at eight a.m. keeping the legs in good shape. She didn't cause him grief, or interfere with him in any way, but she had a series of little practices to let him know subtly who was boss. He was well aware who was boss, and was quite bewildered by her insistence on reminding him.

Must be a completely insecure power maniac. These new-fangled women who model themselves on Demi Moore are a visual godsend, but they're a fierce pain in the arse.

'Hello Deirdre,' he smiled at her, 'here's this week's

18

observations of Dublin pond scum,' half-heartedly attempting a little light banter.

'Excellent. What juicy bits have you got for us this week?' Her face lighting up with a wave of psychotic enthusiasm.

The column was called *Mary Jane on the Tiles*. Colm had inherited it from Mary Jane Murphy, who used to do it. But she had checked herself into the funny farm to dry out, finding the constant round of launches, premières and etceteras too much for her addictive personality. MJM had written *Mary Jane on the Tiles* for seven years, and it was a very successful page. Colm had taken it over temporarily when Mary Jane first ran into difficulties with the straight and narrow. He had been the man in the gap. He had always been fond of MJM and wanted to help her out. She had been a boozing buddy of his, and he knew who all her gossip contacts were, because MJM could not keep the mouth shut about anything. Born to gab. Colm was losing all his boozing buddies. They were dropping like flies, victims of addiction, new age hippiedom, jailhouse marriages, born-again Christianity, this latter a surprisingly common occurrence. Religion was breaking out like a rash amongst his acquaintances.

MJM hadn't emerged from the happy farm as soon as was originally intended. They kept her there for quite a while, but *Mary Jane on the Tiles* continued to be produced every week. Colm, a gifted mimic, copied her style easily. Slightly fey, a light girlish wit, an intimate tone, and a cheerful flirtation with the public. None of the readers noticed the change of hand. MJM had returned to the paper, but refused to take back the gossip column on the grounds that it forced her to do too much socialising, and she couldn't expose herself to the groaning trestles at wine launches and suchlike. She had found a niche for herself as the gardening correspondent, calling herself Mary Greenfield, as she had married her psychiatrist

Dr Greenfield and it seemed to be a rather nifty name for a gardening corr.

'And to think I spent fifteen years hanging round booze-fests trying to find a husband. And here I am all washed up at thirty-seven, riddled with booze and disappointment, and I find an attractive wealthy shrink now throwing himself at my feet. Life sure ain't fair,' she said gleefully.

Mary Jane Murphy no longer existed.

The problem remained about the gossip column, which Colm had been pseudonymously producing for over twelve months. Colm had suggested changing its name from *Mary Jane on the Tiles* to *Colm Cantwell on the Ceiling*. However, he rather liked writing the stuff in MJM's voice. It gave him a sort of delightful trans-sexual thrill to be writing as a woman.

I Tiresias!

He would have found it harder to write it in his own voice. It was so much easier to be idiotic and flirtatious and coy and have no brain when you were supposed to be a woman. For example, you could spend half the column complaining that your new high-heeled Italian shoes were giving you blisters, whereas if you were a man, you'd simply take the damn things off.

I Tiresias!

Women had far more accessories.

The decision was made. He retained the job of writing the gossip column, but it stayed under its original title. All the time Mary Jane was in the detox, it had been kept a secret that her page was being ghosted. The editor of the lifestyle section knew, of course, but generally nobody else did. Colm liked it that way, and after he officially took over he kept it that way. 'I bestow on you my former dissolute personality,' said MJM darkly, as a cheerful malediction. There had been changes in the column under Colm. Mary Jane had become more reckless. Admitted to drinking more, had more sex, lost almost all decorum. As

20

the real Mary Jane got her act together, the fictional one went into a total slide.

The completely insecure Demi Moore lookalike scanned the material for a second or two.

'This looks fine,' she said, pointlessly rearranging a few full stops and commas, and turning subclauses into full sentences in the belief that she might look like she was making an editorial contribution.

This isn't high literature, man. Rearranging the punctuation is pretty pointless, because the typesetters jumble them all together anyway.

'Cornelius is late with the photos. I called down to the lab a moment ago, and he said he'll be ready in a half an hour. Said he was elbowed out of the lab by an urgent news story. They have brill pictures of that suicide off Butt Bridge. A David-Hockney-like collage sequence of shots. I wanted it for lifestyle. I have an article on file about suicide, a very good article, by a psychiatrist or a social worker or someone who knows stuff, you know, full of research graphs and all. I have the article stacked, just waiting for suicide to become topical, and here is the perfect opportunity. But the news desk won't let me have the pictures. I wouldn't mind, but I could run them in colour, and they've only black-and-white in news. I've half a colour page left. Well, I could have half a colour page left if I ditched the piece on the Hospice Ball. So, this is great, Colm,' she said waving his pages. 'Really very very good. Congratulations. You really have a feel for this type of writing, you know.'

'Ah stop,' said Colm.

She's barmy, man.

'You'll have to learn how to take a compliment,' said Deirdre, patting her hairdo and sitting back in her chair.

Colm didn't like this Deirdre person one bit. She injected a phial of tension, of urgency, into the air of the office. This was the nineties thing. People had to behave as though all jobs were brain surgery. Deirdre didn't seem to realise that the *Grub Street Gazette* was a dog. The lifestyle section was a flea on the dog and his gossip page was an amoeba on the flea. Why then, was this Deirdre woman ranting about it as though it had any significance?

'See ya next week,' said Colm as he turned to leave the office, consoling himself with thoughts of his weekly cheque which arrived by magic into his bank account.

'Oh by the way,' said Deirdre. 'A woman came in today looking for Mary Jane Murphy. She was very well dressed. The suit she was wearing cost eight hundred pounds. I know. I tried it on last week in Pia Bang.'

'Oh.'

'Not that I'm quite in the eight-hundred-pound-suit bracket, on my salary' (laughs – haw haw – casts eyes heavenwards) 'but a cat can look at a king's pyjamas, can't it?'

'And what did she say?'

'Just that she must talk to Mary Jane Murphy. She was most insistent and a little rude. She got past the porter by telling some story about wanting to correct some advertising copy – obviously knows her way around. Anyway, I told her nothing, but she gave me an envelope to give to MJM, so I suppose it should be given to you.'

Deirdre proffered a plain white business-shaped envelope. It had *Private and Confidential* written on the corner and the writing was in a neat print.

'Thanks,' said Colm.

Deirdre held tightly to the corner of the envelope.

'Aren't you going to open it? My curiosity is piqued.'

'It says Private and Confidential,' said Colm and gave the envelope a sharp little tug, and once he had complete control of the oblong, he put it into his breast pocket. He enjoyed annoying Deirdre and seized any possible opportunity to do so. The letter was probably a press release or some such irrelevance. Often PR people went to great lengths to put press releases directly into the hands of gossip columnists. Especially young and newly appointed PR people. Give them a few years on the job and they developed a more appropriate jadedness.

Just then, Cornelius the photographer came in with his brown-paper envelope.

'Had to dry them with the hairdryer.'

Colm glanced at the contents, the usual array of cleavage and thigh.

'G'night all.'

I am ashamed to put my name publicly to this stuff. Why is that? Is it because somewhere inside I believe myself to be too good for it? Hardly. I hardly have that much respect left for myself. No, I am simply a snob.

Colm made his way down to Davy Byrne's. He was to meet his friend David there, at six o'clock, for a few scoops prior to going to dinner in some posh place at David's expense. It was four-thirty and he was a bit early. He ordered coffee, because he didn't want to be too far ahead of his friend when he arrived. David was extremely wealthy. His wallet was alive with credit cards. They were breeding. Colm was a strictly cash man. He had this awful feeling that he might do terrible things with champagne in nightclubs were he to possess a credit card.

David Blake had gone to the same school as Colm. Colm had originally liked him because he felt sorry for him. David had one leg an inch shorter than the other, and had to wear special shoes; a minor problem in adulthood, a social catastrophe in a small boy. He walked with a slight limp. Colm and he had fallen into each other's company as a pair of oddballs immediately on entering secondary school. Colm was an outcast, because his granny paid his school fees at this expensive south County Dublin school, but she neglected to pay the cost of the fancy house, the clothes, the sports equipment, the matching socks, that would ensure her grandson fitted into the place. Both boys opted out of rugby, David because he was physically unable, Colm because he couldn't face the indignity of being the last to be chosen for the team, so he happily kept David company on the sidelines. Together they developed a line in ironic commentary. As a duo they were inseparable, and soon became inviolable. David's family was very wealthy, and Colm hung around at their house a lot. Learned how to behave wealthy. By their final year in school they were among the boys whose company was most sought after. Colm had developed a line in chat that would win people over to him fast. Colm schooled himself in guile.

Often they would go sit on the wall up the road from the nearby comprehensive school, and look at the co-ed students as they piled out at four-thirty. They all had raggy jumpers and funny skin and dodgy haircuts, and some were in wheelchairs (the comprehensive was the only school nearby which had been built with wheelchair access). One boy wore an unravelling jumper which day by day travelled up his chest until finally all that was left was a collar and some sleeves. What was a mere limp, mere poverty, to single one out in the context of such marvellous oddities?

And the girls at the comprehensive were great. First of all, there *were* some girls, a species totally lacking in the posh Christian Brothers establishment. Secondly, they were friendly and wore short skirts and smoked cigarettes down lanes. Thirdly, they were impressed with Colm and David as exotic creatures from the posh school with their blazers and ties. Colm and David had had only one serious row in their thirty-year friendship, and it had been over a girl called Emmeline from the comprehensive.

'I'm called after an early feminist and exponent of the rights of women. My old dear is a single mother and proud.'

A very scary girl. Having a single mum was quite something in the 1970s.

Colm had fixated all his developing seventeen-year-old hormones on the cheeky face of Emmeline. However, she had fixated all her self-empowered hormones on the increasingly Byronic-looking David.

'She only likes you because you're a cripple. Girls like cripples because they like playing nurse.'

Colm intended to wound. David didn't say anything, merely got up on his bike and cycled off. Colm had been right. Emmeline had made David take off his clothes so she could poke at his shortened leg. She hadn't meant any harm, was merely scientifically curious. She wanted to be a doctor. No nursing for this namesake of suffragettism.

Their friendship cooled for a while as David dealt with this, the first of his many romantic embarrassments, but they drifted back together. Pragmatism. They knew they needed each other to get through.

David now had loads of dough of his own. He had gone into various businesses and done very well. He owned a couple of nightclubs, a string of restaurants, and recently had diversified into adult recreation shops. Daddy's dough had got him started, but the Christian Brothers had schooled him well, and he was able to multiply. Daddy wasn't very pleased with his choice of businesses, as Daddy was a very religious man, a daily communicant since his teens and a member of Opus Dei. Major rows had ensued.

David was one of Colm's principal sources of information for *Mary Jane on the Tiles*. He was very hands-on in his management style and visited all his establishments almost every night. His staff reported to him the general goings-on, who was in that night, who was meeting whom, and he passed it all on to Colm. Naturally David kept his role very quiet, and Colm kept his role very quiet. So very few people knew that they were being observed when they were lurking in corners of various night-spots around Dublin.

Colm's coffee arrived, and he sat down at one of the tables. Normally he was a barstool person, but he was taking his doctor's advice to sit on chairs with back support. His back had improved quite a bit, the drugs probably, though Colm hadn't had a single shit since he'd started taking them. Eight days ago. The Doc had mentioned the possibility of blockage as a side-effect. He was now full of shit. He would continue to monitor the situation.

He fished out the envelope extracted from the claws (*and they* were *claws; long dark fingernails*) of Deirdre. He opened it, expecting to find some cheap promotional printout or other, but there was a hand-written letter, with a faint whiff of perfume.

Longbrook,
Howth Hill Rise.
Ph 770 9983

Dear Mary Jane Murphy,
    I have been reading your column for many
years, and find it most amusing and diverting. It is
the first page I turn to in the newspaper. I just
love a good gossip, and the great thing about your
page is that it is gossip on a national scale. In fact
it is the reason I buy the paper in the first place. I
love your style, so witty and charming, and you
really capture the lifestyle of the single woman.
    I was out of the country for a few weeks last
month, and returned last week to find that you
had run a story about my husband, James Carter
in the issue of January 11th. All my friends and
acquaintances had cut it out and kept it for me –
ten of them. I would like very much to ask you a

few questions about this matter. I assure absolute discretion, and desperately appeal to your sense of sisterly solidarity.

Please contact me at the above number, during the day if possible.

Yours sincerely,
Sally Carter

Hmmn. This was an odd missive. The MJM column had got many blistering epistles from lawyers over the years, various anonymous threatening letters, the odd indecipherable screed with an address at a psychiatric institution, but nothing as full frontal as this. Colm giggled at the flattery contained in the letter. He wondered was it genuine, was this woman really a complete dip, did she actually *like* the column, or was the enthusiasm put on to encourage a favourable response. He wasn't entirely sure. He put the letter back in his pocket to be looked at later.

David arrived, and hobbled into the bar.

Was his limp getting worse?

These occasional Friday nights they spent together were precious to both of them. David got to show off how successful he was and Colm got to show off how much he didn't care. Uninhibited boasting is the preserve of the thirteen-year-old, and this pair retained enough of their thirteen-year-old selves to be able to get away with the practice. Having a good boast was a delight to them.

'How are you?'

'Great, never better, making a load of dough. The new adult shops are working out great. Just what this country needed, a bit of oomph! A bit of whay-hey-hey!' and David made some suggestive gestures with his eyebrows and arms. 'The restaurants are ticking over nicely. There's always money in grub. I'm thinking of buying a yacht, a nice one, and spending some time cruising the Mediterranean. How about you?'

27

'Fine, a pig in shite, enjoying the world. Just working away on this and that. Doing me bits and bobs of writing. You know me.'

And they got stuck into a few pints. David was a careful drinker, but he reserved all his units for his nights out with Colm. He knew you weren't supposed to do that, but he did it anyway, and spent the next day working off the units on his bicycle that didn't go anywhere. He was in reasonable shape, despite the problem with the leg.

'How's her indoors?'

'Ah, Janet. She's fine, I think. I don't really know. She looks fine from the outside. How's eh, how's eh . . . ?'

'Catherine. Great, you know, really great. We're really getting serious about each other now. I've never met anyone like her.'

David was a major player in the sperm wars. Married in his twenties, he had been presented by the original Mrs Blake with two bundles of joy, now snarling teenagers. A liaison in his early thirties with a Frenchwoman had produced another child, now a ringletted seven-year-old who came to visit Papa twice a year. Adèle was her name. Two years ago, a liaison (*scandalous*) with a nineteen-year-old employee (*waitress*) had produced a little boy, Jason. David honoured all his financial parental responsibilities and some of his emotional ones.

Why can't I be like that? Why can't I happily co-exist with emotional chaos?

David was a reasonably welcome guest in all three households, though the nineteen-year-old, now twenty-one, was the only one who kept the bed warm for him.

'Bigamy suits me. I should have been a Mormon or a Bedouin or some such.'

David had a mature lady, Rose, who came to his apartment, cleaned up and housekeepered for him. Rose was near fifty and was essentially the woman in David's life about whom he was serious. The only woman he was afraid of losing, without whom he could not do.

'You'll have to meet Catherine. She's something. I'd love to know what you think of her. I think she's the one, you know.'

In fairness to David, he was very enthusiastic about all his ladies and was a complete romantic, always showing up staggering under bunches of flowers.

'We had sex for the first time last Saturday, and it was mind-blowing.'

But the women he was attracted to had the prefabricated appearance of women in fashion adverts.

'I had an orgasm that I think was felt by several generations of my ancestors. Catherine is so beautiful, she's like a painting.'

David really wanted to go out with a magazine.

'You know, I'm always very slow to sleep with a girl. I never rush it. Most men make the mistake of rushing things. I take my time, and when I do get round to it, they're gagging for it.'

His record was so bad by this stage that Catherine would have to be an exceptionally dim optimist to be fooled.

The night unfolded, according to the pattern of these nights. They drank a rake of pints in the bar and then they went to a steak restaurant and ordered steak and chips and more beer. And then they went to the Candelabra, one of David's nightclubs, and happily drank champagne in David's office, where they talked about football and about David's love life. David loved talking about his lovers. Colm wondered did he like talking about them more than he liked being with them. The other odd thing about David was that he had no friends apart from Colm. He was in the curious position of having no colleagues, only employees, and therefore work-related socialising always had the drawback of being with somebody who was in his pay. Going for a drink with his staff was fun all right, but he always paid for the drinks and could never escape the sense that they were only tolerating his company in the interests of their paypackets. A form of social prostitution, and David a Goliath of pimps lolling around bars among minions.

Saturday

Colm woke from sleep with a raging thirst, and two junior persons romping round the giant bed. It was Saturday morning and the smallies had invaded. He looked at the clock. 11 a.m. Janet had obviously held them outside until now. Left to their own devices, they'd be in at 8 a.m. They sat on top of his half-sleeping form and played 'jiggy up'. The tandem version. John switched on the TV and changed the channels until he got to *Yukki Teddies* – his favourite breakfast TV programme. June wanted some other thing, *Xena, Lesbian Warrior* or something. John shoved the remote control under the duvet and under Colm. Both children dived under to try and get the 'trolls'. Somebody gave somebody a nip and somebody got their hair pulled and both children started to roar, great pealing crescendos. Colm settled them down, one on either side of himself so they couldn't get at each other, and switched channels until he found a nice nature programme, about otters migrating up and down a river. The children quietened.

He looked at them, June tucked into his left armpit, sucking her thumb, John cuddled against his right side, his bottom lip stuck out in reminiscence of his recent temper. They smelt lovely. They both had their mother's round face, angelic features and big eyes, but were both dark, like Colm.

They have a few signs that I had a hand in their making. John's downward curl of the lip, and June has a flash in her eye which is both attractive and very sly. I have left my fingerprints on them.

Colm loved these children more than he had expected to. He had chosen their names, John after his father and June after Janet's mother, despite Janet's protests. After what Colm viewed as the Cordelia nomenclature disaster, he wanted old-fashioned names which signified nothing but old-fashioned regeneration.

The door opened and in came Cordelia, bearing a huge breakfast tray with four legs which fitted neatly over his form on the bed.

'Mam says to say she's gone to do the shopping.'

A Saturday ritual. Janet always shopped on Saturday. Colm used to go with her. Well, he went to the shopping centre and sat in the Kylemore with a cappucino and an issue of *Hot Press*. He used to help carry the bags to the car, though.

Cordelia smiled scarily at Colm, and left the room.

'Thanks Cordy.'

The breakfast tray was beautifully put together. Colm felt a twinge of gratefulness and remorse. He vaguely remembered coming in last night at about four a.m. and trying to jump Janet from behind. She had just slapped him off. He was a very half-hearted sexual assaulter. He had worked himself up into a lather in the taxi about his lack of conjugal opportunity and decided to resolve the situation right when he got in. It was all David's talk. After a few jars David was like a porno radio station. His tongue loosened up and he started to describe everything he and whoever got up to in great detail. Smutty gossip. Hot gossip. No wonder Colm had come home in a right state and tried to sneak in the back door. And despite this, this disgusting outbreak, Janet had painstakingly put together this breakfast for him with all the appearance of love.

I am not worthy.

Colm had a few days previously reported his bowel

solidification situation to HQ and the breakfast reflected this. There was a dish of prunes and custard. Instead of his usual sugared Frosties, there were bran biccies which looked like little industrially formed turds. No sausies or rashers, just a forlorn-looking poached egg and a grilled tomato on very wholemeal brown bread. But there was a pint glass of fizzy water with loads of ice in it.

For the hangover, which she knows I have. Who would know better than she?

Colm chewed at the breakfast, which was surprisingly all right tasting. He was going to be a better person. He was going to eat more bran. More fibre. He wasn't too mad about the prunes, so he ate a few and then shared them with John and June who scoffed happily, spitting out the stones into Colm's hanky.

'I love spitting,' said John. 'Especially this kind of allowed spitting.'

'Even though I hate John, he is my favourite person on earth after you and Mammy,' said June. 'And after him comes Cordelia and then Ronan Keating out of Boyzone.'

'You're only six. You're too young to be interested in Boyzone.'

'Girls of six get married in Spain. I'm six and three-quarters.'

'No they don't.'

'They did use to in the olden days. Their mammies and daddies picked out a boy for them and married them off but they didn't allow them to go and live with the boy for a while until they were older. Much older. Maybe when they were eight.'

'Who told you that?' asked Colm.

'Cordelia. She read it in a book.'

I can't believe I tried to jump Janet last night. Jesus.

'I'm eight,' said John.

'Part of the reason why I hate John so much is that he's a

boy. I'd like to bury him alive and have him eaten by worms.'

'I hate June because she's a girl, and a cry-baby.'

'Imagine worms eating you and you alive. Imagine it.'

'Stoppit,' said Colm. 'Look at the nice otters. Here's the Daddy otter coming to find the lost baby. Come on, look.'

The children settled and obeyed Colm. He loved that. He loved the way he could effectively subdue them. It was one of the few things in his life he was proud of. His authority over six- and eight-year-olds. They settled peacefully and watched the programme.

'I'm back,' called Janet from below, rustling shopping bags.

'Sweets!' yelled John and June in unison, and they dived out of the bed, across the room and out the door. Delightfully unsentimental.

Colm rolled over in the bed and pulled the duvet up over his sore head.

On Monday I will begin a new life. I will start to work properly. I will sit down and write something worthwhile, anything. I am a better person than I think I am. I resolve . . . zzzzzz.

The next thing Colm knew he was rolling over and felt some major stirrings in his bowel. He could sense the mother of all shits coming on and, mindful of his sore head, he gingerly edged his way over to the en suite for some live hot colon action. And action there was.

Colm lingered for a while on the toilet. He enjoyed sitting on the loo, allowing the air to circulate round his private parts. He got up and looked at himself in the mirror.

Half his left eyebrow was missing. This was a bad sign. He always pulled at his left eyebrow when he was stressed. He looked very lop-sided. Why hadn't David mentioned it? His eyebrowlessness. David's vision barely extended

beyond his own nose, that's why. He heard Janet come
into the bedroom.

'Colm?'

He cringed.

'I'm in here,' he replied.

'Any movement?'

'Yeah, thanks.'

'Prunes. Prunes are great.'

'Yeah, fab.'

'Nothing like prunes to get things moving.'

'Sure isn't.'

'I'm going to visit Marie. I won't ask you to come
because I know you don't like her.'

*Janet's sister Marie is an awful harridan. She's a
bossyboots, bosses her husband, bosses Janet, bosses me.
Bosses the children.*

Colm had this knack of picking fights with Marie. He
insisted on contradicting her generalisations, and rarely
emerged from a visit without suffering and inflicting a few
verbal wounds.

'Fine. Leave me be.'

'See you later.'

There wasn't a hint of rancour in Janet's voice.

This isn't normal. This silence. We'd better have it out.

Colm made his way out of the toilet and looked at
Janet's clear features. No rancour there either.

'Aren't you angry?'

'About what?'

'About last night?'

'What about last night?'

'We-ell,' said Colm.

'You always come in drunk at four o'clock in the
morning after you've been out with David. There's nothing
unusual about that.'

'But what I did? Aren't you angry about that?'

'The Rice Krispies on the kitchen floor? Hardly a hanging crime.'

Oh. He remembered that now. Trying to fix himself some Rice Krispies and missing the bowl each time. And trying to pick them up one by one from the floor, before giving it up as an impossible task.

'The other thing I did.'

'What other thing?'

'To you.'

'You didn't do anything to me.'

'Are you sure?'

'Well, you put your arm around me.'

'And that's all?'

'Colm. You must have dreamt it. Look, I'd better go, I'll take the smallies with me. Cordelia has decided she doesn't like her aunt Marie either, so she's on a work-to-rule. She's got very difficult. Her hormones are at her, I think.'

'You're telling me.'

'She's been strange since her father came to visit. I hope it hasn't dug up too much. Maybe I shouldn't have let her see him. But she said she wanted to and all the books say you should be guided by the child's own wishes . . . I'm uneasy though. Anyhow, I'd better run.'

Janet gave him a peck on the cheek, and was gone.

So, I imagined it all. I didn't try to jump her bones.

He was vaguely disappointed by that and decided on another half an hour under the duvet.

About ten minutes after Janet left, Cordelia came in and sat at the end of the bed.

'Hi,' she said.

She looked somehow different than usual. She wasn't wearing the jingle bell skirt, she had on one of those short minis popularised by gurrrl bands.

'Hello,' he said cautiously.

'How are you?'

She wants some money. She should know that Colm

was not a source of money. Well, pennies maybe. Not serious dough. Janet, der Kommandant, had all the serious dough.

'I'm fine,' said Colm.

'It's a lovely day.'

Small talk!

'Taste this,' Cordelia offered him a peach.

'Do I dare?'

She's probably poisoned it.

'Does it taste funny?'

Colm bit into the peach flesh, and chewed it carefully. The interior of his mouth was less rancid now, after the breakfast, and the peach did taste odd. Dry. Not pleasant.

'Yeah, it tastes funny.'

'How funny?'

'I'm not very good at describing tastes.'

'Does it taste fishy?'

'Yeah. That's it. There's a mackerel taste. Or is it socks?'

'I think they're putting fish genes in the peaches to stop them going off.'

'That's ridiculous.'

'It's February. Peaches are out of season,' said Cordelia, her face concentrated and serious.

'Not in the southern hemisphere,' said Colm brightly.

'I read about it in *New Scientist*. They're putting fish genes in vegetables.'

'To render them capable of swimming?'

'I'm serious,' said Cordelia. A flash of annoyance.

I never doubted your seriousness.

'So, what are you going to do today?' asked the teenager.

'Eh, I dunno. I'll see. I've a few things to check out. What are you going to do today?' replied Colm cordially.

'I'm going to call for my friend Phaedra, and we might go into town and hang round Temple Bar.'

The tragic heroines go to town. Were they best friends because they both had terrible names?'

'Go over there to my jacket and bring it to me.'

Cordelia fetched the jacket and brought it over. Colm opened his wallet and looked in. After a night out with David he usually had money left, because David generally covered everything. Colm's pride used to act up and insist on his share, but he had given that up in the face of David's overwhelming insistence and overwhelming wealth and his own increasingly underwhelming pride. He pulled out a tenner from the wallet.

'Here, teenager. Buy an ecstasy tab on me.'

Cordelia took the tenner and gave him an alarming smile.

'Thanks. I'll buy a CD or something,' and with a cheery 'bye bye', she left the room.

'Bye 'Delia,' said Colm.

How strangely mellow. If this continued it would be great. It would be one of his problems solved.

Gossip

Gossip *gos'ip n.* one who goes about telling and hearing news, or idle, malicious and scandalous tales; idle talk; tittle tattle; scandalous rumours; easy familiar writing. *v.* to run about spreading idle tales.

Colm closed the dictionary.

This is what I am. This is a description of me. I run about spreading tittle tattle. Except run is not entirely accurate. It suggests a dynamism which is absent from my activities.

Thursday at two o'clock was the point in the week when Colm sat down at his desk and wrote his column. During the week he generally collected his titbits and made a few notes on bar mats and bus tickets, and on Thursday he sat down and collated the stuff. He went through his pockets and produced his variegated research documents. Some of the notes were a complete surprise to him, as they were frequently written while pissed. Some he couldn't decipher at all. This week was a little on the quiet side. He phoned Luke Mays.

'Luke, howdy dude. What's going on?'

Why do I sound like an American when I talk to Luke? Luke was a hyperactive freelance publicity director. He and Colm had an excellent system going. Luke bought Colm pints of beer and Colm from time to time plugged Luke's events in *Mary Jane on the Tiles*. Luke had had a book launch on Tuesday and an album launch on Wednesday.

'Colm, Colm. My darling. Am I *glad* to hear from you?'

As camp as bejaysus.

'Could you please do something for me and I'll love you for ever. I have this author who is positively *repulsive* to publicity. She sort of deflects it. She is so boring that there is nothing to say about her. She's middle-class, middle-aged and middle-sized. She's just middling. To begin with I thought she was a dark horse, being evasive. You know me, I have great faith in humanity and couldn't believe anybody's life could be quite so dull. And besides, the novel is filthy. But I was wrong. However, her publisher is my major client with the major chequebook, so I'm stuck. And she can't talk. I tried her out on some local radio gigs, and honestly, I've never heard anything like the silence. I'm not letting her near the national airwaves but if you could put something in, I would appreciate it for ever and ever.'

The surprising thing about Luke was that despite the many fivers that had been put on it over the years, he wasn't gay. He was married with two or three kids. Totally camp, but totally straight. Colm knew this because Colm knew everything.

'I'll fax you over some stuff.'

Twenty minutes later the fax arrived. It was full of lies, Colm knew. There was no way the Spice Girls had been at the launch. And Arnold Schwarzenegger had been in town this week to promote his restaurant, but it was a bit far-fetched to suggest he'd been in Moochies nite club with the boring author crowd.

But truth was a low priority. Normal rules did not apply. His column was sub-moral.

Your diarist was at the launch of self-deprecating writer **Rosemary Hegarty**, author of brand new cracking thriller *Fingerprints*, on Tuesday. I was there admiring her dishy husband, when who should block the sunshine from the windows only the muscle-bound figure of . . .

40

Thursday afternoon was the only bit of discipline in Colm's life. He sat down at two o'clock and got up at five, having efficiently executed the writing part of his weekly employment. He enjoyed doing this immensely, and hated it at the same time. The most complex feelings of self-disgust and humiliated pride gave rise to amazing banalities on the page. It was surreal, the torture inside his mind, and the drivel it produced. When he sat down he made the imaginative leap to become Mary Jane, his nightclub party schmoozer, this lady party animal. He pictured her fully in his mind, the hair, the clothes, the heels. The imaginative act was so intense he could feel the Lycra, smell the nail polish, suffer the cut of the underwired bra.

He hated turning the computer on, yet he felt privileged to be able to make a living like this. In these few hours. Why couldn't he put the rest of his time to profitable use? Well, he had to take into account the whole picture. The writing only took one afternoon, but the research required him to be out in bars talking to people all week. In fact, if he counted up the hours, it probably took him more than the average nine-to-five job. Especially if you reckoned in the time spent recovering from hangovers. And the hangovers were a necessary part of the business. Everybody knows that you cannot get somebody to part with really juicy gossip unless they're well oiled with jar. You have to win their trust, you have to ease them from mere chat into proper gossip. You have to stroke them gently until you hear the magic words, 'Well I'm not supposed to tell anyone, but . . .'

Colm shuffled through his stuff, and amongst his bits of paper he found the letter from Sally Carter. Its perfume rose up to confront his nostrils. He'd forgotten all about it. What to do with it? Ignore it probably. Some crazy dame irate about her husband's carry-on. Colm couldn't remember what the original story was.

He looked up his files. He kept all his columns collated

monthly. He had absolutely no idea why he did this, as he thought he put no value on them. But he did value them. Though worthless, they were proof that he made a living as a writer, albeit shovelling away at the bottom of the dung heap, a writer nonetheless. He found the page from January 11th. Yes indeed, here was the story about James Carter.

> **James Carter**, F&P Lager magnate, bought your diarist a drink when buying a round on Tuesday night (No, not a lager. Brandy and port. I'm fond of my curves) and this single girl thought her luck was in. But just when I was going to go and kiss his feet in gratitude, I noticed somebody had got there before me. He was very intimately chatting, let me say canoodling, with leggy **Anita de Brun** of Models Etc fame. Her legs go right up to her ears, so I felt your diarist couldn't compete, as my legs only go up to my . . . ask anybody . . . I may be a dish, but I'm shallow –

No location. It sounded like a story got from David. Most of his nightclub stories were courtesy of David Blake. He crumpled up the letter and tossed it in his wastepaper bin.

But then, with the full flourish of an act of rebellion, he rescued the crumpled paper and smoothed it. He wrote a note to Sally Carter, in a slightly loopier handwriting than normal, inviting her to meet him, and signed it Mary Jane Murphy. No point in putting his own name on it, because it wouldn't mean anything to her. And besides, she mightn't come, and Colm decided he wanted her to come.

Maybe I could have an affair with her. Maybe the wronged Sally Mrs James Carter is looking for consolation. This is the type of opportunity I need to seize, before I get too old to do it. Before I have no hair. All change now. No more Mouse-man.

The Marriage Bed

The bed was huge, seven foot across and seven foot long. You could share this bed with somebody and hardly notice their presence. You could share this bed with someone and be convinced you slept alone. They had bought this very expensive bed in the first crazy flush of the inherited money. The ceiling in their bedroom was panelled in pine, so he often stared at it and made patterns out of the knots in the wood. He had been trying unsuccessfully to masturbate. Things were getting rough in that department. It was becoming increasingly difficult. He was running out of jizz. When he was young, and suffering the effects of religious terrorism, he had been convinced that he'd go blind/lose his hand/rot in hell as a consequence of this activity. When he was sixteen he did once pull something in his shoulder during a particularly energetic bout. His mother had taken him to the doctor who ominously diagnosed 'repetitive strain injury'. Colm pleaded too much arm wrestling with David, but was convinced that the 'repetitive strain injury' diagnosis was a codeword understood by doctors and mothers for the m verb. The box of Kleenex was removed from his room.

The last time he had had sexual intercourse with Janet was over six and a half years ago, when she was pregnant with June. In the intervening period he had not had sexual intercourse with anybody. He had whacked off an average of three times a week since then, hangovers and privacy allowing. That meant that he had whacked off approximately one thousand and fourteen times. Was it any wonder he was now running out of go?

The reason Janet would no longer sleep with him was because he refused to have a vasectomy. Janet had a terrible time with June. All three of her pregnancies had been difficult in one way or another, but June was particularly bad. Janet's blood pressure skyrocketed and she was rushed into hospital for an emergency caesarean. Colm had to watch the whole procedure, which he reckoned was almost as bad as undergoing it. Both baby and mother had been very weak for a number of months, and Janet came out of the experience thundering 'never again'.

Colm tiptoed round Janet and the baby for a while. Both were making a good recovery, and when things seemed back to normal he tapped Janet on the shoulder and suggested they try going back to lovemaking. That was when Janet suggested the vasectomy. She said she didn't trust any contraceptive – she'd been on the pill when she conceived Cordelia, and they'd been using condoms when she conceived John. She was contraceptive-resistant, a statistical aberration. She couldn't face the prospect of another pregnancy. Colm said he'd think about it.

And he thought about it. And he couldn't do it. It wasn't that he wanted more children, that wasn't the case at all at all. He was delighted with little John, now a toddler, and baby June was the most beautiful creature he had ever seen. And between the two of them and the then eight-year-old Cordelia, he felt their hands were full.

But he didn't want a snip job. And he didn't know why he didn't want it. Janet was furious. She had expected him to acquiesce immediately.

It wasn't more children he wanted. It was the *potential* to have more children. He felt his poor body was enhanced, made magical by this potential. This potential was the root which anchored him to the earth. If he wasn't fertile, where was the buzz? Where was the danger? Where was his link in the chain of regeneration?

'Well if you won't have it done, there'll be no more sex until I'm post-menopausal.'

He suggested that *she* have a procedure done, have her tubes tied or something, and was immediately sorry he opened his gob when her face turned grey with anger. She quietly and quite reasonably pointed out that she had had three children, two of them his. Also, some kidney trouble in her early twenties had necessitated invasive procedures, on top of a burst appendix when she was a teenager, all of which left her abdomen riddled with scar tissue, a veritable war zone. And now he wanted her to undergo further surgery in order to facilitate his desire to resume sex, when he wouldn't have a job done himself.

'Maybe if something came along you could have an abortion.'

He was even sorrier he made this suggestion.

'I don't want that word mentioned ever. I had far too many people trying to persuade me to abort Cordelia, including her recently resurfaced father and both her maternal grandparents, for me to be civil on the subject.'

Poor Cordelia. Alienating people even then.

Colm let the subject drop for a while, and thought he would bring it up again at a later time when Janet was less post-natal. But she never relented and he occasionally thought about having the vasectomy. He mysteriously found a booklet in his desk drawer on the subject called *Still a Man*, women's lib propaganda.

Had Janet put it there, or had he picked it up somewhere while pissed and forgotten about it?

But he still couldn't persuade himself to do it. He waited for a while, and thought that Janet's libido would return and that would make her change her mind. But her libido seemed departed for ever. Nothing like a woman who's had her fill of babies to lose interest in sex. She seemed to be quite happy to do without it. She took up yoga. He'd tried to interest her in other, non-intercoursal forms of sex (blow-jobs), but she was so half-hearted it gave him the droop. And about once a year he reconsidered having the operation done, but always decided against it. So that was why he had masturbated one thousand and fourteen times. It was likely that Janet wouldn't be post-menopausal for another ten years, so that would mean at least another thousand jerk-offs, assuming he didn't slow down too much with age. Ten years wasn't too bad for his next shag. He'd already done six. He could hold out.

It was so long now since he'd had sex, he had even forgotten the memory of it. He often promised himself that he should have an affair. One of David's waitresses or something. Some tacky arrangement involving seedy bed-sits and stained wallpaper. But even if he found a willing lady, he wasn't sure he would be able to do it. Colm was not one of nature's adulterers.

It was after these heavy vasectomy discussions that the no-penis dreams started to happen. And he had started to put on weight. Possibly a natural occurrence as his thirties advanced, but he put it down to the no-sex factor. He was comfort eating. He got his sensual pleasures from biccies and chip butties and jam doughnuts. And pints of Guinness and cigarettes. But he was tired of this.

I am in my prime, well, probably just over it. Mature prime, like cheese. I will have sex. Even just once more before I die.

A Walk in the Park

Colm went in the front door of the Herbert Hotel and immediately knew that the woman in the yellow suit sitting perched on the edge of a sofa in the foyer was his appointment. She looked like she was going to a wedding, smart suit, little hat, gloves, very high heels. And the yellow suit positively glowed. Colm felt inclined to put on his sunglasses. He got closer to her and could see that the curled long blonde hair was immaculately kept. She was a beauty, birdlike, pointy. Tell-tale shoulder pads: a beauty formed and crystallised circa 1984, the year of her marriage. Now in her late thirties, and not moving with the times. He approached her.

'Sally Carter?'

She turned to him and suddenly smiled, like somebody had flicked a switch.

'That's me,' she said.

She reminded him of someone. He couldn't place it. But she was the absolute spit of someone he knew quite well. Was it someone from the telly?

'Hello, I'm Mary Jane Murphy,' said Colm.

Sally Carter looked at him, took in the crumpled clothes, the droopy aspect.

'But I was expecting a lady,' she said.

'I know, but I write the column. I just write it in a lady's voice.'

'Oh. I didn't know.' She looked quite put out. 'I suppose that's the kind of thing that everybody knows except me.'

She sighed, and her posture collapsed a little.

47

It suddenly dawned on Colm who she reminded him of. She looked like one of Charlie's Angels. The small one with the long blonde hair.

'Anyhow, I'd like to talk to you in any case, if that's all right. Shall we go and stroll around the park?'

Colm nodded, and Sally Carter got to her feet.

'Can you walk all right in those?'

She smiled at him. 'I've worn high heels all my life, and I get calf muscle strain if I wear anything else. I even have a pair of high heels to do the gardening in. Bondage to fashion is a thorough matter.'

She's already talking about bondage! A good sign.

They made their way into Herbert Park, which was almost deserted in the afternoon, just a few stray flashers and the odd unemployed youth whiling away the time. The pond was busy with ducks. There were six males in pursuit of a rather small but obviously fetching (if you were a duck) little brown female, who was doing her best to escape. It was now early March. Young male ducks' thoughts turn to gang rape.

The sun came out from behind a cloud, and the yellow suit became a bit much. It sort of vibrated in the sun. Colm put on his Calvin Klein glasses. They were ordinary sunglasses that should've cost eight pounds but cost seventy pounds more because there was a CK on the top of the right lens. Janet had got them for him in the duty free on the way back from a school trip to France. Sally looked at the glasses approvingly. A diamond on a dungheap.

'Thank you for meeting me,' said Sally. 'I know you're probably very busy, and I appreciate that.'

'No not at all. I'm never busy.'

Stupid thing to say.

'I can't believe that,' she smiled. 'I'm sorry if I sound a bit flustered but I was expecting a lady, and I find it easier to talk about intimate matters with another woman. I

48

think women understand women better than men. Don't you?'

'I wouldn't generalise, but if you—'

'– and it is so hard not to think of men as the enemy as they always stick together. Sorry, I'm rambling now.'

'Don't worry, of course it's a bit of a surprise that I'm a man. Even I'm surprised sometimes, ha ha.'

A little joke to soften things up.

'The thing is, I wanted to ask her, I mean ask you, about the piece regarding my husband and Anita de Brun. I challenged him about it and he said he was in Cody's nightclub with Anita, but that it was totally innocent. Which it could have been. But my woman's intuition tells me that it wasn't and it's not.'

They were strolling along the path by the duckpond. She stopped and cast the most appealing big eyes at him.

'I got married fifteen years ago and we've had two kids. Things were fine for the first few years, but frankly, they got dull. And now, we haven't been intimate with each other for two years—'

You too, huh?

'—which led me to the conclusion he was having an affair. I had no proof, but I was almost sure. Hunches, intuitions.'

The little brown duck splattered into the water quite near them, the bucks in pursuit.

'Is there a possibility that it could have been innocent, that he could've been just chatting to Anita?'

Colm was suddenly a little uncomfortable. The simple answer was that he had no idea, as he hadn't witnessed the event in the first place.

'Were they, like, intimate?' She took out a frayed copy of the little article. 'What exactly does "canoodling" mean? Is there such a thing as innocent canoodling? Were they holding hands? Were they chewing each other's faces

49

off? Did she have her hands down the front of his trousers? Were they having intercourse on the carpet?'

Her voice displayed a touch of hysteria and she was pulling a scarf between her fingers with inordinate gusto, her knuckles pure white.

'I'm not sure,' said Colm.

'Well what, precisely, did you see?'

Colm decided the best course of action was vagueness.

'I am a gossip columnist, Mrs Carter.'

A little formality here – might calm her.

'The very essence of gossip is ambiguity. I rarely write about things that are a matter of established fact. The substance of what I write is speculative. If gossip were hard, cold, photocopiable fact, then it wouldn't be gossip.'

'She's my bloody sister,' blurted Sally Carter. 'Anita de Brun is my sister. Her name is Brown, as was my maiden name. But a plain name like Brown doesn't do for a modelling career. Oh no. And now, not content with being successful and beautiful, and driving a Seven Series BMW, she needs to pinch my husband on me.'

If I'd known that he was canoodling with his wife's sister, it would have been a much better bit of gossip.

'Well,' said Colm, 'I wasn't aware of that. The intimacy could well have been the intimacy of a brother and sister-in-law. Different types of intimacy can be very confusing.'

'Tell me what exactly they were doing.'

Her suit was just a tiny bit too tight across her chest, causing a slight stress in the material, and from this angle there was a gap revealing a white lace camisole.

'To be honest, I can't one hundred per cent remember.'

'Was he making the moves, or was she? I bet you it was her.'

'We-ell.'

'Always got what she wanted. Because she was the youngest and the prettiest, she was the pet, and everything

50

she pointed at was given to her. Very bad character training.'
Her eyes narrowed and her soft features became fierce.

*And then the top button of the suit opened and there
nestled a cute white breast in a bed of lace. Not big, not
small. About the right size. About a handful.*

'She just looks at the world like that, as though it were a
box of chocolates, and she chooses and scoffs her
favourites, leaving the dross for everybody else.'

Splash!

Colm hadn't been looking where he was going and fell
arse over snozz into the duckpond. His right leg stepped
and landed firstly on air, and then water, and then he
completely overbalanced and fell head first into the water,
giving his crotch a nasty crack when it came into contact
with the hard edge of the pond. The pain of the bang on
his crotch made him open his mouth and yell 'ow', and in
came copious amounts of duckpond water. The water was
deeper than expected, about five feet. He hit the bottom
gently and clambered back into an upright position,
coughing and spluttering. He hopped out of the pond,
trailing green fronds and slime but, oddly, still sporting the
CK sunglasses which had stuck to his face throughout the
immersion.

Sally was standing there, resplendent in yellow, looking
horrified. And then she started to giggle.

'Oh I'm so sorry, I shouldn't be laughing.'

Colm too started to laugh.

'I'm so sorry,' said Sally. 'I was just about to warn you
to stop walking on the edge there. I had just noticed how
close you were to the water.'

Colm laughed to hide his embarrassment. The laugh got
louder and louder. But then the pain in his crotch set in
and he doubled over.

'Oh dear,' said Sally. 'You'll get your death. It's pretty
chilly.'

Colm rolled around the path in agony.

'What is it?' asked Sally.

'I banged my you-know-whats as I fell.' He couldn't bring himself to say balls.

'You banged your what?'

'My balls. I banged my crotch as I fell in. It's agony.'

'Would you like me to take a look?'

'What!'

'It's all right. I used to be a nurse, before I threw myself away on that bastard. I'm familiar with bodily parts. There's nothing I haven't seen.'

Colm was in too much pain to get excited about her being a nurse.

'Eh, no,' he answered.

'Come with me. My car is parked nearby. I'll run you home, so you don't catch your death of cold.'

She bundled him along the path.

'I'm so sorry this happened. I feel very bad about it. If I hadn't asked you to come and meet me, you would never have fallen into the duckpond.'

He started to shiver now. It was very cold. The early March sunshine made the world look warmer than it actually was. They got to a big silver Audi and she deactivated the alarm. She ushered him into the passenger seat, went to the boot and took out a tartan picnic rug and put it around his body. She then got into the driving seat and turned on the car heating system to full blast. Torrents of warm air swirled around, but Colm kept shivering. His teeth were chattering now.

Sally drove off at speed, ignoring other traffic and mere by-laws. They nearly collided with several citizens. She was a terrible driver, who wrote off a car once every twelve months. It looked like she had never learned to drive, simply one day sat in and pressed the accelerator. Didn't look to left or right once, sailed on trusting in other drivers not to bang into her and on airbags in her expensive huge car to provide that significant gap between her and mortality.

'Will there be somebody at home?' asked Sally.

'I think my wife'll be there. She's a schoolteacher, but she has the day off.'

'What you need to do when you get in is run a hot bath, not scalding. Have a quick bath to get rid of the pond water. Then go to bed with your wife, close together like spoons and roll up in the duvet. The best way to recover body heat is to take it from another body.'

'O-o-o-o K-k-k-k,' his teeth chattered.

They pulled up outside his house. He got out of the car and came round to her window.

'I'll make enquiries,' he said. 'I'll find out exactly what was or is going on with your husband.'

She wrote a number on a piece of paper and pressed it into his hand, the touch of her skin alarmingly intimate.

'I've a new phone. A mobile,' and she closed his hand around the paper.

And he ran into the house, entertaining little hope of the spoons idea with Janet.

Janet was feeling particularly soft-hearted, so she ran a bath for him and put in lots of stuff to make a bubbly lather and stayed with him while he steamed.

'I don't know how it happened. I wasn't looking where I was going and suddenly, I was in the duckpond. Head first.'

Janet's earnest face wore an expression of pure concern.

'You poor thing. It must have been terrible. The water is probably filthy. Water rats live in duckponds.'

'Do they?'

'Water rats pee in duckponds. Marian Jones, the Maths teacher, her son fell into the Liffey and caught Weil's disease. He must have swallowed some fresh rat pee.'

Colm was enjoying the unbridled sympathy. He didn't often get it.

'I was just walking along. I was probably too close to the edge.'

I find myself drawn to the edge of things, desiring to peer over.

When he was a youngster, he couldn't be got down from walking on walls. He remembered putting his mother into a right lather when he hopped up on the railway bridge wall near where he grew up and insisted on walking along it. It was his first remembered act of boldness.

'I like balancing and unconsciously seek opportunities to be at the edge. I am a closet thrillseeker.' He smiled hopelessly at his wife.

I am Mouse-man.

Janet soaped his back, and then his chest. His hairy chest which she used to express a fondness for.

'I inexorably walk at the edge of things.'

She started to shampoo his hair. 'You poor thing,' she said with creeping earnestness.

Don't you find it the tiniest bit funny?

But it was nice to feel her hands on his flesh, the fingers deft with tenderness.

'I hit myself rather badly, in the crotch. Would you like to look at it?'

I'm pushing it here.

He towelled himself dry and lay spread-eagled on the bed.

'Down there, in my pelvic floor area.'

She gently lifted his tackle, and inspected the damage.

'That looks terrible,' she said. 'It's a huge purple bruise. You're lucky it's so low down because if you'd banged yourself a little higher you might have done serious damage to your testicles.'

You wish.

She went off to the bathroom cabinet and returned with some balm. She approached him and went to apply it and was greeted with an enthusiastic erection. An optimistic erection. A desperate erection. A terrible erection.

She ignored it.

Janet applied the balm, which was indeed very soothing. He stared at her, his eyes pleading.

'How're your stools?' she asked, changing the subject which had and hadn't been raised.

'Much better.'

'It's amazing what a small change in diet will do to improve them. That small amount of bran and fibre.'

'My turds are so perfect I'm thinking of exhibiting them.'

No smile.

His erection waned. It was sensitive to subject matter. Janet went out to the hot press and returned with a pair of warmed pyjamas which she threw sharply at him. Colm watched her move around the room, her rounded form dressed dully in a sombre skirt and cardigan, her relationship with gravity a distinctive element. Janet was earthbound, rooted. Colm looked at her coolly.

What is it? There must have been a magic sometime. There must have been some sense of delight at some stage, now gone, not even leaving a ghost.

Her forehead puckered. It was a habit of hers before she tackled any difficult subject.

'I'm worried about Cordelia,' she said. 'Have you ever heard of a book by Valerie Solanis called the *Scum Manifesto*?'

'Yeah. It's some sixties thing. Valerie Solanis was famous for taking a pot shot at Andy Warhol. And she wrote some thing about men being deformed eggs. Some daft screed. She was certifiable.'

'Well, Cordelia has twenty copies of it under her bed.'

'Signifying?'

'I dunno. I just worry about her. I think meeting her

father was a bit of a shock. While he remained a mystery she could always pretend he was great.'

He was a bit of a deformed egg all right.

'She's a teenager. She's supposed to be weird. I remember my mother finding copies of porn mags under my bed and calling the priest to come and perform an exorcism. And I grew up perfectly normal.'

Debatable point.

'She just doesn't look happy. The bounce has gone out of her. Even her hair has gone limp.'

'Don't worry. She's fine. She is, in fact, remarkably stable. She's not even smoking fags or taking drugs. She'll be grand.'

'Hmmn.'

Janet fussed around the room a bit longer.

'I've done the application. I spent most of the day at it. I'm bringing it in tomorrow.'

'Do you want me to throw an eye over it?'

'Probably no need.'

Cutting. There was a time . . .

'I know it's a long shot, I'm the youngest by far of the internal candidates but you'd never know. And being a woman should help. Everybody says that they're trying to increase the number of women principals,' said Janet, battling with her self-deprecating nature.

My wife is going to be a headmistress. Now there's something to get excited about.

Janet went off to do the things that she did to the house. Whenever she had a day off, she spent much of the day spring cleaning. Her standards of domestic maintenance were impossibly high. Everything was always shining and sparkling in an orgy of cleanliness. It was like living in a shop window. Except Colm's study. It was allowed to retain his slob imprint. He was allowed to be happy in his dog basket. He put on his dressing gown and shuffled in there for some comfort.

His study was at the back of the house and overlooked the garden and the mews development that was being built along the back lane behind the houses. He and Janet had recently flogged a tiny portion of the end of the garden to the mews developer and made a stack of dough, which Janet had taken and sensibly spent on the roof and gutters and external woodwork. Every square inch of the inner suburbs was being developed. Colm expected to come out some day and find a duplex perched on the traffic island.

He sat down on his new chair. Der Kommandant had bought him a new chair for his back at a sale of used office furniture. It was a great padded leather thing, with adaptable back support and air-action adjustable height. It swivelled for easy reaching, and had a lever to tilt backwards for relief of back strain. It was the most comfortable chair he had ever sat in. At last, something that was healthy that didn't cause pain. He snuggled into it and immediately dozed off.

When he awoke, about half an hour later, he felt wonderfully relaxed. He decided to try and write. He leant down to his bottom drawer and took out a sheaf of papers. It was a selection of the various first chapters he had started over the years in his attempt to write a novel. Each chapter neatly stapled, the first page of each topped with the optimistic *Chapter One*. He had twenty first chapters. Quite a wadge.

What a waste. If I'd only kept to the same theme, and kept the chapters following one another, there'd be a book there. There was enough physical writing to be a book. But it wasn't a book. It was a collection of twenty first chapters of twenty books.

He contemplated for a moment stringing the various chapters together by writing linking bits. An experimental work, in the mode of eh, neo-Dadaism. A book that made no sense whatsoever. It would be a masterpiece. But then he decided against it. It wouldn't work. He would have to start again from scratch. Seizing his courage in one hand, and the manuscripts in the other, he threw the pile of twenty chapters into the bin. He felt a lot better after that. He felt purged. One of his problems was that he couldn't let things go. He turned on his computer. *Chapter One*, he typed.

And then he went into a trance, and typed madly for four hours. He was gripped by a fever of self-expression. He couldn't get the words down fast enough. They tumbled out, one after another. He felt he was truly on to something. He wrote about a woman in a yellow suit whose husband was having an affair with her sister. A woman scorned. Carla. She had long yellow hair and very high heels. He was content for the first time in ages. He was so happy when he wrote. He loved it.

When the energy burst subsided, he instructed the computer to print and went downstairs to put on the kettle. He *was* a writer. He was a misfit. He enjoyed and indulged his observation of others. He had very few friends. He drank too much and was deeply unhappy. He had been reared by distant and oppressive parents. He had all the writerly attributes except the actual writing. But that was all going to change now. He made himself a mug of tea and went back upstairs.

When he came back into the study with his mug, he decided he'd been too rash and retrieved the twenty aborted chapters from the waste bin and replaced them in the bottom drawer of the desk. They were doing no harm there, nesting quietly.

He took the crisp new pages from the printer and arranged them in the right order. He slurped his tea, and started to read. But the prose was dull. The subject which had fired him so recently had become boring. The main character Carla wasn't credible. It wasn't working. It would never work. He got up from the black leather chair and walked around the study, in the hope that things might seem better when he stood up, but they didn't. He took the new sheaf of paper, eight pages in all, the first page neatly and optimistically headed *Chapter One*, and placed it in the drawer along with the twenty others. Twenty-one now.

Scouting

'I've met his wife. She contacted me and asked me to find out,' said Colm by way of explanation.

'Oh,' said David. 'As far as I know he is a major player. Has always been a bit of a ladies' man. The thing with Anita de Brun is fairly recent, I think. We'll ask Statia. She knows all the gossip.'

'You know Anita de Brun is his sister-in-law?'

'No, I didn't know that. Are you serious? That's gas.'

'His wife's sister.'

'Go 'way.'

'Yup.'

'I can see why she's boilin' so. A husband having an affair with a model is one thing, common as muck really, but when the model in question is your own sister, it's entirely another.'

They decided to go on a nightclub trawl to see if they could run the erring husband to ground.

'How's Catherine?' asked Colm.

'Not so good. I broke it to her about Adèle and Jason. Well, she found out about them. I should've got around to telling her, but I just hadn't. She knew about my first marriage, and about Ken and David, obviously. But I had neglected to tell her about the other kids, and she was horrified. Some busybody informed her. She told me she didn't want to see me for two weeks in order to figure out what she thought about the whole thing. So I'm a bit down in the dumps.'

'She was bound to find out. This country is too small to

60

keep anything quiet. This town is too small. To be an effective adulterer, you have to live in London at least, or preferably New York.'

'I was going to tell her, but I was waiting until I was ready. Bastard busybodies. Damn gossips.'

'Careful David.' Colm gave him a sharp look.

'That's entirely different. It's your income. You're a professional bastard busybody. I don't mind that. There's some purpose to it. I have a problem with people who spread tales idly, just for fun.'

Colm didn't bother arguing with David on this. He was completely inconsistent. Also, Colm agreed with him. He too thought gossiping was a pretty low-down thing to do. It was the lowest of the low.

I am the lowest of the lowest of the low. I hate myself. I enjoy hating myself.

The Candelabra, David's nightclub and one of Dublin's hottest nite-spots, was situated down a mews lane near Stephen's Green. By the time Colm and David got there it was packed, full of people wearing almost no clothes and engaging in mating rituals. The club catered for a mature clientèle. No teenyboppers on e. Folks who were way up the salary scale and whose main line was expensive champagne.

David took Colm to an office at the back of the building and poured him some champagne. They had trawled a number of places and not found James Carter. This place was a last resort. Colm gulped down his bubbly. He loved a good champagne. Thought it was the nicest drink on earth.

'There's something I've been meaning to discuss with you, David. It's very personal.'

'Shoot, buddy.'

'It's Janet. She's stopped sleeping with me.'

'Oh.'

'She's afraid she'll get pregnant again.'

'Oh.'

'So I'm a bit, eh, frustrated.'

'Oh dear, yes, I can see why. How long has this been going on?'

'Six years.'

'What? This has been going on for six years! How have you stood it? How come you haven't told me before now?'

'I wasn't ready to talk about it.'

'How can you stand it?'

'I wank.'

'Jesus, pal, you're in a bad situation.'

'What can I do?'

'I dunno. Can't you make her?' said David.

'Marital rape has been criminalised. If she ain't willing there's nothing I can do.'

'I didn't mean that. I meant persuade. Hold back the housekeeping money or something.'

'She earns more than I do.'

'Threaten to leave.'

'I don't think she'd be bothered.'

'Well, why don't you have an affair?'

'I've decided that's the best thing to do. I've decided it's the only solution.'

'It's taken you six years to figure that out?'

'Yeah. I want to have an affair with Sally Carter.'

'Attaboy. Attaboy.'

'I feel we have a lot in common.'

'It's great you've found someone you find attractive.'

'She is very nice looking, but I don't know if I'm attracted to her or not. I find it very hard these days to know what I think, what I feel.'

'Well, does she arouse you?'

'Yeah, but that's no big deal. The mad lady next door arouses me. You arouse me, David. A dog on the street with a certain strut to its hind quarters will arouse me. I'm hardly a challenge.'

The phone rang. It was Statia reporting the arrival of James Carter and his recent ensconcement in the Drawing Room. Colm went down on his own. James Carter knew David, and he would probably talk to him, and David would have to introduce Colm, which would undermine the anonymity of the situation. The Drawing Room was an exclusive part of the club at the rear. Entry to this room required a membership card which cost a lot of money. Or, if the management liked you, thought you were an opinion former, a mover and shaker, thought you were a honeypot who would attract a buzz, it gave you one for free. Everything has its price. Colm got himself a pint of beer and sat down on the sofa directly across from James Carter. He got a newspaper from the stand in the corner of the room, and ostensibly busied himself.

Carter was a prosperous-looking man, well covered in flesh, wearing a pale-coloured suit which betokened a solid acquaintance with quality dry cleaning. He was around the forty mark, with slightly amusing shoulder-length black hair and a nervous gargoyle-like grin. He seemed agitated, kept shifting around in his seat. One of the floor staff brought him a bottle of champagne and an ice bucket and he ostentatiously gave her fifty pounds and told her to keep the change.

That must be a huge tip. Well maybe not, the champagne in here is probably forty-nine pounds.

Colm continued to pretend to read his newspaper and surreptitiously surveyed Carter, whose agitation seemed to be mounting. Colm was enjoying himself. Part of him had always wanted to be a private eye, but there hadn't been any openings in that area when he was searching for a life occupation. This wasn't a bad second-best. He adjusted his newspaper for a better view. Carter didn't look happy. He called the lounge girl over and had a drink sent to a couple in the corner, who turned around and waved a thank-you to him. He was like an ugly ill-fitting boy in the playground buying friendship with sweets. Colm felt a blast of pity for him. He was a sucker for underdogs. Crawlers. His fellow creatures at the bottom of the evolutionary swamp.

Carter was alone for a further ten minutes and was then joined by a woman. One glance told Colm it was Anita de Brun. She looked very like Sally Carter, but as if Sally had been placed on a rack and stretched, lengthening her legs and neck, thinning out her midriff significantly and obliterating her boobs. Much less attractive, in Colm's opinion. Sally had an endearingly human quality. Whereas this girl looked grotesque. And she looked like she was badly in need of some grub. Carter poured her some champagne.

Colm strained his ears to hear. He had excellent hearing. It was one of his physical attributes, he could hear conversations from across the room. His eardrums had a very fine tuning mechanism. It was an attribute that he had been conscious of from a very young age, when he would hear the bus coming much sooner than any of his pals. He had always wondered to what use he might put this skill. When he did his interview with the career guidance teacher at his posh school, Miss Moon, and she asked him to list his talents and attributes, he put 'good hearing' right at the top of the list. Miss Moon thought it was a skill that was vocationally inapplicable. She was wrong. Being able to listen to other people's conversations was a distinct advantage for a gossip mongrel. It was a writerly attribute too. Another one of those writerly attributes.

Having said all that, Colm couldn't quite make out James Carter and Anita de Brun's conversation, as they were speaking in exceptionally low tones. He noticed that Carter's body language had settled down, he was a lot less agitated. It was very hard to read the situation. They were canoodling all right, but they could have been talking about anything. It could be totally innocent. They could be

64

planning a surprise party for Sally. They could be planning a murder.

They could be planning a murder!

Then he knew his sleuthing was getting the better of him. His imagination was in runaway mode. Too many *noir* movies at an impressionable age. The broad passed Carter her purse, and he got up and went in the direction of the bathroom. She looked around the room eyeballing everybody. A tough looking dame all right. Colm dived back behind his newspaper.

Carter came back from the gents looking a bit more relaxed. It was that bright, unmistakable, chemical-induced relaxedness.

She's a coke dealer?

The two of them got up and left. Colm followed. Momentarily he felt a twinge of guilt about not telling David he was off, but the story had him. His blood was up, he had to follow. He even left half of his pint behind. Out on the street, Carter and Anita hailed a taxi. Colm hailed one too.

'Follow that cab,' he said. He had always wanted to do that.

'Howya boss,' said the taxi driver.

'Howya,' answered Colm, not knowing if he knew the taxi driver or not.

'Remember me?' said the taxi driver. 'Bob's the name. I brought ya home about a week ago. To Candlewick Avenue.'

This would never happen in New York. You probably have a better chance of being shot by a terrorist than of getting the same cab twice in one week.

'Oh, right, I remember now.'

'How did you get on?'

'What?'

'You were saying the wife wouldn't sleep with you, and you were going in to give her a bit of persuasion.'

Oh no. Colm had blabbered to the taxi man. He was getting careless with his tongue, starting to share his gossip. Telling your intimate secrets to someone in possession of a CB radio was a bad idea.

Obviously, having broken his six-year silence on the matter, he was quite happy to talk to complete strangers about it.

'No go,' said Colm.

'My wife wouldn't sleep with me for a while,' said Bob. 'There's no accounting for the peculiarities of women.'

The traffic light in front of them turned red, and Colm's taxi stopped as the one in front just slipped through.

'Hey, they're getting away.'

'S'all right. The cab in front is from my base. I'll phone the base and find out where it went. I know them. She's that model who's sometimes on the telly, and he lives in Howth. I've often brought him home, half cut. Fond of the booze and the little pills, I think.'

'And the ladies?'

'I don't know. If he is, he's discreet. I've never seen him get a cab with anyone except his wife, the little birdy one who rattles around out there in the big house in Howth.'

Shaking her chains. Rattling her cage. My little canary.

Bob called his base and found out where the cab in front was bound, and he sped off in that direction. They pulled up outside a large Victorian pile standing in its own grounds, on one of the back roads of Blackrock. Colm knew the area well. It was where David had grown up.

'That'll be ten quid,' Bob said cheerfully.

Colm parted with the ten quid.

'And the tip,' added Bob.

Colm pulled out another fiver. He had had good value, in fairness. Bob's qualities were exceptional.

'Give us your card,' said Colm as he was getting out of the car. Bob was useful. Bob could be a source.

'Do you mind me asking,' said Bob, 'are you a private eye?'

Colm was pleased at the question, and his spirit lifted.

'No,' he said, 'I am a writer, and I go chasing stories in the night.'

Peeping Tom

After the taxi drove off, Colm stood under an overhanging bush and smoked a cigarette. The house opposite was a two-storey-over-garden-level semi-mansion, with steps up to a grand front door. There was a light on to the right of the front door, probably the drawing room, and the rest of the house was in darkness. Colm was enjoying himself tremendously. He hadn't known that sleuthing could be such great fun. He heard the sound of heels come clicking along the pavement. A lone female walking about at nearly four a.m.? Unusual. The clicks got closer, and Colm could see a young girl, staggering along the path, very much the worse for drink or drugs or violence or something. Colm gave a start, as momentarily the girl looked like Cordelia. He blinked and refocused. It wasn't the Chopper. The girl suddenly saw him, huddled under the bush with his cigarette, and stopped dead.

Oh dear, she thinks I'm a weirdo.

He stood still and continued to smoke the fag. The girl stood still, alert like an animal under threat, and swayed a little on her hopelessly young and skinny ankles. Her eyes opened large and in the lamplight he could see the youth and the fear. How best to communicate his innocent purpose to her?

Innocent with regard to her, in any case.

He thought it wise to say nothing, as anything he said might be interpreted against him. But she continued to stand stock still. Petrified. He was afraid she was going to

scream and give him away. They were each frightened of
the other. She was frightened of what she perceived to be a
potential threat, he was frightened of her fear. He put his
finger to his lips and made a shushing noise, thinking the
oddness of this might calm her. It didn't. She yelped and
ran back in the direction she came, back towards the drink
or the drugs or the violence. Her heels now made a
ferocious clatter. Colm retreated further under his overhanging bush.

In the old house opposite the woman came to the
window of the drawing room and looked out. From this
distance and in silhouette, Colm could see how thin Anita
de Brun was. She was perhaps the thinnest woman he had
ever seen. Like a pencil. Like a spire of smoke.

He puffed another cigarette under the bush and then
made his way over to the drive of the Victorian house. The
drive was gravel and he had to walk along the verge to
avoid announcing his presence.

*I am a grown man. What am I doing in somebody else's
garden in the middle of the night?*

He crept up the wide front steps and observed that there
was a five-inch-wide ledge running around the house. He
could have manoeuvred himself along it and managed to
peek in the window. He could have if he was twenty years
younger, three stone lighter and didn't have a messed-up
back. Luckily he had the sense not to attempt the feat.
Instead, he leaned out as far as he could towards the
window. He couldn't see anything, because he was at such
an angle, but he could hear. He heard the unmistakable
sound of two people making love. Not one person, the
sound he was more acquainted with. Two. The happy
passionate noise of it. The ancient joy of it. And perched
there, on the edge of the steps, he was the loneliest man on
earth.

He listened, like a thrilled voyeur. He waited, observing
the increasing aural urgency, and experienced some relief

when they came. Not as much as them, obviously. And then they started to talk. They started to gab.

'I'll ask her for a divorce. I promise.'

'You've promised it before.'

'I know. It was too soon. I'm ready now. I think we should keep us secret for quite a while after.'

'I find it so hard to be secret. I find I want to tell the whole world about us. It's been going on too long. I know I'm going to blurt it out some time. I sit down with my girlfriends and they know I'm holding back on something. Even Sally. When I'm with her I suffer an irresistible urge to tell her.'

'Jesus, don't!' A yelp of panic in the voice. 'You know what her temper's like.'

'I'm afraid it's just going to come out. I wanted to tell her at the very beginning. I nearly did at that Christmas party when I'd had a skinful of drink on an empty stomach. But I vomited instead.'

'I'll ask her at the end of April. It's her birthday on April the tenth and it's James Junior's on the twenty-ninth, so I'd better wait until after that.'

'Truth is so important, you know. I can't live without truth.'

'I've a cramp in my leg.'

And then there followed an exchange of quite terrifying pet names. Colm decided to leave. He'd heard enough.

He'd used up all his money on the taxi earlier, so he had no choice but to walk home. From Blackrock to Rathmines. Quite a haul. But he was in the form for it. For the first time in a while he was heading home relatively sober. The drink from earlier on had worn off, but the excitement of his activity had caused him real euphoria, given him a major buzz.

The night was becoming morning, and some early commuters were on the road. Colm looked at them, feeling his difference from them. As he got closer towards town, the commuter activity thickened. People heading into town to do proper jobs. He scorned them and he envied them.

A Little Light Lunch

'Aaaargh! Ah, ah. Ow!'

'That's great. Let it all out,' said Frank Ingoldsby. 'Open your mouth wide and keep your eyes open. You have to open your orifices in order to let the pain out.'

Frank turned Colm over and started a little light massage. Frank's hands were very large and very firm. His bright blue eyes were arresting, almost hypnotic. Colm was suddenly conscious of the intimacy of the situation. He was lying there in his y-fronts being manhandled by an ape-like man.

'You seem a lot better,' said Frank.

'Hnnnng!' replied Colm.

'The back is a lot looser. The knots are still there, but smaller. How's the fitness programme? The walks with the kids and the jogging with the stepkid?'

'I'll be honest with you, Frank, myself and the stepkid aren't a swing. She leaves leaflets around for me with titles like "Salvation through prayer" and "The wages of sin is death". She doesn't like me, thinks I'm a moral cul-de-sac. But I shouldn't be bothering you with all this.'

'Oh, don't worry about bothering me,' said Frank, tossing his locks. 'You know, you'd be surprised what I hear. All my clients tell me their worries. I'm a whole-body kind of health consultant. Often the pain in the back might well be a manifestation of a pain in the heart . . .'

It's all new age hippie stuff now. A person can't have a sore leg, it has to be connected to the fact that they failed their driving test last week, or weren't sufficiently breastfed.

'. . . and I have a fairly glamorous client list. You'd be surprised what I know about the rich and famous.'

'Like what?' asked Colm bluntly.

'Well, I don't tell,' said Frank, surprised at the pushyness of Colm. He hadn't taken him for a ferret.

Colm contemplated Frank, standing tall with his long arms doing their trick, and his long head full of juicy information that would go very nicely in his column. It would save him weeks of work. But you could tell by Frank's features that you would get nothing out of him.

Integrity. Pisses me off, it does.

But Frank liked to tease. He liked people to know he knew things. Dropped heavy hints. He liked to hoard his information in a little pile and think about it privately. He was miserly with gossip.

Colm paid up for his massage and Frank presented him with a yellow card of exercises that he was to do now that the original inflammation had settled down. He looked at the card, and thought the contortions thereon looked superhuman. He nodded pleasantly, 'I can't wait to try these,' and left the building.

Frank's clinic was on a busy street in Ballsbridge, and Colm strolled along, heading for town. It was now only ten a.m. His appointment had been at nine-thirty, and he felt a twang of virtue having the show on the road so early this morning. Usually, he was only turning over under the duvet at this stage, with a view to rising at about ten-thirty. He breathed in deeply. The air was somehow cleaner in the morning, more virtuous. He was used to breathing only afternoon air, which always felt as though it had previously been breathed by someone else.

Colm had a lunch date with David, so he went on into town and spent time wandering around the bookshops, looking at books he hadn't written, and fantasising about somehow finding a pile of his own books on a table. *The Heart's a Wonder* by Colm F. Cantwell. *War and Peace* by Colm F. Cantwell. *The Complete Works of William Shakespeare* by Colm F. Cantwell. 'Twenty novels by Colm F. Cantwell. Buy nineteen, get one free'. Bookshops were friendly places now. You were invited to browse and to peruse a book over your cup of delicious coffee. Not like when he was a kid and was chased out of various bookshops for copping a free read. He had read the work of Arthur Conan Doyle by wandering into the bookshops and doing ten pages at a time before he was chased out by a frosty sales assistant. He ordered a coffee and sat himself down to read *The Hound of the Baskervilles* for old time's sake. Time passed. He killed time.

At one o'clock, Colm went into the appointed restaurant and spied David sitting alone, and to some degree forlorn, in the corner. David had phoned and said he needed help and advice, and here he was, looking very much like he needed help. His forehead was frowning and his hair was harassed. Colm sat down opposite his friend.

At your service.

They ordered their lunch. The restaurant was terrifically expensive, the clientèle were well-to-do-looking. Colm happily gave his scruffy threadbare coat to the head waiter, who had a very grand accent. An aristocrat fallen on hard times.

'Careful with that. It's an heirloom.'

David always liked to spend money when he was under pressure. It was how he let off steam. Some people had a few G and Ts. Some people did the gardening. Some people dressed up in women's clothes. David spent a hundred pounds on a few lettuce leaves.

'I'm being sued,' said David.

Colm raised his eyebrows and inclined his head to one side, making a question mark.

74

'Sexual harassment. I got a solicitor's letter yesterday from Drew Ltd, on behalf of Gemma Blake, one of the waitressing staff in the Harbour, accusing me of sexual harassment in the workplace and informing me that court proceedings are to be initiated.'

'And is there any truth in it?' asked Colm.

'Not a word,' replied David. 'I've never sexually harassed anyone in my life. I know I'm a bit of a ladies' man, but harassment? Never.'

'Well, is there any basis whatsoever to the claim?'

'I made a pass at her, but we were at a party, not in the shop. It wasn't in the workplace. She declined. I might have persisted a little, but when I realised she was serious, I gave up. She's an attractive little package.'

'What exactly did you do?'

'Well, my memory is a little hazy, as we all had a few jars on us, but I think I got down on my knees, licked her thighs and told her she was a rare beauty, which she is, unfortunately. But as soon as I figured she wasn't interested, I stopped.'

'That's harassment,' said Colm.

'I don't see it.'

'Of course it's harassment. If you did it to me, I'd classify it as definite harassment.'

'But you're a man. Of course it'd be harassing if I did it to you. You'd find me repulsive.'

'And you imagine your waitresses don't? This is the flaw in your thinking.'

'God be with the days when a man could make a pass at a woman without the law becoming involved. It's not fair. Lots of women have made a pass at me and I don't go whinging to my lawyer. In fact, several staff members have at various stages made advances, but I simply declined them in an adult fashion, instead of whining on about harassment in the workplace.'

'That's because they have no dough. There is no point in

suing someone who has no dough. You are rich. That is why you are being sued. Thicko. Rich men can't just make passes willy nilly. They must pay for every detail. And above all, rich men must pay for being rich.'

'Principles. Nobody has them any more,' whinged David. 'A thing of the past.'

'Have you seen your lawyer?'

'She's coming round this afternoon. She's a new partner in Moore and Kent, which is now Moore, Kent and Smith. Sylvia Smith. A real stunner. Gorgeous blonde. Doesn't look in the least bit like a lawyer . . .'

David was incorrigible. Completely. Too much dough made the brain go soft. His neanderthal impulses were incurable. He would never enter the twenty-first century. He was a lost man, floating unanchored, not belonging to the here and now, not linked into the *zeitgeist*. He belonged in an eighteenth-century novel packed with buxom barmaids and scheming bored wives of aristocrats. For all his ostensible modernity, his mobile phone and this season's Gucci shoes, he was a throwback.

'And Catherine. If she gets wind of this, I'll be finished utterly. I'm already trying to calm her down about the kids. Apparently, she had just got her very religious mother to accept that she was dating a separated man who has two teenage children, and doesn't think she'll ever be able to give her the full picture.'

'She doesn't have to. She should know that lying to parents is a standard procedure. What does she have to tell her poor old mother for?'

'And if I get brought to court and sued for sexual harassment, I'm finished.'

Colm chewed on his squid. Twenty quid a mouthful, and it was a bit chewy. A bit resistant. This squid did not want to be lunch. He spat it out.

'The squid's chewy,' said Colm.

'It's meant to be chewy,' said David.

'I don't care. I don't like it.'

The head waiter arrived.

'Is there something wrong?'

'The squid's chewy,' said Colm.

'It's meant to be chewy,' said David.

'Would the gentleman like something else?' asked the waiter in a surprisingly kindly voice, the sort of kindly voice that can only be purchased with cash. He seemed to understand particularly the tragedy of an inedible lunch.

Chicken pasta was requested from the kitchen. David happily munched on his squid. But David had a bigger jaw than Colm.

Smaller brain, bigger jaw.

David's face was pained, and Colm felt sorry for him. David's personal life was so complex that he would never see a happy ending. He would never arrive at a resolution to life's crises. Never arrive at a safe and calm place. Would be tossed about by time in a state of chaos. Like the vampire who never achieves the triumph of closure, David was stuck in a narrative of infinity. He was so dislocated you wouldn't know where to begin to sort things out for him. Colm hated the disorder of it. David couldn't see it, so he couldn't hate it.

The wine was nice and it slid down easily.

After lunch, fortified with posh pasta and feeling great after his morning massage, Colm strolled out the road home, along Camden Street and across the canal into Rathmines. He managed to avoid going into any of the numerous pubs on the route, but the sight of Brian darting into Maguires on the main street proved too tempting, and he followed the figure into the darkness. Brian had a colleague who minded his stall from time to time. He was branching out, becoming quite the capitalist. Brian went to the pub, drank red lemonade, and dreamed about having lots of magazine stalls and lots of colleagues.

Colm joined him at the bar and ordered a pint. The barman poured half of it and left it to stand on a bar cloth which shuddered a little on impact, as though it were alive. Maguires was the pub that fashion forgot. A pub designed for a criminal clientèle, everything was nailed down: the tables, most of the stools, and the ashtrays were nailed to the centre of the tables, rendering them uncleanable. Even the barman seemed stuck to the spot and moved with leadenness as though, mysteriously, he too was under threat of larceny.

'The Galway girl is not a student,' said Brian. 'She's a young one who's up the pole and got kicked out of home by her parents. She's no friends and no dough and her baby's due in three months time. The father buggered off. Some people have a lot of problems, brother.'

'Sure do.'

'I sent her down to Stella in the basement. Stella was single when she had Ben, so she's been down that road. Stella'll point her in the right direction. She's a nice little thing. I'd say she's barely eighteen.'

Brian liked strays. The more lost the creature, the more he liked it. He saw his house as a place of refuge. Colm ordered a second pint and a lemonade for Brian.

'Fond of it, aren't you?' said Brian.

'What do you mean?' asked Colm.

'Fond of the drink.'

'What makes you say that?'

'Well, I see you sailing down the road, with that glazed look, and I can smell it from you, even in the morning.'

Colm sat up straight, feeling insulted. There was an unwritten rule in Ireland that nobody commented on anybody else's personal habits. You should be able to sit at a bar injecting heroin and have people understand that you need it because of the pressures of your job or the pressures of having no job.

'I recognise the signs, brother,' said Brian, waving his

lemonade. 'I've been down that particular well. But I came back up again. I still like the interior of pubs, though. They're meditative.'

Nothing worse than a reformed alcy for moralising on the subject.

Colm took a long sluice. He no longer felt comfortable in Brian's company. The rule had been broken. Brian reminded Colm of a priest. He'd never seen him with a woman, or with a man, and his attitude to letting 5 Candlewick Avenue was almost vocational. It was as though he ran and managed a refuge. Brian drained his lemonade – 'Gotta go, brother' – and left Colm behind in the gloom.

Colm ordered another pint and used it as a lubricant to decide whether or not to spill the beans to Sally Carter. He pulled the piece of paper with her phone number out of his pocket and looked at it, the handwriting backward-leaning and faint. Would he phone her up and meet her, to tell her that her husband was a bastard and offer her a sturdy shoulder to cry on? He decided against it, decided not to get involved. He wasn't really able for an affair. He should put the whole thing out of his mind. He placed the paper in the voluminous ashtray which hadn't been emptied in a month.

It's all very schoolboy. Really. I am Mouse-man.

And he struck a match with a decisive flick and burned it.

Bouncy Castle

Thursday afternoon. Colm's hours of work. As usual, he wasn't in the mood. He looked out the window, remarking the progress of the mews development. In the small area at the bottom of the garden which used to accommodate two old and craggy apple trees and a compost heap now stood the bones of two townhouses. Four walls, gaping holes for windows, and wooden vaults for the roof, looking like a smart and tidy ruin. Similarly, the next five gardens along. There were ten new houses in all. The builder was a nice fellow, a smart young man with a Kerry accent. He had charmed much of the street into parting with their compost-heap areas. The gardens had been way too big. You couldn't maintain them. Not without a few slaves, and slaves weren't the thing these days.

These mews houses were to be accessed by the back lane. In the original conception and design of these old houses, the back lane would have been used for carriages to access parking space at the end of the gardens, having dropped their charges at the front. Prior to the building of the mews, the back lane fulfilled only the function of being an access route for robbers. The burglars of Dublin 6 knew every nook and cranny of the back lanes, one of the reasons for the eagerness of the burghers of Dublin 6 to flog the ends of the gardens to mews developers. It was like installing a caretaker permanently at the end of the garden. Yuppies at the bottom of the garden. Colm felt sorry for the criminals. Ordinary decent criminals had to make a living somehow. What with the growth in drug dealing, and corruption in high places, being a common or garden housebreaker had begun to look like a pretty decent and almost respectable way to make a living, not to mention hardworking. Unsociable hours. Occupational hazards. No security or holiday pay. The Cantwell family home had been burgled a year previously. They only got a video machine, which would fetch a maximum of twenty quid on the black market. Hardly good money for shinning up a drainpipe in the dead of night. Hardly worth it. The burglars must be in the pay of the giant video retailers to make it worth their while. Manufacturers had built-in obsolescence on their side, but there was also the theft factor. The majority of video purchasers were buying because their previous one had been nicked. Where were all these surplus videos? Who had them?

Colm slapped his cheek and dragged his brain back to work. He switched on the computer, its familiar hum a friendly and oppressive sound. He opened his file for the gossip column, stifling a yawn. He decided to walk around the room to get himself jizzed up.

I can, I will. I can, I will.

He ended up staring out the window again. In the garden next door, the mad lady was out pruning her rosebushes. Colm wondered where she got her clothes. They were so strange. Maybe she went into school uniform shops and pretended to be buying things for her niece, although that sounded a bit too devious for her. She seemed curiously able to cope with life, despite the obvious problems. She had some relations who visited occasionally. Colm had spoken to them as much as possible. He was fascinated and invited them in any time he saw them for chats and tea. There was a matronly-looking sister called Flora with loads of kids, about eight at least, who dressed in a most subdued fashion for fear she might look mad. And there was a brother, Gordon, with a prim wife who looked very far from mad, who came less frequently. They didn't seem to be aware of the voices that occurred at night, but they were of course aware that the mad lady was strange. Angelique was her name. It appeared she had been left the family dosh, her parents having seen that the other two could obviously well manage for themselves. The money was tied up in some complex fashion which allowed Angelique a certain amount per month, without draining the capital. The fortune was only Angelique's for life; after her death it went to the eldest children of the other two. Flora and Gordon took a keen interest in the property, to make sure its value wasn't deteriorating. And the young heirs-in-waiting came and dutifully visited with their parents.

Colm had originally seen Flora and Gordon as vultures, hovering around the damaged chickie, until Flora confided in him over a cup of tea that three of her eight children had been produced by Angelique. Flora and her never-visible husband had adopted them, one by one, as they emerged fatherless from the loins of the mad lady.

'We could never get her to tell us who the father was. It could be the one man or it could be three different men. We don't know. Of course Brian (*horrible husband*) doesn't approve. He thinks that we should have got her committed or at least sterilised after the first baby, but she's my sister. She wouldn't consent to anything, and you can't go locking up your own sister when she's patently no danger to either herself or anyone else, and who's to say that any of us are fit to procreate, apart from the Almighty.'

Colm had to take back his judgmental attitude when confronted with the ordinary decency and concern of Flora, coping very well and quite cheerfully with what must be a very difficult and bizarre situation, obviously with a little help from the Almighty, who featured frequently in her conversation – 'I'll have two sugars please, and thanks to the Almighty.' Colm never had the nerve to ask which of the children were the offspring of Angelique, and it certainly wasn't apparent by looking at them. He had expected some of them to have a nervous tic and a tell-tale partiality for wearing their hair in bunches, to be chattering to themselves and talking to dogs. But each child looked as normal as the next. Colm envied the mad lady her quality of life. She seemed quite happy. Didn't have to work. Amused herself in a very sophisticated fashion each evening by acting out personal verbal dramas for herself. Pottered around in the garden to her heart's content and obviously had a rampant sex-life.

Colm pulled out his scraps of paper and bits of information from his pockets and the drawers into which they had been flung during the week. He reluctantly dragged his brain cells together to focus on the job in hand. He put out the bits of paper on the desk and arranged them in chronological order. On Saturday there was a fashion show; on Sunday a charity garden party. There had been the races on Monday; a book launch on Tuesday; on Wednesday, a very tacky wedding in the afternoon (complete with press releases). He had come home drunk from each occasion and Janet had said nothing to him about it.

She doesn't object to my drinking because she likes to keep me anaesthetised.

Janet used to complain about Colm's drinking, in the early days. She knew when they married that he had a bit of a taste for it. How had he managed to marry Janet?

Colm cast his mind back, but he couldn't remember precisely when he had asked Janet to marry him. It must have happened, but he couldn't remember it, the moment, the words used. It was as though one day he was going along in his normal laid-back fashion, and suddenly, the next morning, he woke up and was getting married to Janet. He had a vague sense that she wanted it and he had gone along to oblige, to not let her down, to not be a shithead. He had married her in order to try and be a better person. Now, looking back, he wasn't particularly sure if he loved her, but he was certain that she loved him. She must have loved him then. She was far too principled a person to marry without love. There must have been some hope for him then. Looking back on the period, it was clear now what had happened. Janet had made him propose to her. He had thought at the time that he had done it of his own free will, but he was wrong. He had been steered into it like a baa-lamb.

Colm first met Janet on the train going into town. He was living in Dun Laoghaire at the time, and caught the eight-fifteen train every morning. At Booterstown Janet, with the then five-year-old Cordelia, got on and always sat in the second carriage. Both of them going to school, one to learn, the other to teach. Cordelia was enrolled in the primary school of the convent where Janet had an impermanent contract. Colm looked out the window for them every morning, and was fascinated by them. The slightly dreamy-looking mother with a face as inscrutable as a Cimabue Madonna, and the calm and centred child. Janet's round face, soft skin and fair hair rendered her features heavenly, and Cordelia's miniature mimicking of these features gave the little kid a cherubic aspect. Colm was idly preoccupied with them. There isn't much to distract you on a busy morning DART. He observed them every morning for about six months. When he finally met Janet it was like he'd known her for a very long time. He saw her sitting on her own in a bar near the train station in Tara Street. Colm was used to nipping in there for a few quickies before he made his way back to his bachelor flat overlooking Dublin Bay. Before he knew what he was doing he went over and introduced himself. Janet recognised him from the morning train. They chatted like old friends.

That night, the first that Colm and she spent together, was Janet's first night away from Cordelia since the birth five years previously. The child was staying with Janet's mother. This invitation had been extended many times, but Janet had always declined it, as her parents hadn't been very supportive of her pregnancy. Once the child arrived, they softened and came round, loved to spend time with their grandchild, but Janet had hardened, and her unforgiving nature was emerging. Only the wounded have an opportunity to be unforgiving.

Janet had paused in the bar for a drink on her way home from town simply because, for the first time in her recent life, she could, happy to have relinquished her responsibilities. She sat high on a barstool, self-contained, savouring this little time. She felt satisfied with herself, felt she had managed a very difficult situation quite well. She had hung on to her career, developed it, despite coping on her own with the pregnancy and the child. She was feeling self-satisfied and a tiny bit smug when Colm appeared at her side.

At the time Colm was going out with a girl called Ginger who took a lot of drugs and was very uninhibited. Well, they didn't so much go out. Ginger wasn't that kind of girl. She was a free spirit who didn't believe in going out. She socialised on her own, drifting around parties and clubs and then came back to Colm's flat (she had a key) like a succubus and before dawn fled to watch the sun rise over Dublin Bay. She had no flat of her own. Kept her clothes in various locations, Colm's place and other friendly abodes. In the summer she often slept rough. 'My people were travellers,' she said, tossing her red hair. 'My granny was the first in off the road.'

He met Ginger again many years later, whilst visiting Mary Jane Murphy when she first started being treated for alcoholism and was going through the screaming ab-dabs in the locked ward. Ginger was a long-term patient in the institution, and haunted the corridors, her red hair dishevelled, her nerves astray. She seemed to recognise Colm, but couldn't quite place him. She was heavily sedated. More drugs than she could ever have wanted. She had never really been for this world; a delicate creature. Colm wondered what contribution his own bastard behaviour had made to her deterioration. Probably a significant enough incident. He had probably been one of the straws. Her life had been a litany of bad things. She had told him many sorry secrets. She was very uninhibited in bed. He would always remember her sad little face when he demanded back the key, a key he gave to Janet. Ginger had become the subject of one of his attempted novels. It was the fate of his failed romances, to become failed novels and languish in his bottom drawer.

So Ginger had been ejected and Janet installed in his life. He stayed over in Janet's place more often than she came to his as they were almost always minding Cordelia. Janet had tired of being a single mum and wanted to be married. She wanted to be married to Colm. She talked of stability and permanence. She took charge of him, ordered him about. Gave him that little shove he needed in order to get anything done, in order to get out of bed. 'Colm why don't you apply for such and such a job? Colm, get your hair cut before you go to that meeting. Colm, I threw out that old suit, you look like a stuffed turkey in it. This was a bargain. Pure new wool. Try it on.' Colm liked having somebody organise him, and soon he developed such a degree of learned helplessness that he could no longer function on his own. He moved in with Janet and when she went away on a school trip, taking Cordelia with her, he searched the entire apartment and couldn't find where she kept the socks.

Finally he must have proposed to her. Somehow it must have happened. He had wanted to buy her a big tacky diamond solitaire to mark the occasion. She didn't want it.

86

Chose a simple white-gold plain ring instead, and also a matching one for him. So there he was, pale spectral band around his wedding finger, yoked to the puritan.

And all the time, riddled with vice, I denied myself.

Colm dragged his reluctant brain back to the matter in hand, the scraps of paper detailing his week. He had enjoyed each of the events reasonably well. He had talked to many people and had a lot to eat and drink. In fact, several of the same people had turned up at several of the events. It was a week-long party. However, most of the people he spoke to he didn't really like. He enjoyed talking to them, but didn't like them. They were liggers who did nothing, achieved nothing. This might sound rich coming from him, who also ligged and achieved nothing, but he was different from them, he was tortured by it. He paid on a daily basis for his life of insufferable non-achievement. He was far from complacent about it. He was eaten up inside about it.

He beat his brain back to the writing of his diary column, after giving himself a stern talking-to. At least this column gave him a chance to make a living. At least he didn't have to suffer the indignity of depending on Janet for his beer money. At least that. But that would come next. Far from improving himself, he was deteriorating, and it was only a matter of time before his brain became too atrophied to even write this tripe.

Being a full time party animal is a lot of hard work, I'll have you know dear reader, and this week was no exception. My diet is working out very well, I dropped several pounds at the races on Monday, where my hat was the envy of all . . . I went shopping in the new BiBi store on Tuesday, where I dropped a few more tonnes on some lemon-yellow silk . . . On Wednesday I dined with my new beau, don't be so surprised, in the lemon-yellow, a new frock for a new cock (*Colm always liked to put in something for Deirdre to remove, just to make sure she wasn't snoozing on the job*), and we ate nouvelle cuisine at Corneille's. Everything was drizzled in green slime, allegedly pesto. This green slime is catching, I tried to eat a humble cheese sandwich last week and was horrified to find that it too had been infected by the pest of pesto. I'm not a nouvelle cuisine kind of gal, but it's a great way to lose weight. Eat nothing . . .

Colm finished his one thousand words and breathed a sigh of relief. It was always astounding to him that he managed to get this weekly task done. He set his computer to print and went downstairs for a cup of tea.

Everybody would be in soon. Janet picked up the smallies on her way home, and Cordelia would arrive on foot shortly after. He set to peeling spuds and vegetables. This was his contribution to the household, and had been the outcome of a major summit meeting a few years back when Janet, absolutely rightly, pointed out how she did everything around the house and he did nothing. The solution of vegetable processing was found, and Colm was quite happy about that. When Janet came home she always found two pots of peeled gleaming vegetables on the stove. She then took over making the food, because she was the architect of dinner, the designer. Colm was merely the labourer. Janet had things numbered in sequence in the freezer, in an unfathomable system, and Colm was neither a gifted cook nor a competent defroster. On the rare occasion when Janet had to stay out late, dinner was fish and chips from Burdocks below in Rathmines.

Colm enjoyed this peeling chore. He liked having a hand in the practicalities of feeding the kids. Once he got over the initial shock of meeting a raw parsnip. He contemplated its shape in wonderment. A nude vegetable. It was shocking. Tuberous. Almost obscene. The slender vowel of

88

'snip' had led him to expect a lesser vegetable. This veg processing made him feel worthwhile. Worth something.

As he was finished, the door opened and in trouped Janet and the smallies. June had a big red face like a tomato. Obviously a tantrum had occurred. Colm's eyes caught Janet's.

'It was left too late to book the bouncy castle for Saturday and they're all booked up,' said Janet, with a grimace. Bouncy castles were the in thing with seven-year-olds. A birthday party without one was social death.

June ran over to Colm and started to blub afresh.

'We're heartbroken and betrayed,' said Janet, 'because we were were promised by our Daddy that we'd have one. But Daddy is great at making promises but not at making booking phone calls.'

So it's my fault. Ah.

'And I promised all the kids in my class there'd be one, and now there won't be one, and they'll think I'm a liar, and I'm not a liar, I just have terrible parents,' whinged June into Colm's knee.

Colm went back upstairs to his study, his trouser leg drenched by June's tears. He rang up Luke Mays who had a lot of contacts with event organisers, as he was a PR man. And if there was a bouncy castle to be had in Dublin this Saturday, Luke would find it. Colm would have to pay, of course. Everything had its price. But Luke's exactions were a simple currency. Exposure. Colm could provide that. And if Luke could provide bouncy castles, then we'd all be in clover. Luke promised to do his best. He said he'd phone back as soon as he had word.

Colm took John and June out for a walk, which he often did just after they came home from school, and left Janet in peace to get on with the dinner. There was a park nearby, in an old square, and it had a few swings and a seesaw. Colm loved this square. It was such a civilised idea, to have squares around the city for children to play in, for drunks to congregate in, and women with buggies to sit down on benches and contemplate their lot. The kids loved it also. They swung about on the swings and played on a twirly machine, and tried to avoid the plentiful dog poo. It was late March and the year was beginning to turn. Colm liked this time of the year. The oppressive cold was gone, but the heat hadn't yet arrived. Not so cold that you had to make a physical effort to stay warm, not so hot that you had to take two showers a day. Optimum weather for slobs.

John was spinning on the twirly machine, yelling 'Daddy look at me, look at me!' He was going through this phase of showing off all the time. He came downstairs at night to display his pearly-whites after they had been brushed, and Colm and Janet and Cordelia had to admire them before he would consent to go to bed. Becoming overly concerned about the opinions of others. Colm would have to educate him out of that. You'd never get anywhere in life if you thought too much about the views of others. Not that Colm had much practical experience of getting anywhere in life, but he had his theories, just like everybody else.

Colm heard the unmistakable jingle of Cordelia and looked around. She was approaching along a pathway, with Phaedra. Both were wearing long skirts, and Phaedra too had jingle bells. Phaedra was a gawky-looking creature with braces on her teeth and thick glasses. In the past year she had shot up in height and she looked much too tall, her spine curling under the ignominy of excessive height in a teenage girl and not enough character to carry it.

'How are the tragic heroines?' asked Colm.

'We're starting a neighbourhood and school project to clean up this park,' said Cordelia. 'It's in a terrible state. It's disgusting.'

Colm looked around at his park. There was litter everywhere and the local disaffected youth had bent a fair proportion of the railings out of shape, making abstract sculptures. The park suddenly changed in his mind from his little mini Garden of Eden to Cordelia's dump.

'Look at all that rubbish, it'll attract rats. And the broken glass by the swings. It's very dangerous.'

There *was* broken glass by the swings, and if June fell off the swing onto it she would get a very nasty cut. He hadn't even seen it. Things like that didn't register with him.

'We're here to do a civics report, and the whole class will come to clean up next Wednesday afternoon.'

'That's great. You are excellent citizens,' said Colm.

'I think you should get Junie down from the swing. It's dangerous.'

Bossyboots.

'The place is disgusting. Rubbish everywhere,' said Cordelia, gesturing to an area under a bush nearby where there were empty beer cans and condoms. Orgy droppings.

'Looks like somebody was having a good time,' said Colm and winked at the two girls. The girls exchanged glances, meaningful glances. Colm wondered what those glances meant. Phaedra blushed. Cordelia remained inscrutable. She was the most poker-faced human-being-child he'd ever encountered.

'Phaedra, you start at this end and I'll go the far side and we'll report on both sides. Don't forget to note how the flower beds are.'

Phaedra obediently went to her corner. And Cordelia went off to hers. Colm attempted to coax June down off the death-trap swing. She refused to budge, still smarting and bad-tempered about the bouncy castle.

'Eff off,' she said.

'June, that's a terrible thing to say. I'm getting very annoyed with you,' he said sternly.

'I only said eff. Eff is OK. I didn't say the bad word,' she said sulkily.

'I don't care, it's a terrible thing to say. And Daddy is cross.'

June's eyes filled with tears and they started to fall down her face. 'I'm sorry,' she blubbed.

The tears on her face stabbed him in the heart. Tears for cut knees he could handle, no problem, but tears because she thought, even momentarily, that he was cross with her and mightn't love her with every fibre of his being, cut him deep. He tried to think of something nice to say.

'We'll go home and see if Luke left a message on the machine.'

This was the magic formula.

'We'll go and see if the man magicked up a bouncy castle,' said June sniffling, more cheerful now that the crisis sparked by using the F word seemed averted.

And on the machine was the high-pitched message: *'Howdy Cantwell, Luke Mays here. Bouncy castle secured for Saturday. Stop. It's eh, an industrial sized one, but you do have a big garden there. It'll arrive on Sat morn at oh-eight-hundred hours with army of technicians to set it up. I offered to pay for it (well, I offered you to pay for it), but they insisted. Live! Event Management Ltd. We owe them. Both of us. Happy birthday, little June. Ciao.'*

'Daddy, can you fix everything?' said June, eyes shining. 'Are you like God?'

I love my children. I love my daughter.

Choo Choo!

Colm made his way in to Castle Grub Street on Friday afternoon to deliver his copy. The production manager, Philip, had tried unsuccessfully to get Colm to send his material in by e mail. He firmly refused to engage with electronic mail. He liked his weekly visit to Grub Street, his little battles with Deirdre, his encounters with the talents of Cornelius, the graciousness of Dan the doorman. Crucially, it made him feel employed.

'But you have to come all the way in here in the middle of Friday afternoon traffic.'

'I don't mind,' said Colm. 'I like traffic. I travel in bus lanes.'

'Oh, haven't the traffic police ever pulled you up?'

'I travel on the bus in bus lanes.'

'The bus!'

For Philip, the bus was an appalling mode of transport. Colm might easily have said he came in in a pony and trap, or crawled on his belly. Philip couldn't get his head around the idea that a trip to the office could be a highlight of someone's week.

I am sad.

Colm had tried to make an arrangement with David to go out later, but failed to contact him. He had nothing in his diary for this evening, but wanted to be home at a reasonable hour so he could be up early to swaggeringly supervise the arrival and setting up of the bouncy castle.

Dan the doorman greeted him with a deathlike throat rattle. The man was a walking ashtray, the cigarette a burning limb. Colm wondered how Dan managed to get through a night's sleep without them. Probably didn't. Probably woke up every hour for a puff. Dan roused himself from his cubby-hole and came out to Colm. Normally he sat there and ignored people. Emitted the odd grunt.

'Rasp, rasp, there was a blondy one in looking for you earlier in the week. Rasp, rasp, rasp, Sally she said her name was, a friend of yours. I told her to come back today, rasp, rasp.' Dan sounded like a choking dog.

'And did she?'

'Rasp, rasp, she's gone on upstairs. Rasp.'

Ah. Silly me. To think she would be put off by the mere fact of me not phoning her.

'Jaysus, Dan, the cough's fierce.'

'Rasp, rasp, rasp,' and Dan disappeared into his snug cubby-hole.

Colm went on up the old staircase. The building dated from the mid-eighteenth century, and the bricks and masonry had settled nicely into bellies and contours. Management often mooted a plan to demolish the place and rebuild it with lifts and sliding doors that went 'ping', but it never seemed to happen. Like a lot of things round here.

Colm went into the office. Deirdre was there, showing off her biceps in a pencil-strap top, her jacket slung on the back of the chair. To the side of the open-plan office, perched on the edge of the visitors' sofa and sipping a styrofoam cup of coffee, pinkie extended notwithstanding, was Sally, wearing a startlingly red dress. Deirdre made big play with her eyes when Colm appeared.

'A visitor for you, Colm.'

'Hello Colm,' said Sally a little breathlessly. A little nervously. 'Your editor here very kindly let me wait for you. I hope you don't mind. I want to talk to you.'

'Eh, fine.'

Colm was a little embarrassed at this development. There was something very embarrassing about Sally, her intensities, her breathlessness, her outfit.

'We'll stroll off for a drink after I finish with Deirdre.'

Deirdre took the brown envelope from Colm's hand and scanned the contents. She read it quietly, with the odd interjection of 'No!' and the occasional little yelp of glee. This was Deirdre's favourite page. Other people's business. She loved it.

'Marian Cooper is engaged! Fancy that. I'd always taken her for a dyke,' whooped Deirdre. 'Colm, you really nose things out. How do you do it? You must have a feel for this kind of writing.'

The woman is a fool.

'There's a few things here we'll have to send to the suits.'

'Fine. I like to do my bit for employment in the legal profession.'

Cornelius came in with his photos.

'I'm afraid the only file picture we have of Marian Cooper is from last year, and it's at her father's funeral. She's wearing a black mantilla and weeping. Probably not good for an engagement story. But maybe it'd be funny.'

'A bit tasteless,' said Colm.

'Taste? When were we ever concerned with taste? The whole story is tasteless,' said Deirdre, 'especially if she's a dyke.'

'Is Marian Cooper a dyke?' asked Cornelius.

'Yup,' said Deirdre.

'I never knew that,' said Cornelius.

'She's not a dyke,' said Sally.

All heads turned in her direction.

'I know her. She's not a dyke. She went out with my cousin's ex who lives in LA, and she wasn't a dyke then.'

'Oh,' said Deirdre huffily, 'My information must be wrong.'

'I still think the funeral pic is tasteless, and it's my page.

My name goes on it. Well, my name doesn't go on it,' said Colm.

'Fine, Colm. We won't use it so,' said Deirdre.

A win for Colm. No victory too small. Yes!

Colm led Sally out of the building, down the rickety stairs, he walking squarely in his flat spongy-heeled brogues, she delicately waddling in her daft shoes. Dan rasped happily in his cubby-hole and didn't acknowledge them as they passed.

'Are you sure you can walk in those?'

They went to a bar called The Bankers which Colm thought might be free of people he knew. He didn't know any bankers. Sally bought them drinks, a pint of stout for Colm, a glass of lager for herself.

'I do hate to see women drinking pints. It looks so like fat,' said Sally.

Stunningly progressive.

It was obvious to Colm that Sally had spent a lifetime battling with her weight. She was an escapee of fat. Whereas he, Colm, was a captive of fat. He had been confronted by weight gain, and ran over to the other side with his hands up. He slurped his pint. A welcome sluice.

'That Deirdre person seems so nice. So emphatic. So empathetic. Whatever.'

'She's a vicious serpent who'd eat you as soon as look at you. You should see her in editorial meetings. She goes out of her way to humiliate people. She's a horror. Especially weak people. She sucks up to strong people. She's one of the worst people I know.'

'Oh. She seemed sweet to me.'

'She's not, believe me.'

'That's typical. And I thought her so nice. I've always been a terrible judge of character.'

'She knows how to turn on the charm, all right.'

'Colm, how've you been since the duckpond? I hope you

96

had no after-effects. I was worried about you.' Sally turned her big eyes on him.

'No, I've been fine. It was no bother. Eh.' Colm didn't want to bring up his discoveries of the Wednesday night right away, though now that she had shown up, he did intend to tell her all about it. 'I've got a bouncy castle coming tomorrow. It's my daughter's seventh birthday.'

'A bouncy castle. That's a great idea. I must get one for Jimmy's party. He'll be ten at the end of April.'

Silence.

'So?' she asked.

'I'm afraid it's true. I hate to break it to you, Sally, but I followed them from a nightclub to a big house in Blackrock.'

'You followed?'

'Yeah. I hopped into a taxi behind them and followed them out to Blackrock.'

'Anita's caretaking some pile out there. It's been bought by a rock star who never lives in it. Half the south side is owned by rock stars who never live there.'

'And they are having an affair.'

'Witch.'

'I'm sorry.'

Sally's face crumpled and she made some tearless crying movements. She hiccuped twice.

'Tell me exactly what they were up to. Exactly what you saw. I want the details. I don't care how gory.'

'Well, I didn't see anything.'

'How do you know, then?'

'I heard.'

'Oh.'

'Sounds of making love.'

'Did he yell "Choo Choo" when he came?'

'Pardon?'

'Probably not. Anita would ridicule him for it. He just

97

pretends to be a choo-choo train with reliable old Sal. Chuffa chuffa chuffa.'

'He pretends to be a train with you?'

'Yeah. It's pretty humiliating.'

How fascinating, how strange.

'And if he's a train, what are you?'

'Oh, a station, or a siding. Sometimes I'm the country-side, with my arms as branches. Sometimes I'm a train wash when we did it in the shower. Chuffa chuffa chuffa.'

'Oh.'

'And sometimes when he'd stopped at a level crossing, I have to do "parp parp".'

'Like Noddy?'

'Just like Noddy.'

'And did you not tell him that you don't like it?'

'No. Look, Colm, I was young when we married and I had no confidence. I was also a virgin. I thought this was normal. He had a huge Hornby train set which he set up in our new house after we got married, and I blamed that. Jimmy Junior plays with it now and loves it.'

'Well, I had a Hornby train set too, but it wasn't a corrupting influence. At least I don't think so.'

'At least little Jimmy has stopped running round the house yelling "chuffa chuffa chuffa". He used to do that when he was younger. And he's the image of his father. Gave me the right willies, I can tell you. Sorry Colm. I shouldn't be telling you all this intimate stuff. It's just I'm distraught.'

'I don't blame you.'

'What'll I do?'

'Well, it all depends on how much your marriage means to you. You could try and hang on in there, or if you're totally fed up, you could get a divorce. But don't do anything rash. It's a big question.'

I sound like an agony aunt.

'Oh, I don't know.' Sally threw back her head dramatically. 'Did you glean anything about their plans?'

'Well, it appeared that he is intending to tell you about it but not until after your birthday and the young lad's birthday, which are both in April.'

'Hmmn. Was she putting pressure on him?'

'Eh, yes.'

'I knew it. I don't absolve him from blame. He's a right bastard anyway. Pardon my French. But I blame her. I would've expected more from her. Imagine that. Your own sister trying to bust up your home. Stealing away the father of your defenceless children. I feel like telling my mother on her.'

'Would that help?'

'No, my mother is dead.'

'Oh, I'm sorry.'

Sally had finished her half of lager, so Colm replenished it and put on a pint for himself. When he came back from the bar, she had tears streaming down her face. Colm offered her a tissue.

'I miss my mother,' said Sally. 'I always miss her at times of crisis.'

Colm gave her some more tissues. He had a big pack in his coat, put there by Janet who had noticed he had the beginnings of a cold.

'My mother died while I was on honeymoon. I was in Florida, and the rest of the family decided not to let me know, to let me get on with the honeymoon. So I didn't find out until I returned and she was already six foot under. So I feel like I missed it, emotionally. I feel I've never really buried her. And it always ambushes me at times of crisis.'

Sally's nose was glowing like a traffic light. Colm indicated the lager in front of her. There was no emotional crisis that couldn't be countered by a glass of booze.

'I'm so sorry, Colm, to be burdening you with all this.

It's just I feel I can trust you. It's like talking to another woman.'

Great.

'Anita would have set out to snare him, but he would have fallen for it so easily. He wants her because she's a model, to gratify his vanity. There is no end to the vanities of men. Women's vanities are superficial, trivial. Like so many things about us. Men's vanities are profound.'

Colm gulped his stout.

Sally's unique and individualistic analysis of gender difference.

'Let's go out and eat. Your kids aren't expecting you home?' said Colm eagerly, gallantly.

'I can phone, we've a live-in nanny, so it's all right. I think she was planning on going to the pictures, but I'll get her to cancel it.'

'Won't she mind?'

'No. I get her to cancel things all the time, and she never minds.'

Colm led Sally to a quiet backroom of a smart restaurant where they had discreet dinner. Sally chose her meal from the menu after consulting a calorie counter which she carried in her handbag.

'I picked this up in LA.'

'You forgot to count the lagers,' said Colm.

'Oh dear, yes,' said Sally, 'thanks a lot for reminding me,' and she added a few thousand calories and subtracted potatoes from her dinner order. Colm took his cue from her and ordered a disgustingly healthy meal, a scrap of trout and some fancy continental lettuce that he knew he would be picking out of his teeth for the rest of the week.

'So, what are you going to do?' asked Colm.

'I suppose I'll have to confront him,' said Sally. 'It won't be easy, I've never confronted him about anything in my life. Or maybe I'll just wait for him to confront me.'

100

I want to ask her would she like to have an affair, but I don't know how. Ride me Sally. Ride me Sally, please.

After dinner, as they were getting their coats, the maitre d' approached them, a thin, tall, Latin-looking chap with sad eyes and a moustache.

'I hope you enjoyed your meal.'

''S grand,' said Colm.

'Perhaps you might mention it in your newspaper column so.'

How does he know I write the column? Nobody knows I write that.

'What column might that be?'

The maitre d' shuffled a little, suddenly unsure of his ground. *'Mary Jane . . . ?* It's just, things haven't been going so well here, and we need a bit of promotion, a few plugs. That's what it's all about now in this business, trendiness.'

Mounting hysteria.

'There was a time when good food counted for something, when word of mouth would fill your restaurant. Not any more. It's all about Swedish chairs, belly dancers and mentions in newspapers. Cooking now aspires to the condition of pornography.'

The man had tears in his sad eyes.

'I love cuisine. It is an art, a vocation.'

'I'll do what I can,' said Colm.

Colm and Sally strolled uncertainly down the street.

'You're famous,' said Sally.

'I didn't know that he would know me. I'm losing my anonymity.'

I'm losing my social immunity.

'It's nice to be famous. Anita is famous. I'd like to be famous.'

Famous for something useful, maybe.

'Maybe I will. Maybe I'll leave James and become someone.'

*

He walked her to her car, which was parked in a highrise carport. It had been there since the middle of the afternoon, and Colm was shocked at the extortionate price demanded by the electronic exit-permit dispenser.

'That's daylight robbery,' said Colm. 'Have you thought about using the bus?'

'Hop in,' said Sally.

She drove him to a carpark at the back of a hotel down the quays.

'Do you want to book a room?' she said boldly, gracefully.

Colm was shocked. As he was trying to screw up the courage to make an approach, dithering, struggling with his maybes and maybe nots, here was Sally, feminine, slightly repressed little Sally, well able to make a pass all on her own. He looked at the hotel. He looked at her. He started to pant like a grateful dog.

Sally booked the room under the name Ms Brown, and paid for it with a credit card of that name.

'I've always kept a private account. My father has often given me money and I put it into this account so I don't have to explain how I've spent it. With my Mrs Carter accounts I have to defend all purchases at a major session at the end of each month. It's like a tribunal. I had thought the whole point in marrying somebody rich was so that you didn't have to bother with economies. But James always says "I didn't get where I am today by flashing money around", which is a bit ridiculous, since he inherited most of it. And he does flash it around. He just likes to think he doesn't because of his vanity.'

They went into the room. A perfunctory anonymous room, clean and spartan, with a big floral pattern on the curtains and bedspread.

So this is to be the site of my first extra-marital episode. It lacks ... it lacks ... significance.

Sally rang room service and ordered a bottle of

102

champagne. Colm got an attack of the guilts. Now that he was in the situation, he was suddenly scared. He kept seeing images of his children bouncing into his big connubial bed at home. He started to sweat. Sally slipped off her clothes, revealing some very expensive-looking lacy underthings. She was in great shape, despite the slight tendency to flesh.

Women nowadays are always in great shape. It's very intimidating.

'Objectively speaking,' said Sally, 'I can see that James is a weak man. He lacks backbone, always caves in to pressure from others. But he has always been able to dominate me, make me do as he says. He suffers humiliations in the world, and he tries to right his equilibrium by humiliating me. I see him in company, crawling about looking for admiration, buying people expensive presents, paying people's bills. And people have contempt for him. But then he comes home to reliable ol' Sal, and throws his weight about. The mistake I made in the beginning was to not make him work harder for my respect, and I've been paying for that ever since. People don't appreciate what they get for free.'

Sally walked across to the bathroom and went inside to pee, leaving the door wide open. Colm averted his gaze and tried to close his ears to the sound. It was all so intimate. He wasn't used to it.

'The problem is,' called Sally from her perch, 'when you get married in your early twenties, you haven't a clue how to behave, how to *be*, and you let all sorts of situations develop which shouldn't. And eventually the time comes when your behaviour and your nature are at odds.'

Sally emerged in a hotel bathrobe. She was very relaxed. Too relaxed. Her relaxation made him nervous.

'Relax,' she said.

'I am relaxed,' he squealed.

A knock sounded on the door. Colm jumped out of the chair and his skin.

'Fuck, what? Fuck.'

'That'll be the champagne,' said Sally. She opened the door and took the bucket from the room service girl, and signed the docket. The girl momentarily looked just like Cordelia. Colm gave a start. But it wasn't Cordelia.

That girl haunts me.

Sally slipped out of the bathrobe again, and poured the champagne.

'To friendship,' said Sally, raising her glass.

'Yeah.'

Colm kept his clothes on and drank his champagne for courage.

'Have you ever done this before?' asked Colm.

'No. I've been faithful to James all through our marriage.'

Colm's instinct told him this was a lie. She was far too comfortable in hotel rooms to be as virginal as she claimed.

'And you?' she asked.

'No,' he replied. 'And I'd better tell you I'm a bit out of practice. I haven't had sex with even my wife for six years, so I'm not sure how the mechanicals are.'

'Oh. Why?' asked Sally, sipping her champagne.

'She doesn't want another kid and I won't consent to having a snip job done.'

Every time he mentioned the snip job, his poor penis retreated further into his groin.

'How strange. But doesn't your wife want to please you? Isn't she afraid you'll stray?'

'I don't think she cares,' and Colm's courage returned.

Seize the opportunity. This is your right. You were born sexual. You have a right to sex.

Colm eventually slunk into bed with Sally, in the flinching manner of a dog who knows his owner is cross with him. They had sex. Sally was very odd. She behaved like she was in a porn video. 'You're so huge, you're so good, do it to me,' were amongst her repertoire of exclamations. She gasped a lot and lightly grunted in a most ladylike fashion. She posed round the bed, as though she had been trained. Colm thought she was putting it on. The false note that Sally struck suited him. He was so used to fantasising about a woman while masturbating, it was very strange to have a real woman there. The tactileness shocked him. He had forgotten that a real woman's skin was so leathery, so unlike the smooth page of a glossy magazine. His fantasy women were all porn queens and suchlike, standard issue back page ads from *Hot Press* and *In Dublin* magazine, in PVC and nurses' uniforms. Sad cardboards. Nothing very original. Not even the occasional animal.

'Do it to me, do it to me.'

The vague unreality of Sally made it easier. Her guardedness made it easier for him to hide. In his thrusting moments, he felt something click and realised that what was wrong with his lower back had suddenly been put right.

He dozed for twenty minutes after coitus, as had always been his habit, and then he woke up with a start, the floral curtains zooming in and out of focus, and he knew he had taken the step that would alter the course of everything.

'We'd better go,' said the dressing Sally. 'Thanks for that, it did me some good.'

'Me too,' said Colm.

Yes!

The Guilts

Colm lay in his bed staring at the pine-knotted ceiling and feeling very bad. He wondered would Janet notice anything different about him. He knew he looked shifty. He felt it in his eyes. He felt a shiftiness had lodged under his eyebrows and at the top of his nose. He went into the en suite and looked at himself in the mirror. He definitely looked guilty. He smelled guilty. He was guilty.

He could hear shrieks and laughter coming from the back garden. He had forgotten. The bouncy castle. He walked over to the window and there it was, like an alien spaceship arrived from another planet, a giant colourful bouncy castle taking up most of the garden, and his newly turned seven-year-old little princess bouncing up and down in the middle of it yelling 'I'm the king of the castle, get down you dirty rascal' at her older brother.

Why didn't Janet wake me up? She knew I wanted to supervise its arrival.

Colm turned on the shower in the en suite and hopped under it, hoping to wash away his sin. He paid particular attention to washing his penis, considering this to have been the most actively sinful part of his anatomy.

My marriage is in tatters. What am I going to do?

He rubbed himself dry with a fresh fluffy towel he pulled from the hot press. The hot press was a picture of pristine domestic administration. Neatly arranged in piles were towels of ascending sizes from left to right. On the extreme left were tiny face towels, then hand towels, then hair towels, and finally huge bath towels. Colm had one day substituted the hand towels for the bath towels to see would this be noted by management. Two days later, the towels were rearranged to their original configuration. No mention was made of the transgressing towels. Everything has its place.

Colm got dressed in neatly pressed clothes which Janet had laid out on the chair near his side of the bed. The selected clothes were Daddy clothes: a nice pair of canvas pants and a colourful striped zip-up top, and matching coloured socks. Today he was to be Daddy. For a moment he thought about rebelling, thought about wearing his usual greys and browns, but decided against it.

I am grateful. I must be grateful.

Downstairs, Janet was going mad stirring chocolate sauce to make Rice Krispie cakes with one hand, and monitoring her food processor which was whisking up sponge cake with the other hand. An array of shaped biscuits dried out on baking trays – snails, cats, rabbits, cut with meticulous care. She went to endless trouble to stick liquorice tails on marzipan sheep. Janet excelled herself at birthday parties. Her food was beautiful, artistic. Little sculptures of dough and sugar. She was far too busy to notice his guilty face, his guilty body.

'Sorry I couldn't send up breakfast, but I'm literally run off my feet.'

''S OK,' said Colm.

'I hope I'll have everything ready by two o'clock. She's thrilled with the castle.' Out the window was the picture of sheer joy that was June bouncing up and down.

Cordelia came staggering in the door laden down with bags of fizzy drinks and crisps, a picture of pure misery.

'Here's all the E numbers and sugar fixes you require. It's all pure poison, of course.'

Janet discreetly raised her eyes to heaven. Colm took a

bag of crisps and opened them. He had a salt craving. And he poured himself a glass of fizzy cola.

'I'm going to call for Phaedra. We're going into town later,' said Cordelia, 'If Carmel phones, that's where I am.' Slam! Cordelia left the room.

'She's such a misery guts, I gave her twenty pounds to go out so she wouldn't pour cold water on the kids' fun. I don't know what I'm to do about her,' sighed Janet.

'She probably fancies some boy and doesn't know what to do about it so is taking her confusion out on all the rest of us. She'll grow out of it.'

'You think so?'

'Sure,' said Colm.

'She told me that she's just started her periods. Fifteen is fairly late to start. Maybe it'll provide some sort of hormonal release for her. I hate to see her so unhappy-looking.'

I think she is a horrible child and her friend Phaedra gives me the creeps.

'I just wish there was something I could do.'

And you've made her horrible with your righteousness –

'Will you carry a few chairs out into the garden, dear?'

– and your sanctimoniousness.

'Sure thing.'

Colm set about his duties, putting out chairs in the garden and getting the drinks cabinet organised in the drawing room so there was something to offer the parents of the junior guests. It would be the usual crew of people, the Parent Gang. He and Janet met them at birthday parties and school open days. He got on a lot better with these people than he had expected to. To begin with he dreaded the gatherings, as he felt that the parenting of a child the same age was rather a slim basis for great social exchanges, but he always enjoyed the events. Watching the subtle competitiveness of the parents, and the open competitive warfare of the children. When people had no common interests to hide behind in conversation, you got a real portrait of character.

He was out of tonic, so he had to go down to the off licence – G & Ts were always in big demand at the Parent Gang rallies. How was it that one was always out of tonic, and never out of gin? One would have thought that the potent part of the combination would be in greater demand.

He set everything up as best he could, and then took himself down to the off licence which was part of the nearby pub. He'd go in for a pint and a think about everything.

Bye dear.

It was early Saturday, so the pub was sparsely populated. A few old guys, retired to a life of glasses of Smithwicks to warm their old bones of a Saturday morning. They had to get out of the house because their wives hated having them under their feet. They all ceased conversing and nodded to him when he came in. He ordered his pint and sat in the corner.

Colm's life couldn't go on like this. He was now a fully fledged adulterer. He was having an affair, well, it was only a one-night stand so far, but it was nearly an affair. But this wasn't the point. He wasn't leaving his marriage for Sally. She was irrelevant. He was desperate.

That's not very nice.

What about John and June? It would be terrible to live without them, only seeing them at weekends or something like that. Taking them to Burger King. What about life without them jumping into his bed in the morning? Maybe he should discuss the situation with Janet, and see what she said.

He ordered another pint, and then another, and soon he began to think he was over-reacting. He was having an affair. So what? Lots of people had affairs and lived away happily in dodgy marriages. Why should he be any different? The marriage was a sham anyway. How could you be unfaithful to someone you hadn't slept with in years? It wasn't logically possible. Despite their drifting apart, despite their lack of communication, there was something between himself and Janet. Something more than dull amity. A certain link. He admired her.

Admiration is no basis for intimacy. I admire Nelson Mandela. I admire Ghandi. Icons. You can't cuddle up to an icon. You can't throw a leg over an icon. Icons are for worship.

Thankfully, the third pint clouded his brain sufficiently to allow him think that it wasn't all that important anyway. He looked up at the clock behind the bar. It was twenty to two. Shit. Janet would think he had disappeared. He bought his two bottles of tonic and asked the barman for a big bag of ice. He did a half-hearted jog home, his three pints of beer swishing around in his bladder, his fat flesh shuddering up and down, and the ice crunching in the bag.

He arrived into the house and went into the kitchen where Janet stood, now in repose, the hum of kitchen appliances silent. She was framed by the most splendid array of cakes and sweets and savoury niblets. The kitchen looked like a child's culinary paradise, and Janet its presiding genius. Her calm face turned reproachful, and then turned to reproach tinged with disgust when he got close enough for her to smell his breath.

'I stopped off for a pint down below. I'd a few things to think about.'

He attempted to inject an air of ominousness into this line, an air of threat, a portent of danger.

'It's five to two,' said Janet, oblivious, the voice emotionless, the brain clogged with dough cuts and sugar snails.

'I'm five minutes early so,' said Colm and winked. He carried his ice and his tonic in to the makeshift bar, and then went out the french doors to the garden.

110

Little June was sitting forlornly on a chair, in a silk party dress her mother had bought her, her head resting on her hands. She had heard Colm arriving with his clinking bottles, and she now jumped up and ran over to him.

'Daddy's back, Daddy's back,' she squealed, and circled him three times before running back to the bouncy castle and resuming bouncing up and down.

Janet called out the window. 'June, stop that. I need you sitting quietly to greet your friends when they arrive. I've told you how to welcome them.'

'Presents, yeah. Hurrah, presents.'

'Stop that,' said Janet. 'People will think you only invited them so they'd bring you presents.'

'Well, that's true, isn't it?' said June. 'Well, some of them I like, but most of them I only invited for the presents.'

'That's a terrible thing to say.'

'But it's true.'

The guests started to arrive. Legions of seven-year-old girls. Roughly half were in pretty party frocks and half in cute dungarees. The butch ones in the dungarees headed straight for the bouncy castle, the femmes for the lemonade table. June ordered all her little friends around and was obviously a bit of a bossyboots. She was small for her age, but developing into quite a tyrant.

The women in this family are all bossy.

Each little girl came with a present and a parent attached, mostly mammies. The odd daddy. They introduced themselves. Hi, I'm Ron Cusack, Linda's Dad. I'm Jennifer, Connies. I'm Sadie. Susie's.

Janet greeted them all, and she seemed to know all the children's names. Maybe being a schoolteacher you got good at learning children's names. 'Isn't Susie's frock lovely. Aren't Connie's ribbons cute. What a nice hat Jenny is wearing.' Colm was hopeless at children's names.

111

He was overwhelmed by the sheer number of them and couldn't tell them apart. They all looked so similar. Apart from his own precious. The daddies approached Colm happily, relieved to find a man in residence, and stuck by him as he poured them large consoling measures of gin.

'I see there's a spot of building going on down the end. The property thing is amazing, isn't it?' said Ron, obviously dragged screaming away from his weekend golf. He was wearing a golf shirt to make himself feel less deprived. Property prices had now replaced the weather as the usual icebreaker at parties. Ron was a balding man, with a nice pink colour to his skin. He looked rather over-washed.

'I'd say you made a tidy sum from the end of the garden.'

'People are making a killing,' said Colm. Ron was his man for the party, he could tell.

Ron likes me.

'My house is earning more money in appreciation than I'm earning with my salary,' said Ron.

'Same here,' said Colm, relishing the irony.

'It's great to have a bit of land to flog.' Ron paused. 'How much?'

He obviously didn't think this question was too invasive. Colm thought it a bit fresh.

'I can't quite remember.'

This was true. Colm couldn't remember. He didn't have a great head for figures. Janet had handled the sale, and had re-allocated the cash. She had spent it on gutters and roofing and paint jobs and put some in an investment fund to pay for schools and college. She was the minister for finance round here. He couldn't remember the figure, except that it was ridiculously high. Was it twenty grand? Thirty maybe?

'Let me guess,' said Ron. 'Fifty K.'

Colm looked blankly at him. Yes, that might have been the figure. Or was it sixty? Ron took this for evasiveness, and would have been offended, had he possessed an offence gene.

'People have made stacks on this Section twenty-three business. Stacks, and it's a bloody disgrace.' Ron shook his head. Colm stared at him, mystified. Sections of finance acts were way beyond him. 'Section twenty-three. They set the maximum square-footage of apartments to qualify for the tax break too low, so all these inner-city apartments are too small for families, and once their single-income owners sell on to move to family accommodation, the premises are destined to become low-grade housing. Slums.'

'Oh. How interesting,' muttered Colm.

Ron took this for encouragement.

'It's already started to happen. Full of blacks and Eastern Europeans. The corporation are now renting from the private sector to cope with the immigrants, and the deterioration has started. The writing is on the wall. Literally. Graffiti in the corridors.'

'That's a bit racist, chum,' said Colm pleasantly.

'Racist. I'm not racist. I just prefer my own race. It's natural. We all prefer our own race.'

'Well, not necessarily,' said Colm. 'What about the attraction to the exotic? The other?'

'Well, attraction, yeah,' said Ron, pulling up his sleeves, and warming to his subject, 'but for breeding purposes it's different. Attraction is one thing, but mating is another. For example. Take a skinny bird, har har. If you're married to a skinny bird, you will of course occasionally be attracted to a curvaceous bird.' His eyes strayed out the doors to Janet, who fluttered about in an uncharacteristically flattering dress which showed off her curvaceous figure.

An ornithological metaphor to illuminate his anthropological point.

'Some people of an adventurous nature are exogamous.

It is only the bourgeois that want to mate with their like,' countered Colm.

'Exo what?' asked Ron. Tax sections were fine, but Greek-root words weren't his thing.

'Exogamous. They seek a mate outside the tribe. Very important for mixing the gene pool. Endogamy has its problems for evolution.'

'Endo what?'

Moron. Moron. He's a moron.

'I'm not a racist,' reassured Ron. 'I don't see anything wrong with other races, except I wouldn't want to marry one. The Sikhs now, they're really racist. Filthy racist. Won't mix with anybody. And who can blame them?'

Colm wished somebody would come and rescue him from the horror that was Linda Cusack's dad, but it looked like they were dads bonding together probably talking about football, and the mammies left them alone. He decided to rescue himself.

Colm abandoned his bar for a while and went through to the garden, where Janet was handing out buns to the children and harassing the adults with spicy drumsticks. She had changed clothes at the last minute after all the cakemaking. June had ordered mammy into the pink dress.

'I want my mammy to look nice in a dress and have her hair out.'

June was tired of her mother's dull navies and A-line browns. Her schoolmarm garb. June wanted a pretty mother, pretty in pink, which was her favourite colour.

We're all dressed to please someone else.

Janet chattered lightly with the other mothers. She did look lovely in the dress, with her hair out, and her adrenalin risen to greet the company, giving her face a renewed animation and cheer. She was a beautiful woman.

A curvaceous bird. Har har.

The children scoffed the buns and slugged back the

lemonade and then went and bounced up and down on the castle to mix it all around.

Little John, alienated by all the froufrou, was playing one of his more disturbing games. He had recently taken to digging an oblong shallow hole at the end of the garden and lying in it on his back, sometimes for hours. Janet had finally persuaded him to tell her what he was doing. He was lying in the hole trying to get a sense of what it would feel like to be dead. Janet tried to coax him out with Rice Krispie cakes, for fear he'd frighten the other children if he decided to explain what he was doing. Or more likely, frighten the adults.

The weather stayed fine for the afternoon, so the juniors worked off all their excessive energy in the garden. Various liquidy combinations of soda pop and cake were regurgitated down the front of party frocks. Two little girls got into a fight over a butterfly cake, and there were screams and tears. Neither would accept a fresh butterfly cake from the kitchen. Both insisted that the one with a bite out of it was theirs. Stand-off. It was a matter of life and death, this bitten butterfly cake. One little girl was overwhelmed and wet her panties. Several dresses were torn. Janet's tulips were trampled into the ground. One child, a nasty bit of work, was slyly pushing other children off the bouncy castle, and when the other children complained, her Mama, who had several on when she arrived, and was stocious now, after Colm's bartending, insisted that darling was doing nothing wrong and left in a huff, the child shrieking in misery. Co-dependency in the making.

Colm took a poor view of this Mama, embroiling her child in her drinking. At least he didn't do that. He never let his kids see him drunk. Drink didn't affect him like that anyway. It never provoked hysteria or personality disorder, it merely mellowed him out. He never got into drink-fuelled rows, merely into drink-fuelled snoozes.

I'm spared psychosis.

115

Colm jollied the parents along, filling up their glasses at a very fast pace. All the children had been given a prize in a mammoth game of pass the parcel. At six o'clock, darlings and mammies were ready to leave, the juniors overtired and cross, the mammies and daddies drunk from Colm's giant gins. The whole house was cleared in five minutes flat. Happy children going home shouting 'I won a prize. I won a prize.' One minute it was alive with yelling kids, the next, silence.

'That's the thing nowadays. Everybody has to be given a prize,' said Colm to Janet, who had painstakingly wrapped all the trinkets in tissue paper.

'It's better that way. Then nobody goes home disappointed.'

'Bad training for life,' said Colm.

Janet looked at him as if about to say something, and then changed her mind.

'My mother,' said Colm, 'always filled some of the parcels for pass the parcel with a lump of coal. The child would eagerly open the parcel to see what they had won, and then get coal dust all over their hands and down their party clothes. I remember one child being so unable to accept the fact that he'd been so cruelly hoodwinked by fate, he insisted he liked lumps of coal and took a bite out of it.'

'That wasn't very nice,' said Janet.

'No, nice it wasn't, but it was funny.'

Colm went out to the back garden to coax John out of his grave. The child was lying there on his back with his hands folded over his breast and his eyes staring at the sky.

'Daddy, do you want to know what it feels like to be dead?'

'No thank you, John.'

He picked the boy up and carried him inside to the TV room. Janet had a nourishing Irish stew dinner ready for them in the kitchen. It tasted great after all the junk they'd been nibbling. Janet had changed back out of her frock, tied up her hair and resumed her schoolmarm aesthetic.

'That was a brill party,' said June, and then fell back in an easy chair into a deep overtired sleep.

Cordelia came in, stomped down the hall to the kitchen, where she poured herself a bowl of stew.

'How did you get on, love?' asked Janet.

'Grand,' grunted Cordelia into the bowl.

'I'm going to try and do a bit of work,' said Colm, heading off to his study, a light clink as he appropriated the gin bottle on the way.

Missing

Janet woke Colm gently at about nine a.m., handing him a cup of tea. He had the mother of all hangovers. A gin-and-tonic hangover, which was a particularly virulent member of the species.

'Colm, wake up. Cordelia's missing.'

Colm tried to wrap his mind round the concept and say something intelligible. 'Hnnnmg!' was what came out. Tea. Tea was needed. He took the mug and had a good big slurp.

'Hnnnmg?' he said again, this time with the intonation of a question.

'I don't think her bed was slept in. It's rumpled, but stone cold.'

'Hnnnmg time is it?'

'Nine a.m.'

'Maybe she got up early to go and clean up the park or something,' said Colm, rubbing his eyes and scratching his head, the urgency in Janet's voice waking him up.

'I don't think so. I have a bad feeling about this. She's been so strange.'

'Janet, don't worry. She's a terribly sensible girl. She's just gone jogging or something. She's a teenager. Teenagers are supposed to get up early and do strange things. Give it another hour and then ring Phaedra and see if she's over there.'

Janet reluctantly agreed.

'When I was a kid her age,' said Colm, 'I used to sleep every night with a piece of string tied round my ankle and

118

hanging out the window so that David could come and pull the string to wake me in the early morning. We always used to get up early and go running off on futile fishing missions. She's off with Phaedra doing something totally delinquent like going to early Mass. Any chance of another cup of tea?'

Janet sighed and went off to fetch the tea. She was so attentive to his physical needs. Some of them. Tea, shirts, clean undies.

I am an adulterer.

The memory came flooding back to him. The breadth of it. Yesterday's Parent Gang socialising had put it right out of his mind. Janet came back with the tea.

I am unfaithful to the woman who scrubs my under-wear. Stop self-dramatising. She throws them in the washing machine. Still.

'Ahhh.'

'I phoned Phaedra's and Kate says Phaedra is gone to her cousin's for the day. She gave me the cousin's number which I'll phone in a minute. I'm so worried, Colm. And there was a weird phone call earlier. I picked up the phone and said hello, and a couple of seconds later the person hung up.'

'Probably a wrong number,' said Colm.

Janet's face had gone a little grey, and her mouth and forehead were pinched. Colm felt sorry for her.

'It's just that Cordelia is obviously so unhappy. It is so painful to watch. There isn't an ounce of joy in the girl. And she's only fifteen. She shouldn't have a care in the world . . .'

But you're so unhappy looking too.

'. . . I've done my best with her. I've tried my hardest to be a good mother, and to make up for the fact that her father took no interest. Everybody said it'd ruin my career, my prospects in life. That I'd get stuck in a poverty trap. But I was determined, and I managed to make a good life

119

for us, without any help from my family, who tut-tutted at every opportunity. As soon as I got on my feet, people were dying to stick their oar in, but I did it on my own. My first job in the convent, I got that because they pitied me. Kind nuns pitied me. And I felt terrible to be pitied and grateful for the damn job. Nobody really understood, until you came along, of course. And you've been so good to her. I know she's very difficult now, but she used to be great with you. Where have we gone wrong? I would give anything to hear Cordelia laugh again.'

Now isn't the time to bring up the dodginess of our marriage.

Colm was fully awake and full of tea by now. Fired by tannin, he sat up and decided to take charge. Janet's obvious sorrow, coupled with his post-adultery guilt, made him feel particularly adult.

I am a man. I can be manly.

'There is no point blaming yourself for doing something wrong. Lots of kids do mad things.'

He took the piece of paper with the cousin's number on it and went over to the bedroom phone. 'I'm just doing this to set your mind at ease,' he said, and patted Janet's hand with a little affection.

Phaedra was indeed at her cousin's, and she energetically disclaimed all knowledge of Cordelia's plans for the day. She did this in such a ham-fisted and awkward fashion that Colm was left with the impression that there was indeed something fishy going on. Phaedra's talentlessness extended to ordinary adolescent lying. He finished the conversation, and hung up.

'I think you're right. I think there is something up. She was very weird.'

'What'll we do?'

'I suppose call the cops and report Cordelia as missing.'

Downstairs John and June, having sniffed the air of panic in the house, were very subdued and playing at the

120

kitchen table. June was absorbed with a scary array of pink toys, which had arrived courtesy of her birthday guests. She had let it be known that this year she wanted nothing but Barbie accessories. She had received a crate of tins of Barbie spaghetti, which she insisted was to be served at every meal.

John was drawing war pictures, with lots of little stick men, their limbs flying off in explosions. There was plenty of red blood and yellow explosions and smoke. Despite all Janet's efforts, John and June were completely gender-stereotyped.

'Look,' said John. 'This body here (indicating decapitated body on left of page), his head has been blown off and it's over here (indicating head impaled on branch of tree on right of page) and look, (indicating brown smudge in shape of sausage cluster) guess what that is?'

'Eh, I dunno.'

'That's his hand.'

'Oh. Very Blakeian.'

'But it hasn't landed anywhere yet. It's just caught flying through the air. What's Blakeian?'

'It's what you're doing, John.'

'And I'm going to have the hand go flying in the kitchen window and land on a saucepan and the mother is going to fry it thinking that it's sausages.'

'What mother?'

'The one in the house there,' he said, pointing at a house on the side of a hill in the centre of the page. 'You can't see her from the outside, but luckily I've done an interior.' He took out another page from under the war drawing and there was indeed a mother, blonde like Janet, and two children, dark like John and June, and a frying pan with the sausage-shaped hand frying away.

Colm didn't know whether to be impressed or horrified.

'And that's a wart on June's face,' he said, pointing to a little black spot on the girl's round cheek.

121

'But June doesn't have a wart on her face,' said Colm.

'Not in real life, but in my picture she does. This is a parallel universe.'

'I think Cordelia has run away,' said June.

'What makes you say that?' said Colm.

'I think she has run away to London on the ferry.'

'You know something?' said Colm.

'To seek her fortune, like Dick Whittington and his cat. Dick Whittington was only twelve. Cordelia's fifteen. That's plenty old enough.'

Janet came into the kitchen, her face white. 'I've called the police. They'll be here in ten minutes. I've checked her room again, and a few of her clothes are missing, and her bank book. But that doesn't mean anything. She often carries her bank book around.' She sat down on a kitchen chair, her shoulders slumped, her spine collapsed. 'There's been so many cases of young girls disappearing lately. And they've never found most of them. The world is full of white-slave traffickers. It would be so easy to snatch her and bundle her into the boot of a car. It's an unbearable thought.'

The phone rang and Janet dashed out to answer it. There was silence at the other end of the line. Colm ran out after her. Janet's face was pure white.

'Cordelia. Cordelia. Is that you?' cried Janet into the phone, her voice tight with panic, the hand holding the receiver white and rigid. Silence. 'Cordelia, say something.' Silence. And then the line went dead. Janet's panic made the hair on the back of Colm's neck stand on end.

'Oh God, no. What are these phone calls about? Somebody has her and isn't letting her speak.'

'Janet, June thinks she's gone to London. I think she knows something,' said Colm.

'Do you know something? Did Cordelia say something to you?' said Janet.

'No,' and June stared at her parents with her calm and

122

serious eyes. 'But I saw her with a map of London in her room. And I asked her about Dick Whittington. So, I think she's gone there.'

'Junie, did she say anything else to you?' said Janet trying to control her voice.

'No.'

'Think hard.'

'We-ell.'

'Well what?' asked Janet, sure now that June knew something.

June looked from her mother to her father. And then looked uncertainly at the floor.

'She said to me that she doesn't like Daddy, and that either him or her has to go.'

Oh Jesus. This is terrible. That's a terrible thing to say to little June.

Janet looked at Colm with her inscrutable expression.

If you hadn't trained her to be so judgmental, she wouldn't have such a negative view of me. Maybe not. It doesn't take a judgmental person to have a negative view of me. I have a very negative view of myself.

The Police

'Madam, I have to say to you that the majority of teenage disappearances are not abductions and in nine out of ten cases the child shows up in a friend's house, or hiding somewhere in the neighbourhood. However, there is always the occasional teenage disappearance which turns out to be serious, so all reports are investigated, so they are. Was there any domestic problems with the wee girl? Rows or suchlike? Discombobulations?'

'Eh no,' said Janet.

'And you're her stepfather, Mr Cantwell. Do you get on all right?'

'Fine,' said Janet.

In Janet's universe, we're all 'fine'.

'Not the best,' said Colm.

Inspector O'Grady looked from husband to wife and back, waiting for some elaboration. Colm stared quietly at them. He always felt awkward with policemen. They made him feel guilty. Student years of carrying around small quantities of dope for personal consumption had acted on his outlook, unreasonably, to make him feel like a major criminal.

'In our experience, it is a frequent occurrence,' said O'Grady, 'that children do not get along great with a step-parent. Teenagers always have problems with their parents and when one of them isn't her blood parent, it gives the child a focus for blame. Very common. Very common.'

'Oh.'

'We're beginning to have a lot of experience dealing

with stepchildren, as the incidence is on the increase now, with divorce and everything.'

He made it sound like a virus.

The inspector's Cavan accent made him sound like a stand-up comedian, but he had a glint in his eye that made him look like a thug. The second policeman said nothing, but took notes.

'A child can take against her stepfather very easily, even though the stepfather may be entirely blameless.'

Which we know not to be the case.

'And you say her natural father showed up for the first time recently? When was that?' said O'Grady, in a more neutral tone.

'Three months ago,' said Janet.

'Would she have gone to him? What's his address?'

'I think he's living with his parents. I'll get the address for you. I doubt if she went there though.'

'Might he have abducted her?'

'Unlikely, possible, but unlikely,' said Janet. 'He is a casualty of drugs, I'm afraid.'

'I agree,' said Colm. 'Doesn't look like he'd get it together to shoplift a Mars bar, quite frankly, let alone abduct an obstreperous kid.'

O'Grady looked at Colm as if to say that shoplifting Mars bars might sound like a trivial act, but it was still a criminal offence. A starter crime. Today Mars bars, tomorrow petrol stations. Colm felt he was not making a good impression here.

'Has she a boyfriend? Often teenagers get it into their heads that they are madly in love. They do *Romeo and Juliet* for their Junior cert, and they lose the run of themselves. Aye they do.'

'No,' said Janet. 'She doesn't appear to be interested in boys yet.'

The quiet guard wrote that down.

'She has a friend Phaedra who probably knows what's

going on, but she wouldn't say anything to my husband or to me. I've spoken to her mother, but Phaedra apparently insists she knows nothing. She has two other close friends in school, Carmel and Veronica. It is of course possible that Cordelia kept her plans to herself, because she's a very stoical self-reliant kind of girl.'

'She may have run off to be an eco-warrior,' said Colm.

'Pardon?' said O'Grady.

'She shows an irrational interest in matters ecological. It's the kind of thing she might do if, eh – ' Colm trailed off uncertainly.

'A lot of young people are interested in the environment,' said O'Grady.

Why does that sound like a rebuke?

'There's been a couple of weird phone calls today,' said Janet. 'The person listens to my voice for a few seconds and then hangs up. I think somebody has Cordelia and isn't letting her speak. I'm nearly out of my mind.'

On cue, the phone rang. Janet looked at the policemen, then at Colm. She dashed out to the hall and picked up the receiver. 'Hello, hello, Cordelia!' she yelled into the mouthpiece. The two policemen lumbered out to the hall. There was a silence, then a click. She flung the phone from her and burst into tears. Colm instinctively put his arm around her, and then felt awkward. Instinctive intimacies were no longer part of his Janet vocabulary. She sobbed into his shoulder.

'Somebody has her,' said Janet.

'Sssh,' said Colm.

The two policemen turned and walked back into the drawing room, treating the emotional display with clammy professional calm.

The phone rang again. Colm and Janet stared at it as it throbbed on the hall table. Colm was now so tense that his shoulders were knotted. Janet cringed away from the phone. Colm walked over to it and carefully picked it up.

'Hello,' said Colm in an uncertain voice.

There was a pause. A breathy pause.

'Colm, darling, I love you,' came the low voice of Sally Carter.

Jesus!

'I loved our night and I've missed you every second since.'

Colm cupped the receiver and made his best shot at a reassuring smile to Janet. He mouthed 'It's OK', then turned back to the phone.

'Sally, did you call earlier?' he asked, keeping his voice as calm as possible.

'Yes but I got your wife both times so I just hung up. She sounds real weird. A real hysteric. She was yelling into the phone, "Speak to me, speak to me". I'm not surprised your marriage is in trouble.'

'It's all right,' said Colm to Janet. 'This is the phone culprit. Go back in to the guards and tell them the phone calls earlier were all right.'

Janet shook her head and went back into the drawing room.

'I'm dying to see you. When can we? I'm dying to touch you,' and Sally's breath accelerated here to a pant, 'I want to eat you.'

Jesus!

'Eh, Sally, I'm having a bit of a domestic crisis here. My teenage stepkid has gone missing. Don't call me. I'll be in touch in a while when she's found.'

'Oh you poor thing. Missing. That's terrible. Is there anything I can do?'

'No. I'll be in touch later. Bye,' and Colm hung up the phone on Sally's protests of helpfulness. 'I'll help look for her. I'll –'

Back to the drawing room.

The two guards and Janet looked at him when he came in.

'That was Sally. She's a girlfriend of David's, wants some advice on how to handle him. I said this isn't really the time. She phoned earlier. So no need to worry about those calls. She was in a phone box and it wouldn't take her money.' Colm lied easily.

'Oh,' said Janet. 'David's never short of girlfriends.' Janet believed easily. 'David is Colm's Lothario friend,' said Janet by way of explanation to the policemen.

'Oh aye.'

The guards looked suspiciously at Colm. His sense of guilt about his recent spot of adultery made him feel overwhelmingly guilty in all aspects of life.

Cordelia said it was me or her.

The silent guard took copious notes, the vocal one spoke to John and June, and they both finally set off. Their first point of investigation would be Cordelia's real father.

'I don't think they'll have much luck there. He was simply never interested,' sighed Janet.

Colm tentatively put his arm around her. Her shoulders felt very narrow, very frail. And he felt a little more adult.

As the afternoon wore on, Janet's family sailed into port. Maria the bossy one came with her two model children, Enya and Cathal. Enya had a birthday present for June. She hadn't come to the party because she had her violin lessons on a Saturday and didn't want to miss them, as she had her eye on a gold medal. June had felt really sorry for Enya when she heard this. A life without parties. How terrible.

Alice, the third sister and the quiet one, arrived shortly after. And then their brother Fintan. Colm helped keep them stoked up with tea. He wondered what useful function all this tea drinking was filling. Shouldn't they be out dredging canals and whacking bushes? It was Janet's family's response to any crisis, to sit down and drink tea. Whenever the flotilla appeared, Janet posed the redundant question: Shall I wet the pot? The death of Janet's mother, suddenly, after a severe flu turned to pneumonia, provoked a mammoth tea-drinking session that went on for a fortnight.

Maria was full of opinions, mostly about the inadequacy of Janet's mothering, and how Cordelia was allowed her head far too much.

'You have all those children spoiled, Jan. From the cradle. I always told you that you shouldn't pick a crying child up immediately, it's the only exercise they get. When Cordelia gets back, she'll have to be disciplined a lot more.'

'Maria, we've discussed this before and you and I have radically different parenting ideas. I don't want a row about it now.'

And the inevitable row happened, inflamed by the tension of Cordelia's disappearance. Janet usually let Maria get away with any old guff, but she was feeling obstreperous today. Maria's two children were impeccably dressed and well behaved.

Unlike our juvenile delinquent and two junior oddballs.

'Excuse me Mummy, but might I have a glass of milk.'

John and June had to be bribed to drink milk rather than orange squash. Money had to change hands.

Alice, the youngest, was sweet and quiet and sad and said nothing, just tut-tutted at her sisters' outbreak of aggressive alternative parenting techniques. Fintan talked about other things, about his job and his new car and his phenomenal scores in tennis matches. He drank his tea with great inappropriate gusto, as though it were a pint of beer, smacking his lips after each draught. He managed to ignore the reason for all the tea-drinking.

Colm set off walking the few streets to Phaedra's house. She lived above in Rathgar. He was sure Phaedra knew more than she was letting on. It was after dinner time now and she should be back from her cousin's. Colm rang the doorbell and the door was answered by Phaedra's mother, Kate Cooper, a tough-looking woman in her early forties, wearing a smart suit and smile. Colm inhaled deeply. The house had the welcome smell of fresh cigarette smoke. Colm had heard the story of Kate Cooper's marriage, and the barring order she had to get against her husband, Phaedra's father. They were well-to-do, her husband a lawyer, a slapper of writs, and handy with his fists. She ran a string of clothes shops. Colm had got all this gossip from Janet, who had heard it from Cordelia. Colm found it hard to believe that Kate Cooper was a battered wife.

Look how stereotyped your thinking is. Battered wives should be in rags and have black eyes and live on high-density unemployment housing estates. They shouldn't be running nice clothes shops in Grafton Street and living in Rathgar.

Kate Cooper dragged deeply on her cigarette.

It's so difficult to feel compassion for the rich.

Phaedra saw her father on Saturdays in town.

'Come on in,' said Mrs Cooper. 'She's upstairs in her room. She still insists she knows nothing. I've just asked her again, and she slammed her bedroom door.'

Colm went up the stairs and knocked on Phaedra's door. It was plastered with Keep Out signs and skull and crossbones and a big red No Smoking sign. Loud music emanated from within. The tinny sounds of the latest girl band sensation. Phaedra flung open the door, probably expecting to see her mother, and gave a little start to see Colm.

'I told everybody I know nothing,' said Phaedra. 'Stop hounding me.'

She really was an unfortunate-looking child. All angles and elbows and knees. A real nervous Nora. No style. No command. Cordelia was a pain in the arse, but she certainly had a bit of go about her.

'Come on in, I don't leave the door open because I'm

afraid of getting poisoned by my mother's cigarette smoke.'

Another one.

Colm went uncertainly into the bedroom. It was painted a blindingly bright red colour and on the wall behind Phaedra was painted 'SCUM' in big black letters.

'What's "SCUM"?' asked Colm.

'Nothin',' said Phaedra.

'It's the "society for cutting up men", isn't it?'

Phaedra looked uncertainly at him.

'It's the Valerie Solanis cult, isn't it?'

'I dunno. It's just a good word. Scum.'

'Where is Cordelia? We know you know.'

'I know nothin'.'

'You do.'

'Honestly, I don't know where she is. I'm not surprised that she's gone though.'

'Why?' asked Colm.

'You should know,' said Phaedra, seizing a little courage.

'What do you mean?' said Colm.

'Nothin'.'

As Kate Cooper saw Colm to the door, she coughed in an embarrassed fashion and said: 'I've a mid-season sale starting next week. Evening wear in particular is excellent value. Any mention of the shop in *Mary Jane* . . . would be greatly appreciated.'

Colm wasn't aware that Kate Cooper knew that he wrote *Mary Jane on the Tiles*.

Maybe everybody knows that I write the damn pages. Shopkeepers. Everybody flogging something.

'Of course, if you can't manage it, that's fine,' said Kate. 'I'm sorry, now probably isn't the time, but I find it hard to switch my mind off from the shop.'

*

As he strolled back from Rathgar, Colm lit a cigarette and inhaled deeply and happily. The evenings were beginning to stretch now and the nip had gone out of the air. It was interesting to observe his reactions to a crisis. He was remarkably calm. He felt that one had to think positively. Until there was other evidence, one had to have optimism regarding the outcome. Janet, on the other hand, was inclined to panic and take the most pessimistic view. Poor Janet. Always easily accessed pain. Born to suffer hardship. Expected it.

Liked it?

He plonked himself down on a bench a couple of blocks from his home. Street furniture. There wasn't enough of it about. He loved this bench, which usually supported a couple of old guys shooting the breeze, one a storyteller, the other a listener, waiting until it was time for them to go to the pub for their nightly bottle of stout. Or a couple of old dears, resting their legs and their wheelie shopping bags, and intently involved in the exchange of information, in gossip. Colm sat alone and lit a cigarette from the butt of the previous, reluctant to return to the tea drinkers. As an only child, Colm didn't quite understand the order and workings of siblings. Didn't understand why they had to keep such close tabs on each other. Christmas was a nightmare for him, as Janet's family started to endlessly visit itself.

From Junie's comment, and now corroborated by Phaedra, Cordelia had obviously developed a real problem with him. He knew she was impatient with him, but was surprised at the vehemence that was being suggested. He was surprised at how hurt he felt by it. He thought Cordelia's feelings wouldn't have much of an impact on him, daft kid that she was. But he was very hurt. He felt truly miserable for the first time in ages.

In the early days she had loved him. He remembered her shining little face above a bright yellow dress when she was a flower girl at their wedding. She preceded her mother up the aisle with tiny grace and dignity. She was so proud that her mother was getting married, as nobody else in her class had that distinction. Some parents were getting separated, all right. Marital collapse was rampant. But maternal nuptials were truly exceptional. She couldn't wrap her little childish brain round the fact that the other mothers were already married. Like most six-year-olds she had no interest in the past, and no great projection into the future. It was all in the here and now. When anybody asked her what she thought of Colm she just beamed and said she loved him. Her refrain throughout the ceremony and aftermath was 'this is the best day of my life.'

He tried to pinpoint the deterioration, but couldn't. He could remember back to when Cordelia was fond of him, but trying to remember chronologically backwards, year by year, it seemed like she had been hostile to him for ever. He could identify no point of change. He thought about having a quickie before returning. One jar. Just the one.

When have you ever had one jar? Who are you trying to kid?

A vaguely familiar-looking silver car was crawling to a halt by the kerb. He absently looked at its occupant, feeling vague and strangely unconnected, and spotted Sally. She seemed so small inside the great metal hulk of car. He was half glad to see her. He was glad to look at a woman with the uncomplicated optimism of not knowing her very well. He pulled himself up from the bench and got in.

Sally drove them to a small bar on one of the quiet squares of Rathgar.

'A small place with an exclusively local clientèle. Nobody will know us there.'

A good spot for an illicit rendezvous. He watched Sally as she went to the bar, and noticed that several heads turned in her direction. Her blue suit was bright and very

133

eye-catching, and with the long blonde hair she was striking. Even now, having an affair, her desire to be noticed in life overruled her quest for discretion.

Hasn't she heard of the colour brown? It's high fashion this year, under the aliases mocha or chocolate. A good stripe for adultery.

From a distance, Sally looked like a girl. She moved with an unspent energy, despite her years, her kids, her problems. It was only when she got close up that you saw the age in her face. She returned with the drinks.

'What are you staring at?' she asked.

'I was just considering that from a distance you look like a twenty-two-year-old, but thankfully, when I see your face you look all of twenty-five,' said Colm gallantly.

'Do you mean I look old?' she said defensively. 'I use half a tub of anti-wrinkle cream on my face every day. It's very expensive, but I think it works.'

She slid in beside him on the couch, and sipped her drink, pinkie finger still extended. That pinkie was so characteristic, it seemed to be the essence of Sally, her poise and affectation, and her physical smallness. Her pert femininity was summed up by that single diminutive digit.

They chatted easily. Thankfully no dramatic protestations of love, which Colm wouldn't have been able for at the moment. She asked him questions about Cordelia and Janet and happily listened to him recounting their history, their story, their 'Once upon a time . . .' After an hour passed, and two drinks were consumed, Colm, sliding into his usual drinking recklessness, was about to order another round, when Sally took charge, led him out to the car and insisted on dropping him home.

'Your suffering family need you now. We'll see each other again.'

She kissed him firmly on the cheek and dropped him off at the corner of Candlewick Avenue, near the traffic island. Colm was thankful for her command. The silver car

134

revved too much and swerved a little frantically as he waved her off.

Women always seem to drive me around. Passengering is my destiny.

He pulled his coat around his shoulders and ambled down the road to the place he called home.

Day Two

Janet hadn't slept at all, had tossed and turned and silently wept through the night. Colm still refused to get panicky. Cordelia was a resourceful and capable girl.

'But Colm, lots of young girls have been disappearing, just plucked off the side of the road and never seen again, spirited away to be raped and tortured for dirty old men's entertainment. Have you ever heard of snuff movies?'

The night's worry had broadened Janet's imaginative powers. In the dark, the full negative possibilities had revealed themselves in lurid Technicolor. Now her brain was a kaleidoscope of horrible imaginings. And Colm could read all this in her face.

'Janet, this appears a little more premeditated than that. She has taken clothes and money.'

'But she could have hitched somewhere and been abducted.'

'Nobody has abducted her. She has run away. She will be found, wherever she has run to, and will be brought home.'

'But why, oh why?'

'Kids do that. It's part of growing up. I ran away several times when I was a kid. Mostly to my granny's, because her larder had more biscuits than my mother's.'

'Yes, but what age were you?'

'About six.'

'See. That's not equivalent.'

'Do you think that June is right? Do you think that Cordelia ran away because of me?'

I know it's true.

'I think she's been abducted. I keep telling you.'

Janet called in sick to work. She didn't want to alarm her colleagues by telling them the real story. John and June were kept home from school. Janet was very short and sharp-tempered with the smallies, her Mammy performance crumbling under pressure. They sniffed the tension and did their own thing. Colm was supposed to attend an afternoon press launch for a new arts magazine and later the opening of an art exhibition. He had promised a rookie PR girl that he'd go to the launch, and she was extremely ungracious when he phoned to cancel. She wasn't the slightest bit concerned by his excuse of a family crisis. Saw it all as a conspiracy to prevent her getting coverage for the mag.

She won't last. She'll have to learn to lick ass a bit better than that.

O'Grady called in the afternoon and reported that Phaedra had broken down under interrogation –

Thumbscrews?

– and had confessed that she knew everything. Cordelia had indeed run off to London. Some further detective work ascertained that Cordelia had taken the ferry from Dun Laoghaire in the morning, arrived in London by train at lunchtime, and had got herself a job in Pizza Hut on Shaftesbury Avenue by teatime. She had walked in during a busy period when the establishment was understaffed, claimed she was eighteen, and found herself immediately wearing an apron and chopping pepperoni. Her announcement to her co-workers that she was homeless had elicited an offer of a sofa in Paddington from an Italian homosexual commis chef, so all in all, she had landed, as it were, on her feet.

137

Leave her there.

Janet was unable to speak with joy. The London police rounded Cordelia up and herded her protesting onto an aeroplane. They issued her with dark threats of reform schools and suchlike, as she was a minor and breaking the law by travelling without parental consent. Janet and Colm decided that it would be better if Janet met her alone, so they could have a little talk. He waved Janet off to the airport, and took John and June down to Rathmines to get some dinner. He was going to head for Burdocks for fish and chips, but decided to take them to Pizza Hut for a change. Give them something to talk to their half-sister about.

Suggested topics: How do they get the pepperoni so circular? Why is pineapple so nice on pizza when it is ordinarily used for dessert? Why is coleslaw nice when it's main ingredient, cabbage, is horrible?

After the pizza, Colm piled the kids into a taxi, and went out to Glenageary to his parents' house. On the rare occasions that he visited his mother and father, he never announced his forthcoming arrival, as it would give his mother a chance to get up some bad mind. He absolutely never came without the kids, whom he used as a human shield.

His parents lived in a small terraced house, a house they had occupied all their married lives. Colm had grown up here, had slept in the front bedroom and woken to the sounds of early morning traffic. He had never asked his parents why they didn't have more children after him, but his granny had hinted darkly at fevers and post-puerperal infections. Though Colm had never been explicitly told, he understood that his mother was unable to have any more after him. Her life had been, and to a certain extent still was, a litany of mourning for children not had. Rather than concentrating on the child she did have, she stared into empty spaces at the shapes of children not conceived.

Colm was a disappointment to his parents. He had not shaped up. His expensive schooling amongst the sons of gentlemen, courtesy of Granny, had not resulted in his parents having a son who was a lawyer or architect, or obstetrician – this latter his mother's favoured profession for him. Rather it had resulted in him developing some of the habits of the idle rich, i.e. an aversion to doing an honest day's work. When he told his parents that he would only go to college to study English Literature because he wanted to be a writer, his mother memorably remarked 'And what might you have to say that's worth putting in a book?' She grumbled every day when he left the house for college. 'Reading books, well it's hardly work, now is it? Just recreation, really. Life's one big holiday.' They couldn't stop him going, because Granny had left money for him to study what he pleased. When he got his first job as a cub reporter she thought he was lying, as his name never went on any of the stories he wrote.

When he called to visit them one day to tell them he was engaged to Janet, his mother memorably remarked regarding Janet's job 'Just as well you've found yourself a laying hen.' When he told his parents about Janet having Cordelia, his mother memorably remarked 'Well I suppose the likes of you can't be too choosy.' He didn't know whether this last was more insulting to him, or to Janet.

Colm didn't visit his parents very often, and Janet absolutely refused to come at all. Mrs Cantwell always managed to serve up some wounding comment with the tea and sandwiches, some vitriol as she passed the sugar bowl, and Janet had, on more than one occasion, returned from the Glenageary terrace in tears.

But she was good with John and June, and his poor old father wasn't too bad, if a bit nondescript, so Colm did make the effort to come from time to time. June was particularly fond of Gran, in her contrary little way. June liked the idea of having a granny, as grannies featured strongly in her favoured storybooks, and grannies seemed appropriate to her view of the world. 'A girl should have at least one granny,' she said.

Even a wicked one.

Colm knocked on the front door, and waited. He knew what was happening inside. His mother would say to his father, 'You get it', his father would grunt behind his newspaper, no intention of getting up, his mother would get out of her chair, shuffle (her slippers made a shuffling noise on the kitchen lino) through the kitchen and hang up her apron, and then pad along the carpeted hallway to the door, where she called 'Who is it?' Little June answered, 'Only your grandaughter who has come through the woods to see you. Trick or treat, trick or treat, have you any sweets to eat?'

'It's not Hallowe'en,' said Colm. 'Behave yourself.'

'So,' retorted June.

His mother opened the door and then opened her arms for the little ones, with hardly a greeting for Colm. They all went into the living room. For a moment Colm couldn't see his father. His presence was so familiar on his chair in his corner that he was almost engulfed by the room. The room had the same wallpaper, same carpet, that it had when Colm was a boy, all greys and browns, and his father over the years had melted into the background, with his own grey hair and flesh and brown cardigan. One day he would arrive and his father would have disappeared into the wallpaper, without trace.

'Hello Son,' John Senior said, abstractly, without feeling.

'Hello Dad,' said Colm.

'We haven't seen you for a while.'

He always says this.

His mother had taken John and June into the kitchen, to explore her biscuit barrel. No matter how seldom they came, she always had a supply of mini Mars and Snickers in. They emerged with their fists full of sweeties and a can of Coke each, and happily settled in the corner with their feast. Mrs Cantwell put a cup of tea into Colm's hand. He was never offered a drink in his parents' house. They had early on figured out his fondness for it – just like your grandfather – and following on from their general practice of never offering him anything he would like, kept the drinks cabinet shut for his arrival. And just when he felt he most needed a whiskey.

'How's work?'

She always asked this.

'Fine.'

He had disclosed to his parents that he wrote *Mary Jane on the Tiles*, and his mother was scathing in her dismissal of it. 'That rubbish in that rag.' He occasionally hinted darkly at mammoth literary projects conducted at great personal cost in dusky rooms, in an attempt to win some approval.

Pathetic, isn't it?

'June tells me that Cordelia has run away.'

Brat. I told her not to mention that. I'm being shopped by my kids.

'It's probably difficult growing up illegitimate. People don't understand how hard that is. Very selfish of women to keep children. Should give them up for adoption. They grow up more normal that way.'

'Mother, we've been through this before, that's very offensive.'

'Oh, lots of people are offended by the truth. Can't spend my whole life saying things just to be nice. Just not to offend people.'

Very little danger of that.

Colm was sorry he came. He was never in his parents' house for more than fifteen minutes before he regretted the moment of soft-headedness which decided him to come. John and June were sitting in the corner, working on a giant jigsaw, a new one which had been bought by Granny. This was their first visit in three months.

'It was little June's birthday on Saturday, wasn't it? I got her the jigsaw as a present.' No reproach, but the tone faintly wounded.

She wasn't all bad. Not *all* bad. They were engrossed in the task, their heads bobbing over the table, pointing out places to each other, a portrait of sibling harmony.

'I've been cleaning out the attic, Colm, and I brought down some boxes of stuff for you to go through. It's all in your room, if you want to take a minute to go through it and save anything you want before I give the stuff to the St Vincent de Paul.'

Colm's room upstairs was exactly how he had left it. Two single beds, one his and the other for guests. A mad wallpaper with parrots on it, now ageing and yellow. An old mahogany wardrobe in one corner. A heavy but small desk in the other. The desk where he had first conceived the half-cracked ambition to be a writer. He sat at the desk, but his legs didn't fit properly under it. The drawer dug into his thighs. He hadn't sat at it in a long time, and it's not fitting any more gave him the creeps. He lay on the bed and stared at the ceiling, its familiar cracks and stains. He had masturbated to this ceiling profusely.

This room had been his universe. It was the larger bedroom. His parents preferred the smaller one to the rear, as it was quieter. He had sat up here and watched the traffic go by out the window. There was an excellent view up and down the street. He kept tabs on the neighbourhood. He had skulked in this room, vaguely ashamed of his parents, their dowdiness, their insignificance, as he had perceived it then.

David and he had hatched their plans to be great lovers in this room. Life had seemed so full of possibility then. He had had so many ambitions. If you had shown his seventeen-year-old self a portrait of his current self, the

142

seventeen-year-old would have scoffed and snorted and muttered: Loser. That was the word he and David had for no-hopers. They practised saying it, varying and colouring the scorn in their voices. Loser. Loser. There was only one decent thing in his life and that was the kids.

And now I'm planning on buggering that up by being an adulterer.

He idly looked through the three boxes which were placed on the guest bed. An old cricket bat. Some schoolbooks. A couple of old schoolbags. A catapult. A broken swingball. And then he spied something he hadn't ever seen before. A beige book, with a ribbon round it. He took out the slim hardback and looked at the cover. *The First Year*, it was called. It was a diary of his first year of life, marking milestones like his first smile and his first tooth. There were a few photographs pasted in, of him as an infant and of his parents smiling proudly. There was a page entitled 'Our thoughts on the birth of our baby', his mother's slightly childish hand, and his father's scrawl. *This baby boy is the most precious gift from God* – his mother's writing – *and I will do my best to bring him up to be a good and fine man. It is the happiest duty I have ever embraced.* And his father's – *I wonder will this boy ever know how much he means to us? I wonder will he ever love us as much as we love him?*

The simpleness was affecting. Colm stood up and walked to the window. He was there and looking down on the street before his vision seemed blurred and he realised that tears were streaming down his face.

I am such a disappointment. Such a loser. My life is so small.

His mother was hovering in the hall like a ghost. She came in, he blew his nose in the clean hanky he found in his jacket pocket.

'I dug this out,' he said, waving the beige book at her.

'Oh that thing. It's amazing how sentimental people are about babies.'

'Yeah,' said Colm, relieved at the dryness and disengagement of his mother. It was a useful way of dealing with life.

We start off so full of passion, and it drips out of us daily until we become like my father below and finally disappear into the wallpaper. Or like my mother here, a husk of bitterness. Or like Janet, who is going the same way. Oh help me now. Help me save my passions.

'So is there anything you want to save?' she asked nodding at the box.

For a moment he toyed with throwing the beige book back into the box. It would be easier to do that, to get rid of it.

'I suppose I'll hang on to this. The kids might like it.'

Normal

Cordelia seemed a tiny little bit happier after her adventure. It had done her some good, the exercise of it. Like a birdy who makes her first foray from the nest, rendering the nest less prison-like, less oppressive. She took secret pleasure in having put everybody to such trouble. Inspector O'Grady lectured her on how scant police resources had been deployed to retrieve a runaway when they should be out catching criminals who beat up on old ladies. This was faintly gratifying to Cordelia. Janet had asked her about her problems, but the girl was evasive. She agreed she would stay at home until she had finished school. When asked about her aversion to Colm, she said she'd try and put up with him.

'What exactly did she say?'

'I'll do my best to put up with him.'

Great.

'And what did you say?'

'I said that she'll have to make an effort. She'll have to learn how to handle personality differences. She's going to meet them in life, and she can't run away from them.'

Marvellous.

Colm avoided Cordelia as much as possible. They smiled stiffly at each other when they passed by. It wasn't that much different than it used to be, they had never been bosom buddies. But the innocence of their aversion was gone, and the knowledge, the statedness, hung between them on the stairs and in the hallway like a screen.

'Pass the remote control, Cordelia.'
'There you are, Colm.'

The Cantwell family settled back to the humdrum of everyday life, its round of lunch boxes, school runs, and the occasional grand crisis of the gashed knee. Janet shopped on Saturday, the presses and freezer were stocked to capacity, the eternal feeding machine of the family kitchen did its thing for the week, and Colm put the bins out on Thursday night. Cordelia concentrated on her schoolwork and her projects and the air calmed a little. Colm tried to be nicer to Cordelia, but his efforts were met with icy politeness.

Janet had been called for interview for school principal, and she wasn't handling the tension very well. She hadn't interviewed for a job since her first interview almost fifteen years previously, and was pretty scared by the prospect.

'I feel so inadequate. I can't think of a single answer to the question "Why should we give you this job?" I keep thinking other people would be better than me. I don't think I have the managerial skill for it.'

'Janet, you have plenty of skill. You're just suffering from the heeby-jeebies.'

'I'm just not cut out to be competitive. I don't feel I'm good enough.'

'You were over-taught the dubious virtue of modesty,' said Colm.

You were over-taught all the virtues.

'Maybe that's so, but it's very hard to learn new tricks at my age.'

'Put on an act,' said Colm. 'You don't have to feel confident, you just have to come across as confident.'

Colm did his best to be helpful to Janet but she was a bit like a gramophone record, constantly repeating her unworthiness for the position, and his patience ran out. Each day she would come up with a new reason why she shouldn't get the job, or a previously unnoticed virtue in one of her competitors.

'I won't get the job because Father Cooney will be on the board and he's never liked me since I insisted that his religious knowledge class sat in a circle to make it more informal.'

A short pause. No answer or comment from Colm.

'Have I told you that Mark Jameson, the Maths teacher, has a very good chance? He's recently done an MA in psychology and discipline skills. It puts him way ahead.'

Colm could keep silent no longer. 'But he's a lunkhead. He can't utter a sentence that doesn't have the words hypotenuse or logarithm in it. He's a sociopath. You'd be much better than him.'

'Better than sociopaths, am I?'

'You know what I mean.'

'And Holly Brookfield, who's also been shortlisted, she's been a principal in England for ten years before she came back to live here.'

'She's too old. They won't appoint somebody who's going to retire in five years.'

'Holly Brookfield's not sixty.'

'She looks nearly seventy. They'll be sizing her up for the gold watch, not a promotion.'

'And Miriam, the history teacher. She's very popular with everybody.'

'Janet, she hears voices. You told me yourself that you found her one day in the staffroom muttering into her teacup to her sister who has been dead for five years.'

'Well, that was an exceptional day. She's generally very on the ball.'

'OK. OK. You've convinced me. Everybody has a chance except you,' said Colm.

'I know,' said Janet.

'I'm just taking the piss,' said Colm.

'I know,' said Janet. 'I'd better do the dinner.'
Saint Janet of the blessed dinners.

'I hope you don't get the promotion, Mammy,' said June, 'because you'll have less time for minding us if you do. My friend Connie, her mum got a promotion and she never sees her.'

'No dear, that wasn't a promotion that Connie's mum got, it was a separation.'

'Oh yes, one of those things. Anyway, Connie has to be minded by the *au pair* all the time and she's afraid that the *au pair* is a child killer, like the English nanny in America.'

'What English nanny in America?'

'I saw her on Sky News.'

'You're not allowed to watch Sky News.'

'I forgot. John turned it on and I forgot.'

'I didn't,' said John. 'She turned it on herself.'

'So Junie,' asked Colm, 'if your mum shouldn't get the promotion so she can concentrate on looking after you two horrors, do you intend to give up working when you're big and have babies?'

'No. After I finish school I'll go on holidays for a few years. Then I might get married to somebody rich. I won't work at all, which means that I'll never have to give it up.'

'No you won't June, you'll get married for love,' said Janet.

'Like you married Daddy? You didn't marry him for money because he doesn't have any. You have it all, in your handbag.'

'That's right. I married Daddy for love,' said Janet, not looking up at Colm.

I wish I could remember. There must have been a moment, some single golden moment, when our marriage made sense. There must have been.

'Who do you love more? Us or Daddy?' asked June.

'I love you all the same,' answered Janet, and she turned

away from the conversation and set about rattling her pots and pans, drumming up her kitchen sink voodoo.

'June,' said Colm. 'If Mummy gets the promotion, you'll be able to go to the cinema more often and we'll all be able to eat in Eddie Rockets every night.'

'Then I hope she gets it.'

My daughter, the impeccable capitalist and utilitarian. Appreciator of the trickle-down effect. Fully psychologically armed to face the twenty-first century.

Cordelia came into the kitchen, her jingle bells a familiar sound.

'What do you think, Cordelia?' asked Colm, continuing his painstaking attempts to be nicer to the Chopper. 'Do you think women should work when they have kids?'

'Yes. They should. Look at Phaedra's mum. If she needed Phaedra's dad for money, she would have had to put up with him punching her about. Women should keep their independence.'

'I don't believe it,' said David. 'I just don't believe it.'

'What, what?'

'Sylvia told me to settle out of court for thirty grand.'

'Phew!'

'Thirty grand. Do you know how long it takes for one of my staff to earn thirty grand?'

'Two hours in a bar with you by the look of it.'

'Sylvia said it was useless to fight it. The case is watertight. The only thing that softens it is the fact that Gemma Blake, the little hussy, was only in the job for two weeks, so loss of earnings aren't substantial and disruption to her life isn't substantial. But I have no defence, apparently.'

'Oh.'

'There was no physical harm done. Even if she was as traumatised as she claims, which I doubt, thirty grand is a lot of dosh for an experience she probably has every Saturday night.

'And the fact that I ignored the letter her lawyers wrote to me seeking an apology. This caused her mental anguish. Mental anguish? What is that, would you mind telling me? Five grand was earmarked for that. And a clause in the settlement for her to keep her gob shut *in perpetua* cost another five grand. Sylvia said we needed to have that in.'

There were tears in David's voice. Colm had never seen him so upset.

'But thirty grand. David, you'll never miss thirty grand.'

'It's not the money. It's just that I'm so disappointed in the girl. It's really made me bitter. And . . .'

'And?'

'. . . And I told Catherine about it and she flew off the handle and gave me the bullet, *in perpetua*. My life is ruined.'

Again.

'So how are you?'

Colm hadn't yet told David his sorry tale about Cordelia's runaway. He was weary of it, and somehow vaguely ashamed. Luckily David wasn't the most probing of friends.

'Grand,' answered Colm. 'You're looking well, David, is there something different about you?'

'You like my hair? Sylvia said it looked better with this cut.'

Methinks Sylvia becomes significant.

Piña Colada

'There used to be a time,' said Sally Carter, 'when I considered the colour of my hair to be a matter of importance,' as she shook out her golden fleece, now showing mousier roots, having liberated it from an uncharacteristically careless bun. Her marital strain was showing around the edges. Her appearance was slightly frayed. The fingernails less manicured. The battle with fat becoming slightly more lost.

'My home life is now intolerable.'

Ditto.

'It's terrible to live under the same roof as someone who has no respect for you.'

Ditto.

'And he goes round the house pretending everything is just the same. D'you know, James pinched my bum the other day. Just absently, automatically. The man has no conscience. Rat. Slimeball. Pig.'

'Oh dear.'

'Weasel. Worm. Slug.'

Stunning command of animal vocabulary.

'Flea.'

Colm and Sally were sitting in what Colm had come to call the Adultery Brasserie in the little hotel in the square at Rathgar. They sat in their pew, surrounded by other illicit types. Drug dealers, prostitutes, bosses and secretaries, bishops and actresses, and various other members of the congregation of the unfaithful.

'Do you like piña colada?' asked Sally.

151

Sally's breathless quality and her determination to speak her thoughts made her voice very loud. Colm wondered might she be a little deaf.

'Keep your voice down. I've never tasted one. I'm a beer man.'

'I loved that song. It was just brilliant.' She sings: '"Do you like piña colada, gettin' lost in the rain, do you like makin' love at midnight, in the dunes by the beach," it's such a great song. You know, their marriage is gone a bit stale, and they both start to look for their fantasy, and it turns out that they are each other's fantasy. Isn't that just brilliant? It's a great, great song. They don't have so many songs with happy endings any more.'

'Happy endings only occur in mindless romantic songs. The thinking person's destiny is tragedy. Or at least ambiguity. We've already had our happy endings, you and I.'

'But maybe we get another chance?'

'No hope. We're too deep in. We can't escape.'

'What do you mean by that?'

'Hmmn.'

'You always say such clever things. Well, we can have a happy ending tonight. Do you like piña colada?'

'I don't know.'

'Right lets go and have some. I know a bar where they make beautiful piña coladas.'

Sally led Colm by the nose out of the bar and into her car and sped off into the night with him. The warmth of the interior of the car, coupled with the gentle motion of the finest German suspension, gave Colm the little nudge he scantly required to fall asleep.

When he came to, they were proceeding along a driveway, a white paling fence flashing past.

'A country club?' asked Colm.

'Not really,' answered Sally, as she screeched the car to a halt on the gravel. 'Home. This is Longbrook.'

'But I thought we were going for a cocktail?'

'Yes. I make them. I used to be a cocktail waitress before I got married.'

I thought she was a nurse.

'I did it while I was training to be a nurse. You can't live on a nurse's training pay. You can't live on a nurse's full wages either. I'd use up my pay packet on my hair budget. I thought it was important to look well when I was nursing. It cheered up the men. I always had this idea that I'd be like Florence Nightingale, raising the spirits of the war wounded, except there was no war.'

'Lucky for us.'

'I dunno. War must be very character-forming. Anyway. Let's go in. James and the kids and the nanny flew to Disneyland, Paris, this morning, so it'll be just the two of us. He takes them out every Saturday.'

The house was white and had four great classical columns reaching from the paved porch right up through the facade to the eaves, and various smaller columns supporting two balconies on the first floor. There was some filigree design in the plaster at the top and base of the house and each window had a lacy windowbox-holder, like underwear. It looked like Southfork. Colm gasped in awe and wonderment.

What a monstrosity.

'You live in a giant wedding cake,' he finally said.

'I suppose it does look like that,' giggled Sally. 'I loved this house when we first bought it. But I've suffered too much pain here, and I hate it now. It's like a prison.'

Sally jumped out of the car and moved swiftly across the forecourt, followed by Colm, who shuffled like a tramp. Her ability to move in those shoes astounded him. Their arrival was welcomed by burglar alarm floodlights which blinded Colm's sleepy eyes. The house was dazzlingly white.

'Come on in,' she said as she skipped in the front door.

153

'This reminds me of when I had a free house as a kid and invited my friends round.' She led him down a corridor and into a huge room which had a bar at one side. The bar was fully stocked, with optics and dusty bottles of wine. There was a little fridge, from which Sally produced a can of beer 'to keep you going' while she left the room to check the messages and 'slip into something more comfortable'.

The lounge was furnished with black matt chairs and stools and black leather sofas. There was an elaborate sound system in the corner which Colm went over to inspect. A CD holder boasted a number of discs, all the artists dating from the early eighties. Duran Duran. Culture Club. Frankie Goes to Hollywood. Sade. Bryan Ferry. Colm slipped on Frankie Goes to Hollywood and the room started to vibrate to the sound of 'In Xanadu did Kubla Khan a stately pleasure dome erect.' The sound system was marvellous, even Colm's ignorant ear could tell that, the music coming from all over the room. Each piece of furniture seemed to be singing.

Sally appeared in an outfit that looked a lot less comfortable than that which she had had on previously, and her dainty mules were four inches high.

'We used to have parties here in the old days, but we haven't for years. I'm the only one who comes into this room now, to listen to music. And the cleaner of course. When I close my eyes I can remember back to a time when I thought I was happy, and I can remember the room full of people enjoying themselves.'

Sally's eye was drawn to Colm's fingering of the CD collection.

'In 1989 for my birthday, James binned all my vinyl and replaced each record with a corresponding CD. I was so upset. I nearly burst into tears. I smiled and said thank you though. I didn't want to hurt his feelings. He had gone to so much trouble to source all the discs. Or his personal

154

assistant had. But a decade later, I still weep for my vinyl. I miss the scratches.'

Colm's instincts told him to leave. Sally was not reliable. He knew that being here was going to cause him trouble. He was going to have to pay for it.

'I shouldn't be here. I think it's a mistake, Sal.'

'I love it when you call me Sal,' she said, sashaying behind the bar and getting out a cocktail shaker and the ingredients. Colm knew he should go. He was so used to being driven places that getting up and walking down that long drive seemed beyond him. He tried to relax, but couldn't shake the feeling that he had been captured by Sally, who had enlisted his inertia as an ally.

'It's not a mistake. I'm entitled to have friends here. It's my house too. James had Anita here sometime last week. I found her earring in the hall carpet.'

Ah! I'm an elaborate tit for tat.

Sally was now shaking her cocktail machine up and down and doing a little dance, singing 'Yes I like piña colada.' Colm sat himself into a comfy chair. Her jacket had slipped from her shoulder and she was smiling at him, and looking pretty great.

'I'm so glad I met you, Colm. You have really made me think about life and I'm now on a learning curve. I have never challenged myself, you know, asked myself the hard questions.'

We have a lot in common.

'Questions like?'

'Well, like, do I love my kids? I look after them all the time, with help from the nanny of course, but I have never asked myself do I love them. And now that I've asked myself that question, I find that I don't. There's too much James in them. I was never strong in the home so I didn't influence them very much, so they've both turned out like James. They look like him. He must have stronger genes than me, as well as a stronger personality. His thick upper

155

lip pouts out of both their faces. But anyway, now that I think about it, I don't like them.'

'Sally, that's terrible.'

'Terrible but true. I'm so glad that I met you because you've really made me think. You write so cleverly in your column about human nature. You really say things.'

She poured the pink scuffed liquid into two tall glasses and made little arrangements with red and green cherries and umbrellas for the top.

'People expect women to love their kids automatically. Nobody bats an eyelid when a man pays no attention to his children. But some women are simply not maternal. I'm not. I've just been pretending to be. I heaved such a sigh of relief when they all set off for the airport this morning and was glad to see the back of them.'

'Sally, you're just upset about your husband. You do love your kids, you do miss them.'

'Nope. The old Sal would have pretended but this new Sal isn't going to have any more emotions she doesn't feel.'

Sally came round the bar and delivered Colm his cocktail on a little tray with a napkin, like a professional.

'From now on, I'm going to be a genuine person. Then maybe things will change for me and I'll have a better life. For example, I'm stopping being nice to my sister Anita. I haven't returned her phone messages. She's screwing my husband, and yet she rings me up to see will I go shopping with her. I'm simply not going to talk to her any more. I'm finished with all this niceness.' Sally delivered all this in a tone of vehemence, and dug her pearly teeth into one of her cherries with near viciousness.

'When I met James he was ugly and awkward and a misfit, but rich. I thought he was lucky to get the likes of me and he'd be grateful. I was considered pretty then. I thought he'd never have an affair, because he used to say "I never thought a girl like you would look at me." I had the power then. But it all changes when you have kids. It gives a man a hold over you.'

'And vice versa.'

'Huh?'

'It also gives a woman a hold over a man.'

'I don't see it like that. I used to be a goddess to him. Now I'm just the woman dumb enough to be the mother of his children. They used to say that a man loses respect for you when he makes love to you. He doesn't. He loses respect for you when he impregnates you. Making love isn't such a big deal any more. It used to be, in the nineteenth century, or in the fifties. But now, screwing is just so common.'

She then smacked her lips. 'What do you think?' she asked raising her glass in the question. 'Do you *like* piña colada?'

'It's lovely,' said Colm. The cocktail was cool and very strong, and Colm had began to relax and to stop worrying about his surroundings.

I'm up to my neck in it. So what.

Sally wove her spells and danced him up to bed. He hesitated on the threshold of the master bedroom, a fleeting wisp of discomfort at occupying the place of another man. The word cuckold danced through his brain, a word he had always liked. A momentary shudder of regret when he thought of Janet and the kids and then a lightness of head at the fondness of touch, and at last, he again began to feel no pain.

They dozed for an hour afterwards. Colm felt great. Felt like he'd just been for a jog, except he'd enjoyed it. Sally seemed to be happy too. She entered the bedroom with two steaming mugs of coffee. 'Dawn is breaking,' she said. 'I wonder why they always say that dawn breaks, while dusk falls. It makes me think that dawn is a time of breaking hearts and dusk is a time for falling in love.'

I'd better get out of here. I'd better get home.

'Am I terribly shallow, Colm?' she asked in a serious voice. She stared honestly at him.

Oh no. She's getting real.

'We're all shallow, except for great people like Gandhi or Nelson Mandela. But you're not the shallowest, because if you were you wouldn't have asked the question.'

'I sometimes think I don't deserve to be happy. And that's why I'm not.'

Colm got out of the bed and stretched. For one moment he forgot to be self-conscious about his body, but then he suddenly remembered and hurriedly dressed, pointlessly holding in his tummy muscles as he did, his mind racing ahead to the main road and the taxi he would get back to Candlewick Avenue and its normality.

'Are you my love?' she asked.

'Your friend,' he answered.

Promotion

My *name is Colm Cantwell and I am an adulterer.*
Colm went to imaginary AA meetings. Adulterers anonymous. Where everybody confessed their affairs, articulated their promiscuity, put words on deeds. Dusky parish-hall-feeling rooms full of the guilty. Men with their collars pulled up, sitting alone and bone-chilled, smoking cigarettes.

Colm sat at his desk, attempting his weekly task of writing his column. His eyes were so heavy he could hardly keep them open. He was so bored with this column. It really cheesed him off. He felt like an old man. The thought of having to write it made his limbs go lank. Even his fingers felt leaden as he fumbled with the keyboard. His fingers felt like they had put on weight. Hadn't had much exercise. Had eaten too many doughnuts.

Out the window, the effects of the advancing spring were evident. Trees were beginning to leaf, early flowers were emerging. The mews at the bottom of the garden were almost finished now, roofs were slated and windows glazed. Birdies were tweeting on the branches. And the mad lady was naked, and weeding with great concentration one of her many flower beds. Colm was too jaded to remark on the peculiarity of this particularly. He sighed, a heavy weary sigh which came from the depths of his being. And when the air was gone out of his frame, his body felt like a husk, and the energy required to breathe in again seemed far more than he had available to him. He wanted to do something. To confess.

Tell Janet?

That would be the obvious thing to do but he hadn't the nerve. She would look at him with pained subliminal contempt, and he felt that her face could wound him more than he was willing to allow himself be wounded.

I am Mouse-man.

Perhaps he should talk it over with David? But David, though Colm was fond of him, would never understand. Because he was so multiple in his affections, so general in his loves, he wouldn't understand what a quandary Colm was in, how bad Colm felt about shafting his marriage. For David, things were black and white, but Colm could only paddle about in moral greys.

Perhaps talk it over with Brian? Brian had seen a lot of the world, and had a priestly vibe about him. This was it. This was the problem. Colm's conscience development had been shaped by the availability of the confessional, and hence the need to speak about his transgressions and the optimism that the act of speech would bring him relief, along with some vague intangible post-modern forgiveness.

Or maybe I should just go to the pub.

Terrible. This was the problem. Rather than face up to things, he went to the pub. This was where he always went wrong, because after two pints the world seemed much more manageable. It all seemed rather absurd. The comic possibilities seemed more evident.

But then he had an idea. He opened the Gossip Column file on his computer and started to work. Get some damn value from writing the damn thing.

Your diarist is involved in some naughty shenanigans, dear reader, which she must tell you and only you about. I am having an affair with a married man. So far, we have had two trysts, one in a hotel and the second in my home. His marriage is dead (no action!), but he has a couple of children (evidence of action past!). The world is full of married men, so the saying goes, especially when you get to my age, you often have to leap aboard on the return journey. But dating a married man has its share of heartache, dear reader, and your humble narrator is very down in her spirits.

Our trysts are naturally non-public, so I was unaccompanied at the lunch to launch *Cool! Magazine*, the latest offering to aim for the attention of the under fives, sorry, the under thirty-fives. Novelist Howard Haines told me about his new project, to build a quality salmon farm in Connemara. Superior spoils, no pesky riffraff. Sounds a bit fishy to me . . .

Colm started to feel better. Not cured, mind you, but marginally better. It gave him some relief, these little utterances. It made him feel that he was confronting things, dealing with life. He detailed the tiling and bathroom showcase he had been bribed to go to; an exhibition of disturbingly attractive still lives that he'd wandered into by mistake; and another fictitious launch full of mega-stars courtesy of a fax from Luke Mays. He printed out the thousand words. It was so difficult, this column, and so tediously easy.

Then he made a list.

Options.
1: Stop seeing Sally and resume empty disastrous life.
2: Continue seeing Sally and stay at home saying nothing, living a double life crammed with deceit.
3: Continue seeing Sally and tell Janet and see can something be sorted out.
4: Move out of home and into a flat: reassess life by taking it in a whole new direction, perhaps taking

Sally on board, perhaps not, depending on how one felt when one's desk was cleared, so to speak.

He decided to do nothing for the moment. Masterly inactivity. His speciality.

He went downstairs idly. No vegetables to do today as the kids were going to their aunt Marie's after school, but he was a creature of habit, and was used to going into the kitchen at four in the afternoon. He sat at the kitchen table with a cup of coffee and smoked a cigarette. Today was Janet's interview day. She had gone off this morning looking very dry-cleaned, her hair recently cut and a little more crimson on her lip than usual, the lip unusually quivering.

He sat and waited for her, genuinely curious to see how she had got on, to see how her personality had survived the ordeal. He heard the key in the front door, then the pad pad pad (rubber soles) of her shoes on the tiled hallway, the light familiar clunk as she put down her schoolbag, swish as she put her jacket on the hallstand, disturbing the wax jacket which hung on a peg, eternal and unused. She appeared around the kitchen door, the face as unreadable as usual.

Then she did a strange and unpredictable thing. She produced a dusty bottle of white wine and put it on the table. She went to the drawer and fetched a corkscrew, took two glasses from the press and poured them both a glass of wine.

'I need this,' she muttered and sipped.

Colm took up his glass and slugged. He treated all drinks as though they were beer. The wine was absolutely excellent.

'So?' he asked.

'I don't know. It went all right. I didn't fall on my face or anything, but it may have been too easy. They didn't

162

ask me any tough questions. I couldn't shake the impression that they were just humouring me.'

'When will you know?'

'The chairman will phone us all this evening, after dinner.'

She sipped the wine in a more enthusiastic fashion. 'So I dropped into the off licence and bought the wine because I thought it might help pass the time.'

Colm looked at her. Perhaps now was a good time to confess. Her mind was busy, so perhaps her brain would have less space to accord much importance to his adultery. Or maybe this was a very bad time. Maybe in the middle of all this promotion business, it would be very unfair to upset her with his carry-on. Maybe wait and see. If she got the job, then, afloat on a wave of elation, he could tell her and she'd hardly notice.

Darling I got the job.

Great, I'm having an affair.

That's nice for you dear. I hope it's a good one. I got the job!

'It's nice to have a break from the kids, isn't it?' she said, absently smiling. 'They're a delight, but I get tired of managing them all the same. Don't get me wrong, I love them, but a break is nice.'

The closest Janet could bring herself to saying anything selfish.

'Yes, they're a handful.'

Colm was conscious of this being one of the first times in a long time that they were sitting 'chatting'. Usually, Janet was whizzing about doing something. Meals, ironing, washing, repairing broken things with superglue. He hadn't seen her take her ease in ages.

'Your hair is nice. The cut suits you,' he said.

Janet grimaced at him. She had always hated compliments. Even in the beginning, she had stiffened whenever he mentioned her earthy beauty, and he had loved going on and on about it.

'You need a cut yourself, darling. Your fringe is getting very long. And now that it's beginning to grey, it looks better shorter.'

Colm had noticed his brown hair peppering. Janet's own silky blonde was also beginning to turn. It wasn't very noticeable, but it was there nonetheless, when you looked at her closely. The grey was catching. They both lifted their wine to their lips, middle age wrapping itself round them, like a vine.

The phone rang. They jumped in unison and both spilled some wine, creating two little puddles on the table.

'You get it,' he said.

She moved, her body language a mixture of haste and dread, out to the hallway and lifted the phone.

'Yes, this is Janet Cantwell.' Pause. 'Thank you. Thank you for phoning,' and then she hung up.

That didn't sound too good.

She reappeared round the doorway, tears now pouring down her face, her shoulders shaking with sobs. Colm got up to put an arm round her, to comfort her. He was surprised she was taking it so badly. He hadn't thought her that bothered.

'I got it,' she sobbed.

'Then why the tears, Janet? Why are you crying?'

'Because, because I can handle everything except success. Haven't you noticed? I'm only able to cope when I've a struggle on my hands.'

She wiped her eyes and sniffled some more.

Here is Janet, traumatised by fortune. Now isn't a good time. No siree.

Janet took a cloth from the sink and wiped the wine spills off the table, leaving a wet smear. She threw the rest of her wine down the sink, and airily announced 'It looks like rain,' before dashing out the back to rescue washing from the ominous weather.

Colm steadfastly sipped his wine and refilled his glass from the dusty bottle. Nectar. He watched Janet out the window, deftly removing washing from the line, as the rain broke and the skies started to spit. She returned to the house smiling, the overflowing basket across her shoulder like a turf creel, her housekeeping destiny clinging to her with all the damp sheets.

Puzzles

Deirdre had changed the colour of her hair. It was now a strange dark purple colour. Very unnatural. An all right colour for plums, maybe, but a disaster on a human head. She turned a very chilly eye on Colm as he approached her desk with his brown envelope.

'Aaah Colm. Thank you. A word. Sit down.'

Colm obeyed the command and settled himself on the small and uncomfortable and low-down chair that was on the near side of Deirdre's desk. He looked up at her.

'Colm. I'm thinking of shrinking the gossip page.'

Colm felt decidedly shrunk on his perch.

'It's getting a bit passé. All the newspapers are doing it, and to be honest, Mary Jane is a bit tired.'

Exhausted.

'I thought that maybe, we could keep the item, because the concept is fundamentally good, but just run it in a panel on the side of the top half of the page. About eighty words, maybe?'

Five sentences.

'A sort of summary. All the newspapers have started gossip columns, and I'm not saying that they're doing it any better than you, but certainly our page is not as distinctive as it was. I say *our* page as I feel it belongs to all of us, Colm, and we'll all feel sorry at its demise. Gossip is finished, Colm. We're post-anecdotal. Nobody *talks* any more. It's all the Internet now.'

I hate writing the damn thing but now, that I'm being

166

threatened with its removal, suddenly it's important to me. Mary Jane . . . is a large part of my life.

'And space is at a premium at the moment. The property supplement in the weekend section has gained a page, so I've lost out to that. Not to worry Colm, I've plenty of other stuff you could do. I need a restaurant reviewer, that'd be up your street. Connie's given it up now she's pregnant, she can't eat a thing except bananas and fish fingers. And I need somebody to set the crossword. Have you ever done that kind of thing? Somebody who's good with words like you, who's got a dynamic lexical feel, that's exactly the type of person who is great for crosswords.'

I am to be put to pasture doing puzzles.

'Colm, you're not saying anything. Is this all right? You never liked the Mary Jane column anyway, you always said it was a dreary task.'

Colm sat there, looking at plum-head, and he felt that his stomach had just dropped out. He wasn't going to put up a fight for the page. But it was still unpleasant to be getting fired, which was essentially what was happening here, no matter what gloss was put on it. Deirdre smiled malignantly at him. He had always been polite to her, but the woman was no eejit, and sensed his dislike. She reckoned he wouldn't take the crossword, reckoned he wouldn't be able to humble himself that much. He decided to say nothing. He put down his copy on the desk, battled with gravity to lift his weight from the too-low chair, turned and walked out of the office. He made his way down the rickety stair, saluted Dan the doorman, and went out into the Friday afternoon bustle and energy of the city.

I have just been fired. I am now unemployed.

It was quite a shock to Colm. He simply hadn't ever imagined this situation occurring.

Dodgy hubris.

He wished he had seen it coming. He wished he hadn't

left himself so psychologically unprepared for it. He wished he'd built up some psychic armour.

I wish I'd tendered pre-emptive resignation. My speciality.

He walked along the street and made his way to Davy Byrne's. David was there to greet him for his Friday night session.

'You look shook,' said David.

'I've been fired,' said Colm.

'Fired? But that's ridiculous.'

'The new editor doesn't want the page any more.'

'Can't you take it elsewhere?'

'No. It wouldn't work. Get me a pint, me old segoshia. I now rank amongst the unemployed.'

'Don't be ridiculous. I'll give you a job.'

'As a bouncer? I've often thought I look like a bouncer. Whenever I go to a black-tie do, people are always handing me their coats.'

'No, as a manager or something.'

'David you are a real friend, but I'm afraid it wouldn't work. I'm a scribe. For better or worse, that's what I am. I know I'm not the very best, but it's the only thing I'm able to do.'

'Colm, there's plenty of things you can do if you want. You're one of the brightest people I know.'

'I'm a bum, David. I've just been fired. I'm the droppings of the Celtic tiger. Just as well Janet has been made headmistress. It's a good salary hike for her, which she'll need more than ever now. Now that she's married to a complete bum.'

'In school, when we were kids, you were by far the cleverest in the class. Everybody agreed. If we had taken a poll to elect the person most likely to succeed, you would have won hands down. You were always a star, Colm. And I was grateful to you for being my friend, so I could glow a little in the refracted light.'

168

This was a very unusual speech from David. Colm was stunned by it. David had never said anything like this to him before. And he wasn't usually that eloquent. Had he taken up a creative writing class? Once Colm got over being stunned, he started to feel sorry for himself once more.

What went wrong? Why have I done so little with my life?

'Don't worry, Colm. You just have to go through this bad patch, and then things will pick up. You hated writing the column. You were always giving out about it. In fact, you whinged non-stop.'

'I know, but it paid the bills.'

'At what price? At what price do you pay the bills? You're better than that, Colm. You know you are. Here, let me get you another.'

David took Colm's rapidly emptied glass to the bar for another pint. He leaned on the bar, Byronesque with his black curls, and placed his order. David was a man used to giving orders. Command suited him. Colm looked at the manly figure of his friend. A success. Fulfilled potential leaned against the bar, cosy and elegant in a new cashmere sweater, subtly signalling the barman's attention with a crisp twenty-pound note. Whereas Colm was an under-achiever. Unfulfilled. Recently fired, wearing three-year-old trousers and ancient underwear. It was funny how time had gone by and changed himself and David. Colm didn't agree with David's views on anything. David had gone straight into business and become quite right-wing, whereas Colm had become a lefty, dabbling in student politics as much as his irresolute personality would allow. But the friendship had survived everything, and now it seemed that David was the closest person to him on earth. Closer than Janet, closer than Sally. David was the brother that he never had, whom he loved and was loved by despite all the evolved differences. David came back with the drinks, the limp so expertly managed its tremor was barely noticeable on the surface of the pints.

David sat down beside Colm and clinked the glasses together.

'To the future, which will look up for you Colm, I promise.'

Colm thought of Janet and of how he would break the news to her. She would be disappointed. The fiscal ease to be provided by her salary rise would be eroded by this latest development. The presence of his contribution to the household finances was hardly felt, but its absence would be. Colm's face became hot. It took him a while to figure out what was going on. He was ashamed. His face was hot with shame.

'Look on it as an opportunity to reassess. If you really want to continue with *Mary Jane. . .* , I'm sure one of the other papers would take it. That woman only cut it out of malice. It's a popular page. You could place it somewhere else, no problem, and probably get better money. Or you could write a different column.'

David was an entrepreneur, and saw problems merely as opportunities to think up solutions.

'It's only by encountering obstacles that you learn how to soar.'

David had become startlingly lyrical. He didn't used to talk like that. Probably the new girlfriend Sylvia. David had this way of acquiring some of the personality traits of his girlfriends. When he was going out with the French-woman he was given to exclaiming *Mon Dieu!* and *Zut alors!* like someone from a comic book.

As the second pint went down, followed by the third, Colm began to imagine other columns. Better columns. Political columns. Sociological columns. With his own name at the bottom of them. He would become a proper commentator and make a really good contribution to debate. No problem. After the fourth pint, he was going to start up his own magazine, financed by David, and run the whole show himself. Full of all sorts of columns. David could afford to underwrite a magazine for a while until it got off the ground. No problem. By the fifth pint, Colm was in better form than he'd ever been in before in his life, and he went trotting off with David to have steak and chips and then on to David's nightclub for nightcaps and more breeze-shooting and more plans and more columns. Taller ones. Ornate ones. Corinthian columns with grapes and palm leaves reaching right up into a shiny cloudless sky.

Headline

Colm felt like his skull was ripped open, and its gooey contents were spilling out, all over the pillow and sheets. He groaned and clutched his forehead. John and June were in the room, dancing around and singing and laughing. He groaned some more and put his head under the duvet. John came over to his side.

'Is there something wrong with you, Daddy?' asked John.

'I'm just tired, love, I was out late.'

'Well, you're always tired on Saturdays, and it's a bit of a bore for us because we've no school and Mammy won't take us shopping any more because we're too bold.'

This stirred Colm a little, and he struggled to the edge of the bed and hauled his legs out. He wasn't in his pyjamas, just a vest and underpants. He had obviously fallen in to bed the night before. His trousers were standing puddle-like in the middle of the floor, a squat concertina parody of his lower body, the belt holding the shape together. His shirt was hanging from the curtain rail, one sleeve snagged on the hooks, raised as though hailing a taxi, which was the last thing he remembered doing.

How had that ended up there?

'Did you know that our mammy is a headmistress?' said June.

It all came back to Colm. His conversation with Deirdre the day before. His unemployed status. He slithered back into the bed, and under the duvet.

'Go away children, play somewhere else.'

'You're boring, Daddy,' said June.

Lovely talk.

Colm went back to sleep. It was safer there. His nightmares were kinder to him, softer on him than his life.

He woke again a couple of hours later. John and June were in the bed with him, also asleep. They were snuggled into his back, a little pile of breathing humanity. He felt marginally better now. He struggled over to the en suite to have a piss. Afterwards he looked in the mirror. The face was terrible. His skin was mottled and grey and there were bags, suitcases, under his eyes. He looked fifty. He washed his face with cold water, then got into the shower. His physical strength seemed to have deserted him, his legs couldn't hold him up, so he sank on his haunches and sat in the shower tray, leaning back against the tiles, and half-heartedly rubbed shower gel on his hairy chest. He sat there for about ten minutes, until he felt he had some chance of being clean. He then struggled up onto his legs, got out of the shower and dripped on the floor. With a supreme effort he assembled his things for shaving and set about the task, hoping the shake in his hand wouldn't carve up his skin.

How am I going to tell Janet that I've lost my job? She will be so disappointed. She'll look at me with scorn.

It was even more of a challenge than telling her about his affair with Sally. That was chickenfeed by comparison with this. He needed time to think. He got dressed, leaving the smallies asleep, went downstairs and spied Janet in the kitchen, singing along to a tune on the radio as she unpacked the bags of shopping. She loved shopping, all those aisles of products, all that domestic order.

She didn't see him in the doorway, and he observed her unnoticed for a few moments. Her face was serene and contented. Janet was fine. Her ability to be contented was incredible. She rarely looked thrilled, but she had this

173

indefinable happy thing about her. The same expression as members of religious cults. A smug saved look.

I'm going to heaven and you're not.

'I'm going for a walk. The kids are asleep upstairs.'

He went out the door and down the street. The year was beginning to warm up a little. There was pep in the air. Colm had a raging thirst. He went to the newsagent's and got himself a can of Coke. He knew what he had to do. He had to take Deirdre's offer of the crossword and restaurant review. He would have to rave about ravioli. Cast aspersions on asparagus. He had no choice. It would be less money, but less money was better than no money. He simply couldn't have no job at all. He couldn't be totally unsupported. The vision of Janet kindly slipping tenners into his jacket pocket so he would be able to buy himself fags was too much, her face pained and self-sacrificing, yet beatific. Fags. He needed fags, so he turned and went back into the newsagent.

He didn't know how he'd overlooked it the first time, but screaming from the front of the evening paper was the headline CARTER MISSING along with a picture of the man. Colm picked up the newspaper and scanned the article.

James Carter, lager millionaire, was reported missing yesterday by his distraught wife Sally. Apparently he left the house on Thursday with the words: 'I'm going out for a walk,' and has disappeared. Sources say that criminal elements have targeted big businessmen for kidnapping and extortion scams, but no ransom note has yet been received by the family. Carter has two young children and lives in a mansion, Longbrook, on Howth Hill. Known for his sometimes outlandish generosity, Carter had few enemies, and sources confirm that the police are keeping an open mind about the situation. A tearful Mrs Carter appealed to her husband to come home if he was able.

At the bottom of the page was a small portrait of Sally. A very attractive and posed one.

Famous now, Sally. Famous now.

This was a bit of a turn-up for the books. Colm knew it meant trouble, and specifically trouble for him. He knew that whatever was going on, he was going to become up to his neck in it. And he was going to have to pay.

This is all I need.

He strolled on down to the bench with his Coke and his paper and his fags and sat down. To phone Sally? Or to wait for her to phone him? To tell Janet about the affair? To blab, or not to blab? Do nothing, it's safer. He opened the body of the evening paper to look at this organ's crossword and restaurant review. He had no choice. He would have to do them. He could survive on very little, but he couldn't survive on no dough.

The Galway girl appeared and strolled down the road towards him. She was visibly pregnant now, and the pregnancy made her youth even more startling. She smiled shyly at him and passed on by, her smock dress swishing in the wind, her youth leaving a faint trace behind her in the spring air.

Janet had been beautiful pregnant. She had been so shy about it, so delicate, but the joy had shone out of her. Her giving nature happily embraced the nurturing role. She had been so careful of her diet, of getting enough rest. She had depended on him more, needed his protection more. Occasionally, in the night, she would throw her arms round him for comfort. She had been so sensual then, so touching. She had had sex with him then with abandon. But towards the end of the second pregnancy, she had started to be ill and that was the last time Colm could remember any real happiness with Janet.

She must have loved me then.

Colm looked at the photograph of Sally on the bottom right-hand corner of the front page of the evening paper. Her hair styled and falling around her ears with a studied casualness, her lips holding a pout which she often forced when she thought she was being observed. Poor vain little Sally. She'd be happy with the photo. It showed her in what she would consider to be her best light. Colm wondered had James finally run off with Anita. Was Sally destined to have to endure a very public ditching? He felt sorry for her, and for himself. It was sad to have got so much wrong in life.

He flicked through the rest of the newspaper and found that paper's Saturday gossip column. Yes, it was the same old guff he himself wrote. Deirdre did have a point that it was all becoming a bit jaded. Colm persuaded himself that he did indeed want to compose the crossword, and write the restaurant review. It would be a bit of a relief, frankly, to be able to wind down the lounge lizard act. He decided he'd better go home and discuss the change of plan with Janet.

Along the way he passed a coinbox phone and dialled Sally's mobile. Sally answered, her voice taut. 'I can't really talk now. The police are here. Things are very tense.' And the line went dead. Colm didn't know had she said tense or intense.

The Body

Colm told Janet about the rearrangements of his duties for Castle Grub Street. Janet was quite pleased.

'That's great. It'll leave you with a bit more time to do your own thing.'

This was the closest Janet came to encouraging him to write. 'Your own thing' was her euphemism for Colm's literary ambitions. She'd never interfere with him, never try to dictate to him what to do. It was against her principles to be overly didactic.

Instead of giving me the root up the arse I so badly need and indubitably deserve.

'The dough won't be as good as it used to be.'

'Fine. That doesn't matter one bit. My salary hike means we don't have to worry about that. I'm thrilled, in fact, Colm. You hated doing *Mary Jane on the Tiles*. You were always giving out about it.'

Did I moan that much?

'Janet, while we're talking eh, I have to ask you, are you happy with the way things are going?'

'I couldn't be more thrilled. I know I had a funny reaction the other day, but truly I'm delighted I've got the headship. The kids are fine. Cordelia's a good deal improved. She seems more settled in herself. We're all fine.'

'And us?'

'Us?' She said this last as though she wasn't sure who 'us' was. Wasn't sure if 'us' existed. 'Oh. We're OK, aren't we?'

177

'Well, we're not exactly intimate, are we?' said Colm as gently as he could.

'Oh, that old chestnut.'

Our sex-life – a chestnut.

'Well, I thought that had gone right out of your mind, it's been so long since you've mentioned it. To be honest, I've totally forgotten about it.'

'It'. Our sex-life – an 'it'.

She moved her hands awkwardly and tidied a stray hair behind her ear. Her eyes darted about and avoided him. She really didn't want to talk about this. Her face had a slightly affronted look, as though he was being ill-mannered. Her nose rose in the air as if she was getting a bad smell.

'You know what you've always had to do. That has never changed. But you seem to have gone off the idea as well. You haven't mentioned it in ages. To be honest, I'd forgotten about it altogether.'

'It' again. Go on, you coward. Speak. Tell her you're having an affair.

'I'm eh, Janet I'm – '

'What?'

'I'm dying for a cup of tea. Will you put the water on?'

'Sure.'

Janet made a delighted swoop on the kettle, sensing the conversation was now to be terminated.

A few days later, Colm hadn't heard from Sally at all, and working on his first crossword while simultaneously listening to chat radio in the afternoon, he heard the sombre crocodile tones of the newsreader announcing the finding of James Carter's body, washed up on Portmarnock Strand. Gobsmacked, while being quite an excellent word in its own way, was inadequate to describe how Colm felt.

19 across. So surprised, he was hit in the face –
[*gobsmacked*].

Colm was amazed at how much he enjoyed devising the
crossword. He spent the afternoon with his Chambers
dictionary, digging out words and meanings of words, and
produced a dinky little puzzle which had a nice local
Dublin feel, a few topical references to tribunals and
brown paper bags and such like, and he felt quite pleased
with himself. He had his appointment to go eat in a new
Italian restaurant, and now that he was over the trauma of
being reassigned without consultation, was quite happy
with his new professional arrangements. The cheque in his
bank account would shrink, but it would be enough to
keep him going. The weeks ahead were now endlessly
lacking in activity, and various of his PR contacts were
heartbroken. Having spent years buttering him up, they
now had to go and butter up somebody else. Luke Mays
almost wept.

A waterlogged James Carter turning up on Portmarnock
Strand was a pretty nasty turn of events. Possibly a
suicide? Colm would certainly have thought James Carter
to be a bit of a nervous Nora, going by the body language
and behaviour on the night when Colm followed him and
Anita out to Blackrock. He was fond of the booze and
drugs, by all appearances, and Sally's descriptions of him
made him sound emotionally peculiar. His desire to please
people wasn't normal behaviour, and certainly a sign of a
lack of self-esteem. The pressure of the affair with Anita
maybe took a toll on him. Or maybe he was out walking
and had an accident. Colm wished Sally would phone him
and put him in the picture.

She didn't phone.

After a couple of hours he phoned her mobile and was
diverted to voice mail, and decided not to leave a message.
He began to get quite agitated.

Colm stayed in at night now that he had no reason to go

to the three receptions he had in his diary. He sat watching the television, feeling the effects of his sobriety. His brain, usually occupied with alcohol-induced hyper-thoughts, now observed the quotidian. Janet never sat still all evening. Colm thought her afraid to give him an opportunity to bring up 'it' again. She hoovered under his feet in the living room, though the carpet was clean to begin with. She was uncomfortable and awkward in her movements, as though she felt she was being watched. Colm offered to help, but Janet declined.

'That's OK thanks. I'm used to it, it'll be faster if I do it myself.'

Tonight's special project was polishing the light switches, and when Colm offered to help with that, she called back from the hall, 'No need, it's just done.'

When she was finished, she sat at the dining table with a mountain of essays to be corrected. The scrubbing had been a mere preamble to the *real* work of the evening.

'I'll be glad when I'm head next year, I won't have to do all this correcting then.'

A complaint from the saint? How odd? How relieving.

Cordelia came home from swimming and moodied round the downstairs for a while. She was naturally surprised to see Colm sitting in watching telly. She looked at him with puzzled distaste, as though someone had left a refuse sack on the armchair. Colm smiled back at her. She put on her Walkman and sat reading magazines for a while, angled on the chair so her back was firmly facing Colm. Janet asked Cordelia a few questions about her day which the teenager couldn't hear, her head bobbing in time with her personal stereo. Finally she retreated to her bedroom with a mug of cocoa, and Janet raised her eyes to heaven and shook her head, exasperated, before returning to her copybooks and the comfort of the mundanity therein.

After a couple of hours, Colm couldn't stick it any

longer and went out down to the pub below in Rathmines, got himself a pint and phoned Sally from the coinbox. This time she answered the phone and spoke for quite a bit. She sounded strangely calm and unflapped. She detailed how the policeman had called at her door that morning and reported the finding of James by an early-morning jogger on the beach. How she had broken it to the kids then and how difficult that was. How she had phoned her family, including Anita, and told them. Anita had reacted very badly, naturally, but Sally had paid no attention, afforded her no particular notice. She said the guards had been terribly sympathetic, everybody was very sympathetic, very, very kind, but she was sort of numb and didn't know what to feel. Except when she told the kids and saw their reaction. She didn't feel numb then. The funeral was to be delayed as the state pathologist had to examine the body. It didn't look like suicide, as there was no note and nobody felt that James had been heading that way. She cut the line rather abruptly, promising she'd get in touch again in the next day or two. Colm returned to his pint.

Sally's voice had lost the naive breathless quality. It sounded colder, much more grown-up. And there was a great deal of pain in it. Major pain. The pain of someone who had lost something very, very valuable. Sally's reassuring self-centredness was gone. People's lives were complicated. Colm wondered what it would feel like if Janet died. Though the marriage had failed, he would be devastated. He knew that. He slurped his pint, an uneasy edge of anxiety mounting in his soul.

Funeral

The funeral arrangements for James Carter were listed in the newspaper, and Colm decided to go. He wasn't quite sure why, as his better judgment was telling him to stay away, but he couldn't help it. He was drawn to it. Attracted to it. He couldn't resist.

He got one bus into town and then hopped on a second out the Northside. It rained all the way. Great sheets of heavy wet rain came pouring down. Appropriate weather. He found the church, a very large cruciform job in a vast carpark. He sidled in the back entrance, secreting himself in a low-key pew to the rear. It was a posh funeral. You could tell by the ladies' hats, which were crisply fashionable as for a wedding, though all dutifully funereal in colour, and the mounds of expensive-looking bouquets which filled the air with a heavy and sweet perfume.

Colm muttered along to the intonation of the Mass, the words so ingrained in his brain they were unerasable. The responses came out as a reflex action. This was the first time in a long time he'd been to a church. Janet had insisted on a church wedding and on having the children baptised, and Colm had gone along as it suited him to have someone take charge of family matters spiritual. He just said 'I do' and 'we do' and 'go for it' in the correct places. Janet wasn't a Mass-goer, but she liked to have that department looked after.

When the funeral was drawing to a close and the incense-waving priest led the coffin down the aisle, Colm positioned himself at the edge so Sally would see him as she passed by. He wanted her to know that he had come, to offer her some support. The coffin was ornate and shiny and expensive-looking, and was borne by a number of swanky undertakers, their faces a study in mute agreeableness. Then followed Sally as chief mourner, with her neatly-dressed children held, one in each hand, by her side, their black leather shoes shiny as hooves. The little fella was indeed the image of his father. Sally's face was still and firm and brave, and her hair golden and pretty against the black. Colm caught her eye as she passed, and a flicker of Sally's eyelash told him that she'd seen him and was grateful. He was glad. The other mourners followed. A very sad-looking old couple, probably his parents; the man was tall and had the tell-tale fat lip, and the woman was delicate and pretty and immaculately coiffured despite her age. She hadn't passed on any of her looks to her son, but was the source for his taste in women. They were followed by a bunch of over-tall fat-lipped middle-aged men and women, obviously siblings. They looked like a race apart. Their height, their fat lips. Then other people. More distant family, the fat lip more sparsely scattered. And there were some children, struggling to copy the adults' sobriety, though suppressing some fit of amusement which had secretly taken hold. Colm had a pang as he thought of June. She was the kind of little girl who would find the fun in funerals.

The crowd passed on by out into the rain, and Colm was about to slip out when he spied Anita. She was being supported by a young man, her body contorted in an expression of pure grief, her face blotchy and red. She wore a black mantilla, and her eyes were hidden by dark glasses, her hair straggling down her shoulders in rats' tails. The man was helping her walk, and she was barely managing, as though each step was as excruciating as the mermaid walking on a thousand knives. Colm was a bit taken aback. It was startling, this grief, and very conspicuous. Too conspicuous. Colm looked around him to see were people noticing. All the black hats and the perfume of the flowers and the heavy incense, not to mention the superfluity of widows, made him feel he was a spectator at an Italian opera. A participator. And the drama between these two sisters was screamingly obvious for all to see.

Outside people moved quickly under great black umbrellas, and the odd flowery pink one, and hopped into cars to go to the cemetery. Colm wanted to go, wanted to see out the event to the end, but decided against it. It wouldn't be appropriate. Sally might find it difficult to deal with. He hung back in the porch of the church and watched the people disperse. Naturally, he had no umbrella, so he waited for a while to see if the drenching would ease before rushing off to his bus stop. He lit a cigarette and puffed on it. Cigarettes always tasted nicer in the rain. A man in an anorak jumped into the porch. He too had no umbrella and his hair was wet.

'Can I have a light?' he asked Colm.

Colm lit the stranger's cigarette with a match, trying not to singe the hair which fell forward into the flame. Colm liked matches, their simplicity of design. He hated lighters. Was always mistrustful of them. When he had a lighter in his pocket, he was always conscious of carrying about a little container of paraffin. Couldn't get it out of his head that it might explode or something.

Drips of rain were falling from the stranger's hair and making his cigarette soggy, but he was managing to smoke it all the same.

'Terrible accident,' remarked the man, shaking his head, his ferrety features full of sympathy.

'Terrible,' agreed Colm.

'A terrible tragedy. Just out of the blue like that. Terrible.'

'You never know for whom the bell tolls,' said Colm helpfully.

'Did you know him well?' asked the man.

'Hardly at all,' said Colm. 'And you?'

'I hardly knew him either. Just what you'd read about him in the papers. The bits and pieces of stuff in the gossip columns.'

There was a silence which Colm inexplicably felt the need to fill.

'I'm friendly with his wife,' he blurted out.

'Oh yeah? She's a nice-looking lady. It must be terrible for her, and for those little kids.' He pulled heavily on his soggy cigarette, trying to keep it going.

'If you don't know them, why are you here?' asked Colm.

'I'm a policeman,' he said with a sigh. 'We always have to take a close look at death by misadventure, especially where the individual is wealthy, like Carter.' He yawned and threw away the butt of his cigarette. 'Loadsa dough. Oodles. Hey, you don't know anywhere good round here to get breakfast?'

'I'm not from round here,' said Colm.

'I suppose I'll just look down towards the village,' muttered the guy, and he pulled up his collar and hopped out into the easing rain. Colm watched him go, and lit another cigarette. He didn't know what he would do without cigarettes. He was the only person he knew who wasn't trying to give them up, who liked smoking, enjoyed it, relished every breathful.

Big Trouble

'I don't believe it,' said Colm, and drank a huge slug of his pint and lit another cigarette, despite the fact that he had one already burning in the ashtray.

'It's terrible,' said Sally.

'Terrible is an understatement.'

'And I'm sure I'm going to be caught.' She too downed her drink with the vigour of the damned. They were sitting in the adultery bar.

'You'll have to confess. You'll have to tell them.'

'They'll never believe I didn't mean it. I can't tell them. I'm in big trouble. What'll I do?'

Colm took another long drink of his beer. He felt as if he was in a dream, and any moment now he'd wake up and things would go back to normal.

'Tell me again why you didn't call for help?'

'I just didn't think of it. All I could think of was that I was going to be blamed. I don't have a strong character, you know. I'm not by nature heroic. I'm a mouse, a scuttler. When things get tough, I scuttle for cover.'

'And you didn't for a moment relish the thought that he'd be dead?'

'I swear not for one moment. I'm not a murderess. My nature isn't tough enough for that. You need to have firmness of purpose to be a murderess. You need a strong character for that. I told you, I'm lily-livered.'

Colm sat back against the support of the bar sofa. He was flummoxed.

'I'm the sort of person that things happen to. I never

make things happen. I never take control. That's my problem.'

Ditto.

'And if I did take control, my life would have turned out much better. I didn't ever want to marry James, it just turned out that I married him. I just ended up married to him. I suppose I was young. I remember a few weeks before our wedding day, I bought a dress. He didn't like it, said it was trollopy, and without asking he repacked it and sent it back to the shop. At the time, I thought it was very commanding and masterful and charming of him. I must confess I found it more than a little attractive. But now I'm not so sure.'

'Sorry to interrupt, Sally, but we'd better cut the reminiscences. We have a very serious situation on our hands.'

'I know we do.'

'I mean you do.'

'I know I do.'

The problem was as follows. Sally had gone out with James 'to talk things over'. Despite the drizzly rain, they had driven to a carpark on the hill of Howth, and got out of the car to go for a walk. James had told her everything, that he had been having an affair with Anita, that he wanted to divorce Sally and marry her sister. 'Though I'd been forewarned, though I knew all about it, I was still very shocked to hear him say it, and I got very shaky. Tears were streaming down my face, and I couldn't properly see where we were. In a fury, I just lashed out at him, punched him in the face. I hurt my fist, you know. Anyway, he stumbled backwards and overbalanced on the wet grass, and started to slip down the side. It isn't sheer or anything at that point, it's sloping, and it doesn't look like you would fall. But I think it was the rain which made it more slithery, and I watched as he skithered and bumped along. It seemed to take ages as he was trying to get a handhold on the surface as he slipped. At one stage he came to halt, and he went to grab onto a shrub, but that came away in his hand and he started slipping again. Finally, he went over the edge. And the terrible thing was that my overriding feeling was fear that I would be blamed. It never occurred to me to wonder how my kids would feel without a father. I was just afraid for my own self. And that goes to show what a disaster I am as a human being. It proves it beyond doubt.'

Sally played in an agitated fashion with her fingers, the knuckles white with tension.

'So I went back to the car and jumped in and drove home and I cooked dinner on the Aga for the kids and myself. Then I got worried about my footprints and I threw the shoes I had been wearing into the Aga and incinerated them. I never decided *against* calling the fire brigade or the coastguard or anything. It simply never occurred to me. I didn't once think of James after he'd gone over the edge. It was a real case of "out of sight, out of mind".'

'You're going to have to confess,' said Colm.

'Why? What good will that do anyone? It'll make things worse. At least now my kids only have to contend with a dead father. If I confess, they'll have to contend with a jailed mother, and the notion that their mother allowed their father to die because she was lacking in the necessary backbone required to phone the emergency services. And that is the most charitable interpretation they might put on it. They'll always suspect that I did him in. They're given to the macabre, those two. What good will it do anyone if I confess?'

Colm had no answer for that.

'I thought I'd get the funeral over with first and then see what I was to do. I thought I'd talk to you and see what you advise me to do. You're good at dealing with life.'

Colm groaned.

'Or death, I should say.'

Colm groaned again.

'The police asked me a lot of questions, but they were very nice and they believed everything I said. Because it was raining, there was nobody out walking, so we weren't seen on the hill. I was wearing an old wax jacket with a hood, so even if somebody saw me, they wouldn't recognise me. I looked terrible.'

'I think you should confess,' said Colm again.

'I don't see the advantage. I'd be a jailbird and my kids would have no parents. Besides, confessing is a strong, noble kind of thing to do. A weak person wouldn't confess. I have all the disadvantage in life of being weak. Let me at least have the one advantage.'

Colm knew he was advising her to do what he wouldn't himself have the nerve to do. Well, he wouldn't have been in the situation in the first place.

'I'm going to do nothing. It's safer,' said Sally. 'If they catch me, well and good, I'll fess up. But I'm not going to make it any easier. I owe that to my kids. Anyway, enough about me and my problems. Here I am wittering on as though I was the only person in life who had troubles. How about you? How's barmy Cordelia?'

Sally. Your troubles are pretty spectacular.

Colm wanted to escape. He wanted to put a lot of distance between himself and Sally. Her having told him the whole story made him an accessory. He was fond of her, but he didn't think the fondness extended as far as being an accessory to husband erasure. He needed time to think. Time to get a handle on the facts. He believed that Sally hadn't done it deliberately, but was he being a sap? Was Sally a scheming manipulator? She came across as such a ditz, but maybe she was a smooth operator with a ditzy veneer. And maybe, just maybe, he was being taken for a ride.

Ride, Sally, Ride.

Colm dragged deeply on his cigarette. Sally. Salacious Sally. She sat there in a state of agitation. But Colm knew that a bit of time would pass and her dread and fear would be blunted, and she would go back to her normal routine. No long-drawn-out tormenting from her conscience. She could and would put it all behind her.

'You know, I thought my life was in a bad way before,' said Sally, 'but in retrospect, it was fine. It's only when you get into a *real* pickle that you realise what had worried you before was very small beer. I had thought that it was a disaster when I found out that James was having an affair with Anita, but it was a far preferable state of affairs to his being dead and me being responsible.' She sighed and took a deep draught of her beer, calorie counts for once disregarded.

'Anita is apparently throwing a right wobbler. She's holed up in the Blackrock mansion with a crate of whiskey and has missed several work appointments. The only time she's appeared was for the funeral. People are starting to talk. People are beginning to say she's more cut up than expected. I've been saying that she has a nervous disorder to make her look less strange, but Alice the nanny said that she'd heard it said that Anita was a special friend of James. She's a nice girl, Alice, but very loose-tongued, and that is just what you *don't* want with a nanny. A nanny needs to be discreet. The kids are howling day and night, and the noise of them would break your heart. It makes me feel so wretched.'

Sally drained the last of her drink and held out the glass, soundlessly requesting a refill. Colm got up and went to the bar to get more. Reflected in the mirror behind the bar Colm saw a man who he knew was familiar, but he could not place. Someone from the town, from receptions and suchlike probably. A novelist-cum-screenwriter. Or a poet and critic. But then the man lit a cigarette, and from the way his hands cupped it and his fringe almost fell into the flame, Colm suddenly recognised him. It was the guy, the ferrety policeman, whom he had met in the porch after the funeral. The breakfast eater. He was sitting there, doing the crossword, minding his own business. A pint of beer was unhurriedly being consumed, its head dissolving away to nothing. He was wearing a lemon-yellow wool jumper, and he looked decidedly off duty. That's a coincidence, thought Colm. He must live around here. Must be a local. Dublin is such a small world. This was always happening. You'd meet someone in a certain context and they'd pop up in another. Colm thought about saying hello, but decided against it. The man was very absorbed in his paper.

He returned to Sally with the drinks.

'There's a guy over there I met at the funeral.'

'Who?'

'A policeman.'

'A policeman?' exclaimed Sally.

'I met him in the porch at the back of the church, and he asked me for a light. Said he was a cop.'

'Point him out to me.'

'There,' and Colm pointed at the back of the lemon-yellow jumper sitting at the bar. The man wriggled his shoulders, obviously to relieve backstrain. Those barstools. A killer on the back.

'He must live round here. It's only ever locals who come into this pub. Nobody else knows about it,' said Colm.

'Don't be silly,' said Sally. 'This means trouble. He must be my tail.'

'Your what?'

'He's tailing me.'

Of course. Why didn't I think of that?

'It means trouble for me, and for you. They must know about us. That means that they don't believe me. That means they suspect me, that means I'm in big trouble.'

That means I'm in trouble.

Dúirt bean liom go ndúirt bean leí.
(A woman said to me that a woman said to her)

Glup glup glup glurrup. James Carter's body drifts down through the water in slow motion, his face distorted with agony, bubbles escaping from his bluish lips. Strands of seaweed float by. A school of little fishes dart past. An octopus glows in the eerie dark. A jellyfish does a loop-the-loop with a starfish, their colours caught in shafts of underwater light. The drifting body gets nearer and nearer but the eye is drawn away by a school of formation-dancing blonde fishes singing 'I'm gonna wash that man right out of my hair'. Then everything goes fuzzy for a while. Then a sensation of diving deep, plunging into the turquoise water and at the sea bed, caught in seaweed, there is a wreck of a boat. A head suddenly falls out a hole in the hull. Just like *Jaws*. The head is James Carter's. The features blur in the water and when they clear again the face is Colm's own.

Colm woke with a jolt, covered in sweat. It was only a dream, but it had been totally vivid in a Disney Technicolor kind of way and it really startled him. It was late morning, judging by the colour of the light coming in the window. His head wasn't atrocious this morning, as he had been too worried by Sally last night to get very drunk. It would only be a matter of time before the police came to interview him. Colm was sure of it. And if they asked him,

192

he couldn't spill the beans on Sally. He would have to persuade her to confess. It was the only right thing to do.

He hauled himself out of bed and into the shower to clear his brain.

Boy oh boy, are my troubles getting worse. I'm having an affair with a husband killer. I'm going to be arraigned as an accessory after the fact.

Colm made a firm decision that he was going to tell Janet. He now had no choice. It was all going to come out. Everything would be discovered. Probably in two-inch-high headlines in the evening papers. He had to speak. Today was Wednesday, and often Janet came home at lunchtime on Wednesdays because the kids did sports or drama or gym or something. The smallies wouldn't be home for a while after that, so he could talk to her on her own. He would sit her straight down and tell her, before she could start talking about anything else. Or start doing the housework or start sticking broken things together with superglue.

Colm went down to the kitchen and made himself a cup of coffee. He sat down and waited for the interminable hour to pass before Janet appeared, slightly earlier than her normal early time. She didn't do her usual routine of hanging up her coat and stuff, but came straight down to the kitchen and burst through the door. She looked totally grey, and immediately Colm knew that something was up. She flung her bag down on a kitchen chair and slammed her armful of copies down on the table and turned to Colm, her eyes red-rimmed and wild and her hair escaping all over the place.

'Is it true? Tell me,' she asked, controlling her voice.

Colm stared uncertainly at her. She looked him squarely in the face.

'I know by your face it's true. You look guilty.'

Colm's eyes fell to the floor.

'You bastard,' she whispered in a frozen voice.

She knows. Someone has told her.

'You miserable worm of a man. I want you out of the house right this minute.'

Colm stared at Janet. This was an odd reaction, this tempest. He had expected her usual pained dignity. In fact, he had thought that the role of wronged wife would suit her quite well. She would bear it admirably, sporting her usual long-suffering mien which he had always found inexplicably attractive. Even now he thought that. But this reaction was very out of character.

'Janet, sit down and let's talk about it, rationally, like adults.'

'You expect me to be rational? You expect me to sit down?' screeched Janet. She was holding her hands out in front of her, and they were shaking wildly. She looked like a person who was restraining herself from doing violence.

'I'll make you a cup of tea,' he said, and went over to the kettle to fill it.

'Tea?' screeched Janet, uncontrollable now. 'Tea? You think I can drink tea? I blame myself, you know. If I'd kept on sleeping with you, it wouldn't have happened, you bastard. And I should have sensed something was up when you stopped putting pressure on me to sleep with you. I should have sensed it.'

She slumped down at the kitchen table, and her shoulders started to shake.

'I didn't believe it at first, it seemed out of character, but I can tell that it's true by your reaction. I thought she was making it all up. And now suddenly it seems to me that I don't know you at all, that I've never known you. That you could be anybody.'

Colm went over to her and put an arm across her frame. She jumped as though she'd been caressed with a red-hot poker.

'Don't touch me,' she said in a deadly voice.

Colm made two cups of tea thriftily from the one

194

teabag, and threw the used teabag into the sink. He saw Janet notice this, and her instincts go to reprimand him for sink-dirtying and slob-acting, then she stopped herself. He milked and sugared the tea and put it in front of her. She drank it, helplessly.

'Who told you?' asked Colm.

'Kate Cooper. I find out from Kate Cooper. And she told me with a distinct hint of prurience and malice. I don't like her. I know she's had a hard life, but that doesn't excuse her being gleeful at the troubles of others.'

'How did she know?'

'Phaedra told her.'

'How did Phaedra know?'

'Well, Cordelia told her.'

'And how did Cordelia know?'

'What are you talking about?' Janet got up and put her hand to her forehead, the tension there obvious from the lines. She turned round three hundred and sixty degrees distractedly, and sat down again. 'I need to speak to Cordelia, but she won't be back from the school trip till tonight. I want you out of here before she comes back, and then I'm going to decide whether or not to call the guards.'

What's Cordelia got to do with it?

'The guards already know,' said Colm.

'How?'

'Well, they suspect. They followed her when she was meeting me.'

'What? They followed Cordelia?'

'Cordelia. What's Cordelia got to do with it?'

Things are suddenly ceasing to make sense. Red alert. Red alert. Sense deficit.

'What are you talking about?' asked Colm gingerly.

'What are *you* talking about?'

Colm sat down at the opposite end of the table from Janet and cradled his mug of tea. It now seemed to him that whatever else was going on, Janet didn't know about

195

Sally. Momentarily he felt some relief, then regret, as it meant that he would have to tell her, then a rising panic regarding what was actually on Janet's mind.

'What are you talking about?' asked Colm again.

'I'm talking about you sexually harassing Cordelia.'

Colm laughed. The notion was ludicrous to him. Then Janet's face told him that laughing wasn't a good response.

'I never speak two words to her. She flees when I enter a room.'

'Naturally.'

'Janet. What exactly did Kate Cooper say to you?'

'She said Phaedra said that the reason Cordelia ran away was because you were always making passes at her. That you are always trying to get her to take ecstasy tablets and drink gin and smoke cigarettes, and that you're always discussing condoms and contraception. That every time you pass her in the hallway, your hands stray and feel her up. Cordelia told all this to Phaedra, but made her promise not to say anything to anybody. Phaedra told Kate in confidence shortly after Cordelia came back from her runaway episode. Kate decided to discuss it with Father Jack, her confessor up in Rathgar, and he advised her to tell me, which she did with glee.'

'It's balls.'

Janet was less sure of her ground now. Colm had seemed so guilty when she came in. But now he seemed not guilty. She was sorry she hadn't had a chance to hear Cordelia's side of the story.

'It's total balls. The only grain of truth in it is that I do occasionally give Cordelia money and tell her to buy an e tablet on me. It's a joke based on the absolute certainty that Cordelia will never take drugs. I also offer her cigarettes, but that too is a joke. I do it because she is totally anti-smoking and I know she will never take one. As for anything sexual, it's total nonsense.'

Janet drank her tea. She was confused now. She hadn't

believed it at first, she had received the report from Kate Cooper very coolly. Kate had phoned her at school, and she'd met her in an espresso bar, and over two steaming lattés Kate had calmly related her tale. Janet's first reaction was that somebody was making it up, it seemed so unlike Colm. But then, as she'd deliberated over it during the next few hours after returning to school to finish her classes, she thought it was far beyond Cordelia's or Phaedra's imaginations, and there must be something in it. By the time she got home, she had decided again that it was nonsense, but Colm's reaction when she came in the door had persuaded her there was some truth in it.

'What were you talking about when I came in?' she asked. 'Why did you react like that? What did you think I was talking about.'

'Aaah! Well, I'd better tell you. Janet. I'm – eh.'

Colm started to cry. Tears descended his face and after a moment, a trickle had turned into a gush. His nose started to run. His face was streaming with liquid, and he grasped at a box of Kleenex to halt the deluge.

'I'm so sorry Janet, but I'm having an affair,' and the tears kept on coming down his face, and splashed onto the table. He collapsed forward into his hands and wept Niagaraously, for himself, for Janet, for the dead love that hung in the air between them.

Janet stared at him as he struggled with this tidal wave of emotion.

'For how long?' she asked quietly.

'A couple of months,' he wiped at his face with the tissues. 'Oh Janet. We are at a terrible place if you could believe that of me.'

Janet slowly nodded.

'I would never harm Cordelia,' said Colm firmly. 'I know she doesn't like me, and I have to tell you that it hurts me so much. I've hoped she'd grow out of it, but she doesn't seem to be, and now it seems even worse than I thought. When I first met you, Cordelia was like this little fairy that accompanied you everywhere, and she occupied part of my heart. I'd never *known* a child before, properly known. And I had such fun with her. And now she hates me.'

'Who is the affair with?'

'Nobody you know.'

'Where did you meet her?'

'She wrote to me about the column.'

'What's her name?'

'Sally Carter.'

The name rang a bell with Janet.

'Is she the wife of the guy who just drowned?'

'Yup.'

Janet looked at him coolly for a moment and considered.

'Did she do him in?'

Colm paused for a long time, and then said, 'I hope not, but I think she might have and we're all in big trouble then.'

'And do you want to leave us and be with her?'

'No. But I want to do something because you and I, Janet, cannot live any longer in this empty marriage. Because I am so lonely here with you.'

He got up and went out into the hall, returning with his overcoat on.

'I'm going to go out now, maybe see can David put me up for a while,' said Colm. 'You'd better sort out Cordelia. Either she's making it all up or she's deluded. Either way she probably needs to talk to a professional, not gawky Phaedra whose reactions probably exacerbate the problem. Probably ghoulishly eggs her on. I'll go away for a while, and then we'll see.'

And his tears started again. Janet stared at him, his face beetroot from the emotion, his hair greasy and lank and misshapen. He turned to go out the door, his shoulders hunched and defeated. No spine. He was hopeless in her eyes, so lacking in all the qualities she admired, but somehow she looked at him and she couldn't help but love.

The Study

Colm felt exhausted as he walked down the road from the house. He decided he'd go for a pint first and then phone David's various establishments to try and run his friend to ground. David would surely put him up for a while. Colm's energy was very low. He had this thing lately where all his limbs felt like lead. He felt like they were trailing the ground after him. He passed the flotsam house and his eye was caught by a familiar sign in the front window. 'Room to let'.

A little shot of adrenalin reinvigorated his muscles and he skipped up the steps and rang Brian's bell, the second bell down in the stack of eight. A few noises, like stomach rumblings in a great beast, from inside the building, and Brian appeared.

'I want the room to let,' said Colm.

Brian looked surprised. He raised his eyebrows and shrugged and beckoned for Colm to follow him. 'It's a bit on the small side,' he said. 'People think it's too small, so they rarely stay in it for long. Only the very desperate want this room.'

'You're looking at the very desperate,' said Colm.

Brian went up the stairs, stopped outside the door to the room on the return. This was the equivalent room to Colm's study in his own house. Brian selected a key from his huge keyring, opened the door and allowed Colm pass though. The room was exactly the same in shape and dimension as Colm's study. It had an eerie familiar feel. There was a desk in this room also, in more or less the same position as where his own desk at home was. And the view from the window was very similar. Except there was no mews development and no mad lady. There was an iron bed against one wall, and a little two-plate cooker in the corner. It was amazing what could be fitted into a fairly small room. It felt right, this room. It had a snug womb-like feel. It was small, but it felt like the amount of space he would currently be able for. It was like when he was a kid and in trouble, he would hide in the wardrobe, not trying to evade detection, but rather trying to reduce the world to manageable proportions.

'There's no en suite, so you'd have to share the bathroom in the hallway with the guy in number five, but he's pretty clean and tidy. The communal bathroom rule is that you keep your shaving and toilet stuff in your own room. You put a small sum of money into a kitty every month, and that covers loo-roll and bulbs for communal areas.'

I could move into my study, and that would solve a lot of my problems. It would be like moving into my own head.

Colm fell to his knees and wrapped his arms around Brian's legs and said, 'I need this room. I need it so badly,' and the tears started again.

'You're in a bad way, brother,' said Brian, and he tore up the 'Room to let' sign and put it into Colm's hand. Colm went over to the bed and lay down on it. The mattress was ancient, and had lumpy contours and hillocks like the topography of County Monaghan, but he snuggled into a drumlin and, closing his eyes, fell off into a deep and restful sleep, the torn 'room to let' sign crumpled in his hand. Brian shut the door behind him and went downstairs to his own room, the equivalent of the Cantwell family kitchen, feeling surprised that Colm of all people would need his refuge. He never ceased to be amazed at the sheer range of people who topple out of respectability.

Colm felt like he had been asleep for hours, but in reality it was only an hour and a half. He opened his eyes and for a moment he had no idea where he was, then the little window told him he was in his study, then when his eyes focused on the rest of the room he remembered he was in number five and was now a fully fledged flotsam. He had always felt an affinity with this house, and he had been right. He did belong here. With the single parents and the Bosnian and the *Big Issue* seller and the magazine magnate. It was funny, but it was as though he had always known he was destined for here.

He decided to phone David, and try and round him up to accompany him on his debut restaurant review. But there was no phone in the room. Colm went out into the hallway, hoping to find a callbox, but there was only a gap on the wall where a phone used to be. He went on down to the kitchen, or rather Brian's pad, and tapped on the door. Brian's room seemed cavernous by comparison to his study.

'The kettle's just boiled, brother. How about some brew?'

'Thanks mate,' said Colm and sat down as a mug of tea was prepared and put into his hands. Brian's room was meticulously ordered and clean. There was a slatted divider half-heartedly separating the living/sleeping area from the cooking area. Every square inch was utilised by some essential appliance. It registered with Colm how wasteful of space it all was at home. In his old home.

'Is there a coinbox in the house?' asked Colm, and Brian smiled.

'We got rid of it. It just attracted vandals. Here.' Brian passed him a mobile phone. 'When you're homeless, the first thing you need to get is a mobile.'

Colm ran David to ground and arranged for him to join him for Italian dinner that night.

'Do you want to talk about your troubles, brother?' asked Brian. 'I don't mean to pry but if it would help, my ears are yours.'

Dying of curiosity. Dying for gossip.

'Not right now,' said Colm, 'but maybe in another few days. I'm going to talk things over with my friend David. We've been friends since we were eleven.'

'That's good,' said Brian. 'Keeping friends for a long time is a sign of good character.'

Colm couldn't help feeling patronised.

This is the trouble. People are very nice until you get to know them well, then you realise that even good people are terrible.

Colm set off to catch the bus into town. He left the house feeling weird, as he was approaching the same road as he always approached but from an entirely different perspective. He was nearer the bus stop now, though. *That* was an advantage. He came out of the front gate, and was heading for the main road, when Cordelia appeared coming towards him, dragging her hockey stick and sports bag, her head gloomily bowed and her eyes glued to the pavement. Colm thought of passing her, but his courage failed and he ran back into the front garden of the flotsam house, his home, and hid behind the dustbins until she went past. He couldn't adequately hide his bulk from the road by crouching, so he lay down, amongst the muck and litter that lay around the bins, stray evidence of neighbourhood cats. He peeped out and watched Cordelia as she went. Truly she was the most sorrowful-looking child he had ever seen. He was frightened of her now. She was so hostile, and now he knew she was saying all these things about him, the depth of her enmity was clear to him. She hated him. And there was something so potent about that. It wasn't the mild languid dislike of middle age. Nor the weary contempt of later life. It contained the pent-up energy of adolescence. Like a river dammed, the deluge enormously powerful in its threat. And it frightened him. And he didn't know what to do about it. The fact that her stories weren't true didn't make it any easier to sort out. It meant that the kid was in really deep trouble in her head. She must *really* hate him to have made it all up.

Cordelia was safely past, and Colm got up and dusted himself off. He really was a sight, having slept in his clothes and scrabbled around in the dirt. He had brought nothing with him from home, his old home, not even a comb, and he would have to go back tomorrow when everybody was out and retrieve a few essentials. He went on down to the end of the road and hopped his bus into town.

Colm arrived into the Italian restaurant to find David seated with his napkin attached to his neck like a baby's bib and absently chewing cheese sticks, while drinking something long and white. The napkin was huge, of Alice in Wonderland proportions. Colm gave his crumpled coat to the waiter and approached the table and before he sat down, David blurted out, 'God, I am so glad to see you, I really need to talk to someone. I'm in terrible trouble. Sit down, sit down.'

You took the words right out of my mouth.

'You remember Gemma Blake. The kid who sued me.'

'Yes,' said Colm.

'Well, something terrible has happened, and I feel really bad about it and I couldn't sleep last night. She's dead. I just feel so guilty.'

'What happened?'

'She died in a car crash.'

'Hold on, I don't get it, why do you feel guilty?'

'She bought a Porsche nine-eleven with the lawsuit money and has apparently been driving it around at high speed, and she crashed it into a tree in the south of France where she was holidaying with her boyfriend, spending the remainder of the money.'

'Hold on, hold on, so why do you feel guilty?'

'Well, it's my fault. She wouldn't have been driving round the South of France in a fast car if it hadn't been for me harassing her. She'd be still working in the Harbour Bar earning three-fifty an hour, and there's very little trouble you can get into doing that.'

'That's ridiculous, David, you can't be held responsible for what people do with money they obtain by suing you.'

'And, eh, I hoped that things would turn out badly for her. I cursed her a few times and said I hoped that the money would do her no good. And that's exactly what happened. And I feel I caused it by thinking bad things.'

Oh, the luxury of having imaginary problems.

'David. This is daft. You are perfectly entitled to have been annoyed with her. It's entirely human, and you can't be responsible for how she spent the money.'

'Then why do I feel guilty, so? Why couldn't I sleep last night?'

'Because you don't have any real problems, so you make a few up to give your life a bit of texture.'

David was outraged. His face took on a purple colour. The first course arrived. Pasta. It slithered down Colm's gullet and he hardly noticed what it tasted like. David chewed his portion bad-temperedly, venting his annoyance on the fettucine.

'Colm, I listen with great sympathy to all your problems, and I think I deserve a little more care when I have troubles of my own.'

Colm sighed. He could see David's point of view, but he hadn't the energy to engage with it. He knew he should try to be sympathetic and patch things up, but somehow his patience was gone, and he coolly said: 'It's egocentric in the extreme, David, for you to think yourself responsible for Gemma Blake's accident. You are not the centre of the universe, and destinies do not revolve around you. They have a dynamic all their own.'

David looked hurt. He took off his giant napkin bib and placed it on the table and got up. He summoned his coat and left.

And Colm was alone.

It was not ten-thirty. Janet would by now have spoken to Cordelia about the Kate Cooper story. Colm wondered should he have stayed and been there for the confrontation. But he would have hated to be there. He couldn't imagine anything more painful. Would she admit she was fibbing? Or maybe Phaedra made the whole thing up. If Cordelia insists it's true, Janet will probably believe her. Colm ate his main course, and washed it all down with a gullet full of expensive wine. He ate and ate and ate until he felt like bursting, until he felt his trouser-band tight against his tummy. And when he could fit nothing more in, at last he was satisfied.

The Internet

Colm let himself into number thirty to retrieve some stuff. It was mid-morning and everybody was out. He felt like a burglar. The most important thing was his computer, as he had to write up his restaurant review and print out his crossword in order to be able to deliver them the next day. He went into the bedroom and got his shaving and toilet things from the en suite. The bed lay large and accusing in the centre of the room. He missed the bed. Even after just one night.

He remembered vividly the day they'd bought it, how he and Janet had bounced on it like kids in a furniture warehouse in Kildare. He had gently shoved Janet down on it, wondering would the respectable teacher in her protest, but she had been carried away by the moment and rolled over and over kicking her feet in the air, shrieking with laughter. He had bounced on it too, the plastic shop covering creaking underneath, and rolled over on top of her, until her protests overtook her laughter.

'Newly-weds?' asked the middle-aged shop woman who stared on indulgently.

'Not yet,' answered Janet. 'Two weeks time. Saturday fortnight.'

'Enjoy it while it lasts,' she said as she went off to do up an invoice. Colm and Janet had paid no attention to the woman, who was good-humoured and smiling at them, the tone of her comment benign. But the shop woman's line remained in Colm's memory as a part of the episode of bed-buying, only the sweet tone of the woman had become

207

sickly. It had seemed so impossible then that their relationship would founder. But founder it had. Colm lay down on the bed for a moment, to feel it for one last time. He tried again to remember his proposing to Janet, but he couldn't summon it. He fished about in his brain, but it wasn't to be found. It had disappeared out of his mental record. It was strange. He could remember buying the bed, he could remember viewing and buying the house, he could remember so many things, so many irrelevant details, but he couldn't remember that. The delete button had been pressed.

Colm carried the computer hard disk out of the front door and was overwhelmed by the feeling of being a burglar. A couple of passers-by glanced in his direction and he felt that they looked at him most suspiciously. But he persevered. He *was* a burglar. He was burgling his old life to furnish his new.

He got his bedsit well set up. All his files from the study in number thirty were moved in and stacked under the bed in number five. Now he *really* had manuscripts under the bed. He took a brass-framed picture of John and June on John's First Holy Communion day from the drawing room. John looking concentrated and holy, and June grinning devilishly. He hesitated a moment, and looked at a mother-of-pearl-framed family portrait taken shortly after June's birth. Cordelia aged eight and looking sweet as sugar, John a toddler. A tired-looking Janet clutched June who was a tiny baby. And Colm stood in the centre, looking so proud, his smile shone from the photo like a lighthouse beacon. A proud *pater familias* in a proper family. He popped it into his swag bag, and scuttled up to number five with his spoils.

He put his photos on the windowledge of the bedsit and felt marginally better. It made his new existence less of a shock now that he had some pictorial evidence of his past. It helped the transition. He sat down to do his bit of work on the computer. It was dead handy to have the kettle there in the room, he didn't have to go so far for his cup of tea. He worked away, colourfully describing the meal he ate the previous evening, though he hardly remembered a thing about it. The review was a rave. Colm was sure he would have noticed if anything hadn't tasted right.

Colm finished the task in no time at all and pressed 'print'. He was sorry it was so rapidly finished, because now he would have to think about things. He would have to think about talking to the smallies. He would have to talk to Janet and see what had transpired with Cordelia, the teenager from hell, and he'd have to tell his parents he'd moved house and wrecked his marriage. It was all too much. And as for Sally, he really didn't know where to start dealing with that business. And unfortunately, he'd pissed David off so he was now officially friendless.

He lay down on the hillocky bed and literally put his head under the pillow, groaning and hoping everything would go away. A knock came on the door. It was Brian.

'I found this TV in a skip below in Rathmines. It works perfectly well now I've changed the fuse in the plug. It's amazing what people are throwing out these days. Celtic tiger my granny. The television stops working, so the owner buys a new one. Changing a fuse in a plug is more hassle than going to an electrical store and forking out two tonnes for a brand new TV. Do you know that one time I found a Waterford crystal vase in a skip, totally undamaged? Someone had just gone off the look of it, and discarded it.'

'Maybe they were throwing out their wedding presents.'

'I never thought of that,' said Brian. 'Do you want the telly?'

Colm nodded. 'Great. Thanks mate.'

Brian put the television on top of the wardrobe, which was the only remaining clear surface. Once Colm had moved all his stuff in, the room had started to look a lot smaller.

'I'll hook you up to the cable.' Brian opened the window, reached out rather dangerously and pulled in a flex, which he attached with gaffer tape to a wire at the back of the TV. 'I'm the official recipient, but I hook up everybody elses on the quiet. So if anybody from the cable company calls, whatever you do don't let them inside the building if I'm not here to disconnect everybody.'

Criminal activity. I knew I'd end up a criminal. I've always felt a vague calling to criminality.

'Is that not illegal?'

'Of course it's illegal. You will be thieving television programmes. The alternative is to allow them to rob you blind by charging the earth to the individual members of this multi-dwelling. The privilege of living within the law is the preserve of the rich, and it is therefore all the more surprising why so many rich people break the law.'

'Have you got Sky Sports?' asked Colm.

'No, sorry.'

'Only kidding,' said Colm, and he tried to laugh.

Brian paused. 'I met your wife on the road this morning, and she asked me did I know where you were. I said that I didn't. Do you know, that is the first time she's ever spoken to me? I had no idea she knew who I was. Did I do the right thing?'

'What do you mean?'

'In saying I didn't know where you were.'

'Yeah, I'm going to tell her soon. Later on. Maybe tomorrow. Or after that. Mañana. Mañana.'

Brian left the room. Colm's newly acquired TV satisfactorily jingling about something or other. He lay back down on the bed and put his head under the pillow once more. He never wanted to go out again. He decided he no longer wanted to make his Friday trip into Castle Grub Street. He wanted to stay safely in his bed.

An hour passed and he just lay there, with a blank brain. A knock came on the door.

'What fresh hell this?' he asked, the hint of melodrama suggesting his humour might be restoring itself.

It was Brian, with a cup of cocoa. 'Here, have some of this,' he said. Colm obediently took the steaming mug and sipped. He knew that Brian was keeping an eye on him, making sure he didn't come to any harm, wasn't doing anything strange with ropes and chairs.

Do I seem that ragged?

Colm decided he'd better pull himself together, start trying to function. He really didn't want to go out. He didn't want to meet anybody he knew. He was terrified that he'd meet Cordelia on the street again, but he couldn't stay in for ever. He transferred his crossword and his restaurant review onto a floppy and, carefully pulling up the collar of his jacket and wearing an odd tea-cosy hat belonging to Brian, he went down the town to the Internet Café. It had opened about six months previously, and Colm had often passed it, averting his gaze in the manner of a vegetarian passing a butcher.

The Internet Café was full of seated individuals who didn't look to left or right, but expertly keyboarded in fervent communication with 'out there'. On instruction from the gentle giant behind the counter, Colm acquainted himself with the delights of electronic mail. He sent in his material, relieved that he might never see Deirdre again. He could just click on 'send' while he sat here and drank too-strong coffee and smoked a fag. He would send in his copy electronically, and they would send him his cheque electronically. He needn't exist in real space at all, he could be a cyberworker. Nobody need know where he was. Mysteriously, without his noticing, his coffee cup kept refilling. He sat back, slightly mystified by how easy it all was. He had paid for half an hour on the machine, so he decided to stay and observe for the twenty-eight minutes remaining.

'How are you getting on?' he remarked to the young person on his right, a skinny bespectacled youth who looked studenty, and was ferociously typing in messages while snorting and sighing. It seemed like high drama to Colm. The boy glanced up from the machine, his eyes glazed.

'Pardon?' he asked.

'Just wondering how you're getting on. Are you having trouble, like?'

The bespectacled youth shook his head and returned to his machine.

'Talk about weird. Geek city,' he muttered under his breath, leaning his head on his left arm, thus shutting Colm out of his line of vision and glued himself more fervently to his screen.

Colm didn't know the etiquette. He was a dinosaur. He ruffled his scales, shook his tail and left the Internet Café.

My scene, not.

He went to a strange bar, afraid that somebody would come looking for him in any of his regular haunts. He didn't want to be found. He didn't want to see Janet, not for a day or two, or a year or about that, and he didn't want to see Sally at all. Cordelia needed to attend a professional before he could communicate with her, and the smallies he would have to talk to and explain everything. But not yet. He wasn't able for it yet. It was around six-thirty and the bar had a light buzz, a few groups having a drink after work before they rushed off home to their responsibilities. And there were as always a few men drinking alone, like him. You never felt out of place in a pub. He nodded in a friendly fashion to the lonesome men, and sat up at the bar. The pints slid down easily, and he heard a lengthy dissertation on how a man just missed a treble in Cheltenham from a loquacious pint-

212

swiller at the far side of the bar, who appeared to be talking to the barman, but was happy to include anybody who might listen in his storytelling ambit. Colm sent a few encouraging nods in his direction. Anonymous chat about horses. It was just what he wanted. Just what he was able for. Colm relaxed with his new friend, and the hours passed gently until closing time.

Colm climbed down off his barstool feeling a slight twinge in his back, despite the anaesthesia of the drink. He headed for home, feeling comfortable and almost brave in the darkness of the inner-suburb streets. He stumbled along, substantially pissed, and went down Candlewick Avenue. His mind a little absent, autopilot brought him to number thirty. He got to the gate, and was about to go up the path to the front door, when he realised and stopped himself.

This isn't my home any more. I don't live here no mo'.

He looked up at the big gloomy house, a light on in the master bedroom. Unusual. Janet normally had it turned off by eleven. Probably big family conferences. Hopefully Cordelia was getting reprogrammed.

Hopefully she'll see sense and admit the story is bullshit. If she insists it's true, Janet will probably believe her and then maybe she'll stop me seeing the smallies. And then my life, which is a bit low on point anyway, will become totally pointless.

Tears came to his eyes. He took out a small precautionary bottle of whiskey from his pocket and had a slurp. It burnt his innards and cheered him up somewhat. He turned on his heel and headed back to number five, doing a little shuffling dance. A dance of the damned.

Number five was lit up like a ship. Every flat had a light on. Nobody went to bed early in this house. This was a house of the undisciplined, the irregular. Colm let himself in and made his way to his bedsit. It felt better, coming home here. He felt more in charge, more adult. He felt like it was his own roof, whereas number thirty always felt like Janet's house. Though it had been bought by dead Great Auntie Julia's money, it had always seemed that it was Janet who procured it and fixed it up.

He fell into his bed, and was drifting off to sleep, when through the haze of tiredness he saw Brian gently open the door and peep in, register he was asleep, and creep out again.

He is kind, Brian. A guardian angel.

And Colm was asleep.

Disguise

Aknock on the door. 'What fresh hell this?' called out Colm, and Brian popped his head around the jamb.

'I've brought breakfast,' he said, and came into the room with a freshly cooked breakfast on a tray. 'I'm just looking after you for the first day or two until you get settled and into your stride.'

Colm felt vaguely narked by this. It was all a bit much, but he was dying of thirst, and the orange juice followed by the tea did the trick and the sausages were amongst the nicest he'd ever tasted, so he swallowed his annoyance along with the breakfast and sat up.

His shirt from the previous day was lying on the chair, and even from this distance it was obvious that it was pretty manky. He was about to go out to the hot press to fetch another when he remembered where he was. He'd have to let himself into number thirty to get shirts and undies from the hot press. Today was Friday. Usually he spent Friday morning getting himself ready for his trip to town in the afternoon to deliver his copy, but now that he was a cyberworker he didn't have to do that.

But it was niggling in his mind. How did he know that the copy had gone in? Maybe it had gone somewhere else. Maybe his crossword was floating round the World Wide Web and would be published in Tokyo. How did he know that 'send' icon was reliable? It seemed so paltry. He didn't trust it.

Brian sat by his bed and drank a mug of tea.

'Are you going to tell them at home where you are?' he asked.

'Stop hassling me,' said Colm.

'They'll be worried. They'll think something has happened to you.'

'Something has happened to me,' said Colm.

'Do you want to talk about it, brother?'

'Naw, not yet.'

Brian left him to it and he carefully mopped up the yolk of his expertly cooked egg with bread, diligently chasing every last yellow dribble around the edges of the plate. He wiped the plate clean with another piece of bread. Details. He could cope with details.

He decided the next course of action was a shower. One step at a time. When he confronted the entire day it seemed far too much for him, but when he considered the next twenty minutes, he felt equal to the task. He got out of the bed and a mild ache in his back told him he had spent an imprudent amount of time on the barstool the previous night. He went down the hall to the communal bathroom, and looked all around for a shower attachment. There was a bracket on the wall, and a fitting on the taps, but no attachment. He resigned himself to a soak in the bath, and turned on the hot tap. There was no hot water. A sign on the wall suggested you put three 50p bits into a slot machine to generate enough hot water for a bath.

No way. I'll stay stink.

He boiled up a kettle in his room, and thereby acquired enough hot water for a shave and underarm lick, which would do him to be going on with. He carried the kettle of water down to the bathroom to do the shaving job. There was a tiny cracked mirror which made him look like a Picasso, exactly how he felt. He got no overview of his face, which was probably a mercy. Feeling slightly better, his jaw nice and smooth, he went back into his bedsit and pondered his situation. He thought about getting a clean shirt and underwear, but was afraid to go back to number thirty to collect stuff, as Janet might take the day off school and lie in wait for him. She would know he'd been in yesterday. Truly, he couldn't face her. He'd go to Dunnes Stores and buy some cheap undies and a clean shirt to keep him going. And he'd get some cheap strange clothes as a disguise, so he could go out and not be recognised.

He sat down at his computer, which seemed the only safe thing to do, and he opened his creative writing file and started to doodle and dawdle and dribble, and thought about actually climbing inside the computer and finding a safe haven in there, his mind occupied with writing, and therefore too busy to allow anything else get into his head and cause him trauma or oppression. The writing had suddenly become a way of shutting out everything else.

He sat and worked for over three hours. He didn't print it out at the end, left it locked inside the machine, secret and safe, where he'd find it again when he needed it next. Hunger arrived, lunch hunger, so he decided to go down to the centre of Rathmines and get something to eat. The Corner Cafe was still busy, though it was way past lunch hour. Halfway through his totally tasteless quiche and beans, the worry about whether or not his crossword and review had arrived came back to plague him, so when he finished he went over to a callbox and dialled Deirdre.

'Colm!' said Deirdre, with more enthusiasm than felt right.

'Deirdre, did the copy arrive on the e mail.'

'Colm, the crossword is fantastic! It is the best crossword I've ever seen. Totally great. Totally fine. You really have a gift for crosswords.'

'Thank you, Deirdre.'

'Eh, Colm, where are you?'

'I'm in Rathmines.'

'Your wife dropped in, looking for you, and also the blonde woman, Sally, is that her name? I said I wasn't expecting you as I'd already received the material by e mail. But, eh, why is everybody looking for you?'

'Deirdre, I've disappeared. I've become a cyberworker. Logged on, tuned in and dropped out. Just keep sending the cheque to the bank, and I'll keep sending in the material. Oh, and I'll forward the receipt for the dinner by surface mail, with a stamp on it. I gotta go. Bye.'

'But Colm, is there something the matter?'

Dying to know. Her nose growing inches by the minute.

'Bye Deirdre, there's a mad guy hammering on the glass wanting to use the phone, Bye.'

This is much better than going in. This way I can terminate the conversation.

Colm was short of money so he went to a cash dispenser and got himself a few bob, avoiding his own local bank in case someone was lying in wait for him there. He bought himself some cheap undies first. After paying for them at the cash desk, he went into a changing booth and put them on, discarding the old in a large tubular ashtray. The old grey y-fronts sat on top of the ashtray, an installation in elastene and fag ash.

If I was a conceptual artist, that'd be art.

Colm felt uneasy as he left the store, thinking that the security people might think that he'd put them on without paying for them. He went out the exit, expecting a long arm to land on his shoulder, and didn't feel comfortable again until he was fifty yards down the street.

He went into Oxfam and bought some second-hand clothes which were a totally different look than he normally wore. He bought some tight pants and a red and black striped T-shirt and a fake leather jacket. He also got some old cowboy boots with a heel, as he'd remembered somewhere that one of the most recognisable features of a person was their walk, and an unusual shoe could disguise that. As a final touch, he tried on a big leather belt and a cheap pair of sunglasses. He looked totally different, his beer gut protruding to the front like a trophy rather than hidden under a sloppy jumper, the cowboy boots giving his legs a bowed appearance, and his walk a certain slouchy rhythm. Nobody would recognise him now. He looked totally different. Except the haystack. That needed radical work. He went to the hairdresser's, where a training session was in full swing. They'd do his hair for free so long as he didn't mind a student hairdresser under supervision.

'No probs,' said Colm.

'What do you want done?'

'Something very different.'

The students set to work. They dyed it black and permed it, and when he looked at himself in the mirror two hours later the transformation was radical. The student stylist went to endless trouble to get a lock of hair to fall annoyingly over one eye. He looked like Phil Lynott in a trick mirror. Poor Phil Lynott. So young. Tears came to Colm's eyes.

I'm going to have to get a grip on myself.

As a test, he went down to Brian's magazine stand and bought a paper off him. Brian took his money and gave him change without a hint of recognition and went on to the next customer. Colm took off the sunglasses.

'Brother, you look totally different. I didn't recognise you! You've done something to your hair?'

Great. Now I feel safe.

Colm put the sunglasses back on and they made him feel invisible. It was a wonderfully comfortable feeling.

'So what do you think?' asked Colm.

'You look like a sleazebag, or a pimp. You definitely don't look like yourself,' said Brian.

'Fine,' said Colm.

'Colm, tell me this, are you in trouble with the law? You don't have to give me any details, but do tell me anything that I need to know.'

219

'I'm not in trouble with the law. I just need to disappear for a while. It's a mental health strategy.'

'Fine, brother, fine,' said Brian. 'I understand those mental health strategies. I'll ask no questions.'

Colm hung around the magazine stall for a while, serving the odd customer and feeling very brave to be out in the open. Brian took advantage of his presence to head off and do a bit of business. Magazine selling. It was a pleasant way to make a living. Especially on a fine day like today. Brian returned and the customers were glad to see him. He was like a part of the street furniture. Colm left the stall and wandered off, savouring his new invisibility. It was Friday, and the pubs beckoned, but he wasn't in the form and he had no company, so he returned to number five, confidently strolling down Candlewick Avenue, happy he wouldn't be recognised if he was spotted. He idly read the newspaper for a while, until he felt hungry again, and went down to the nearest chippy for a steak and kidney pie, which he brought back to his bedsit and ate with his fingers. He had no cutlery. Keeping himself fed was a bit of a chore with no Janet-stocked fridge for him to graze.

With nothing else to do, he had no choice but to pass the time at his computer, writing, composing, doing his own thing.

Right and Wrong

The weekend passed and Colm stayed mainly indoors, reading and writing and lying low and attending to the endless demands of keeping himself fed. He knew he'd have to contact Janet, but he still couldn't face it. He went out for a walk to try and get his courage up and thought he'd maybe phone her from down town. He turned into the road with the bench, and there was perched Sally. She had been driving round looking for him for some time, had given up and decided to sit there and see would he appear, her huge silver car parked two foot out from the kerb, causing an obstruction. She was sitting on the edge of the bench, and she was wiping tears from her eyes and powdering her nose. Colm spied her from the end of the road and was torn between dodging down a side street and doubling away from her, and talking to her. She looked so lost, so forlorn. He would be blowing his disguise if he talked to her, but it was mainly Cordelia he was hiding from. He dodged down the side street, took about ten steps, then changed his mind and turned back towards the lone blonde figure sitting on the seat.

He approached her and she took no particular notice of him. He sat down beside her, and soundlessly lit a cigarette.

'Fuck off creep,' she said without looking up. 'I don't believe that I'm going have to deal with kerbside creeps as well as all my other problems,' and she moved a foot further away from him on the bench. 'You wouldn't have sat yourself down there if you knew what a problem person I am. So just go on your way and find someone else to harass. Jesus!'

'Sally, it's Colm.'

'Colm?' she exclaimed, turning to look at him. He took off his sunglasses.

'It is you.'

He grinned at her.

'You look like, I don't know what, some kind of sleaze or something. What have you done to yourself?'

'It's a disguise. I don't want people to be able to recognise me. I want to disappear.'

'Stand up and let me look at you.'

Colm obeyed the command.

'Yeah, you look like some kind of aging playboy. All you need is a medallion. But it's kind of nice. It's sort of sexy and repulsive at the same time. Why are you wanting to disappear? You look like Dennis the Menace. It's the T-shirt,' said Sally.

'It was the only T-shirt in the shop.'

They got into the car and drove off aimlessly. Colm at first liked being on the move, but then Sally's driving started to make him nervous, when she swerved to avoid a cyclist and almost hit an oncoming truck. Sally honked her horn. 'Those damn juggernauts act like they own the road. They're safe perched high up in their cabs, and they just bully all other drivers out of their way like fascists. Bloody Nazis.'

'Pull in here,' said Colm as they passed a pub in Booterstown. He'd never been in it before and thought they might be safe there.

'I've been trying to contact you for days,' said Sally. 'I called into your office and spoke to Deirdre, and I've been on the phone and talked to David. I didn't phone your home, but David told me he'd been trying to get you there with no luck.'

David's been trying to get me?

222

'I've moved out,' said Colm. 'Big problem with Cordelia.' He paused for a moment, trying to think of some introductory sentence to describe the Cordelia problem but couldn't think of anything, so he just ploughed ahead. 'Janet told me that she'd been talking to Kate Cooper and – '

'Who's Kate Cooper?'

'Phaedra's mum. Janet says that Kate says that Phaedra told Kate – '

'Who's Phaedra?'

'Cordelia's best friend. Well, Cordelia told Phaedra that I keep coming on to her, so I moved out. I'm in a flat.'

'Coming on to her? What do you mean?'

'I mean, you know, coming on to her. Sexually.'

'Wow. That's terrible. And weird. You aren't a "coming on" sort of guy. Slightly repressed in that department if anything.'

'Yes. That's what I thought.'

'Here, let me get this straight. Janet said that Kate said that Phaedra said that Cordelia – '

'And I told Janet about you.'

'Oh my God, you're in the soup.'

'So I'm in a flat.'

Sally rocked back and forth for a moment and started to sniffle.

'You've left your family for me, it's so kind, and I don't deserve it because I'm such a disaster.'

I didn't leave them for you. Please don't get that into your head.

Colm went up to the bar again, his gait so altered by the heel on the cowboy boots that he was listing from side to side like a ship. Sally looked at him and giggled when he returned.

'I can't get over the change in you. You look totally different. It's like an entirely different person.'

Colm was getting quite self-conscious about the tight T-

223

shirt. It seemed to be shrinking as he wore it and was starting to ride up his belly.

'Is that policeman still following you around?' asked Colm.

'No. But they've interviewed me extensively. And questioned me about my whereabouts, but they don't have an exact time for the "event", so they can't pin me down without an alibi. They do suspect me, I'm sure of it. I had to tell them about us, you and me, which they knew about in any case. It's made them a bit less cautious in their treatment of me as I'm a bit less of the grieving widow in their eyes. But I also dished the dirt on Anita, so I think they went off to Blackrock to harass her, which gave me a bit of a breather.'

Sally seemed to have calmed down a lot about the episode. She was taking everything alarmingly in her stride. The overriding objective seemed to be to evade detection. Thou shalt not get found out. And now, by listening to her, he was colluding with that. He tried to go along, but his instincts worked against it.

'I think you should confess.'

'And leave my kids parentless? No way. You've got to be out of your mind to suggest it. I wish you'd stop saying that. It's not going to happen. It's illogical.'

'It's not illogical. It's moral.'

'Moral? What do you mean, moral? How is it moral when it does no good for anybody?'

'It would do you good. You would 'fess up, and you'd be jailed and pay your debt to society and then you'd emerge with a clean conscience and start anew.'

'I haven't got a debt to society. I have a debt to James, perhaps, but when you add it all up, abuse for abuse, it's just about even. All the shit I've had to take from him over the years is just about equal to one fatal push over a cliff.'

'Sally!'

'It's true. Anyway, when I meet him down below, I'm

224

sure he'll give me a sound thrashing. I'm not confessing. And that's that. You're very old-fashioned, Colm, in your notions. Morality is all about pragmatism now, not abstract principles.'

'And what about right and wrong?'

'The right thing to do is not to leave my kids parentless. I know in my bones that's the right thing to do.'

Colm felt he was losing this argument. Sally was being very persuasive. And he was enjoying his drink and moral principles went into an inevitable slide on the third pint.

'What's your apartment like?' asked Sally.

'Well, apartment isn't quite the word. Bedsit describes it better. It's a back room at number five on Candlewick Avenue. It's the equivalent room to my study at home,' and he corrected himself, 'in my old home.'

'You're just down the road?'

'Hence the disguise.'

'You're dead lucky to have found a flat. People can't leave their marriages any more because of the property crisis. I know several people who are in terrible marriages, but they can't split up because they can't afford a flat. It's doing more to keep marriages together than all the archbishops.'

Sally went home to her kids after a couple of drinks, but at about ten o'clock she met him in a small pub in Rathmines and accompanied him back to his bedsit, having stowed her ostentatious car in the supermarket carpark.

'I've never been in a bedsit before. When I was a nurse I always lived in accommodation,' she said as they went in the door of number five and up to his room. 'I've always thought of them as kind of romantic.'

Colm opened the door to his little room.

'It's eh, fine,' said Sally. 'It's amazing how you've fitted so much stuff in here.' She flopped down on the bed, and Colm opened a couple of cans of beer from his tiny fridge and handed her one. She took it and held it uncertainly, unused to drink coming out of anything other than glass.

'Here's to things improving,' said Sally, and clanged her can off Colm's.

'Yeah,' said Colm.

Hours later, after a lot of chat and with a curious mixture of reluctance and enthusiasm, he took her to bed in the landscape of County Monaghan and they did a very good job shutting out their troubles as they ducked and dived and manoeuvred their way around the drumlins and hillocks, and finally she came and he came and they slept.

While he was drifting off, he noticed Brian open the door an inch and peer in and see the company he had and smile with satisfaction and leave.

When Colm came to, Sally was pulling on her clothes and cursing, 'I'm late, I'm dammit late,' as she pulled on stockings and a skirt and ran a comb through her hair. 'I need to be there when the kids wake up. They wake at six-thirty. Early birds.' She straightened her clothes and smiled at him.

'Things have a way of working out for the best. I'm a widow and you're officially separated, so that's nice. At least we don't have to worry about *that* being morally wrong. Not that it would stop us, but it's nice to not have to worry.'

Colm was yawning and rubbing his eyes, slowly coming to.

'Those damn detectives are coming again this morning. By the way, have they been in touch with you? They said they were going to give you a call.'

'They wouldn't be able to find me. I've disappeared.'

'That probably doesn't look too good.'

She rushed out the door in a flurry, leaving Colm very confused. He didn't approve of Sally, but he couldn't get away from her. There was something that bound him to her. Something inexplicable. She seemed to have a right to walk into his life and make claims.

Digestives

Colm woke to an unpleasant smell, and it was only when he got out of bed that he realised it was himself. The sun was high in the sky, the afternoon well on. He made his way down to the bathroom armed with a few 50ps, and put them into the slot machine. He ran a big deep steamy bath and hopped into it and lay back, and the water caressed his back and sucked some of the tension out. He'd never enjoyed a bath so much as this. He closed his eyes and relaxed and imagined for the first time in a long while that he was at peace. He knew that he'd have to contact Janet today. Before she put out a missing persons notice on him. Janet had had a good few days with Cordelia, so hopefully something would be sorted on that score. He gave himself a good scrub in the bath and started to feel much better. Renewed. Refreshed. Washed. He hadn't put the kettle on for his shaving water, so he shaved in the bath, something he hadn't done for a long time. Janet had forbidden it as it left too much scum in the bath and was in danger of clogging the ancient plumbing. With the Victorian architectural aesthetic went the Victorian plumbing problems. He had obeyed. So much of his behaviour was in fact under orders from Janet. Now that he had escaped from her, he felt strangely incapable, yet exhilarated. He had become institutionalised. Rendered incapable by the institution of marriage to Janet.

He went down the town to get some supplies, digestive biscuits, apples and cheese, the basics of his between-meals snacks. There was a small newsagent and sundry shop on the near side of Rathmines, which he used regularly for papers and fags. But it stocked other basics deep inside the shop, where he normally never went. He stared at the rows of various digestive biscuits. Fat free, low salt, chocolate chip, nutty or cheap, several different brand names of each type. Whilst he was contemplating the glory of variety, much to his consternation, Janet pulled up with the kids and Cordelia, and all four of them got out of the car and came into the shop. Colm stood frozen in his aisle, momentarily forgetting his disguise and thinking they'd greet him. They walked in and didn't give him a second glance as he stood staring, his mouth open.

They don't recognise me. It works!

He moved over to the magazine rack and grabbed a magazine, shoving his head into it. Janet selected some drinks and apples. She looked so neat and tidy and schoolteacherly. There was no evidence of her domestic crisis to be seen in any detail. Her voice rang with the usual commanding chirrup as she exchanged pleasantries about the weather with the shop lady. Her movements were strong and confident.

You hardly expected her to be going round in laddered nylons and clutching a gin bottle, did you?

Once Janet became engrossed in her weather chat with the assistant, June and John spied their opportunity to get up to mischief. Getting a leg up from John, June climbed up onto the freezer to procure her favoured ice cream. She had to lean over to reach in and lost her balance, falling in head first. Her legs were shaking in the air like a trapped insect, her shrieks emerging muffled by the freezer chest. Colm almost went to rescue her, but John was on the case and had her hauled out in no time. Colm ducked back into his magazine, and observed through the side of his eye that June had emerged successfully clutching two fantastically wrapped ice lollies.

'They're too dear,' said Janet. 'I said you could have a Super Split, not a Magnum.'

'And I nearly killed myself getting them,' said little June. The fall into the freezer had given her a fright and she was close to tears. Janet spotted this and relented. A couple of foolscap jotters were Cordelia's purchase, and Janet bundled the lot of them up and into the car. Colm had a good look and could see her face was a little pale, but otherwise normal. He watched them go. It was like looking at a picture that he used to be in, but was now outside of. His point of view had changed utterly. He felt very dislocated.

A shop assistant sidled up beside him. He started.

'You're not supposed to read the magazines,' she said in an unpleasant nasal voice.

'I'm not reading it,' said Colm. 'I'm looking at it.'

'This isn't a lending library.'

The woman took the magazine from his hand and put it back on the shelf and tidied up all the magazines. Colm felt stung by the unnecessary rudeness. They were normally nice to him in this shop. Then he realised that they didn't recognise him as the local and regular he was. To them he was just another dodgy-looking stranger. A Dennis the Menace-Phil Lynott hybrid, strolled in off the high road. He decided against making his elaborate digestive biscuit purchases there, and went on down further into Rathmines to a bigger shop where he was in no danger of blowing his disguise. A shop where he would be faceless and served by the faceless. A shop full of indiscriminate hostility. A shop full of even more varieties of digestive biscuit.

He went to a strange bank and got a mini statement from a machine. His funds were running low. He would have to phone Deirdre. She would've received his restaurant review receipt this morning.

I need that dough. The price of that meal is enough to

keep me going for a fortnight of food from the local café and chippy.

'Colm!' The tone was hard to read. Enthusiastic, yet guarded.

'Deirdre!' he replied.

'Where are you, Colm?'

'I'm in a callbox somewhere on the southside. I'm phoning to see if you could sub me the money to pay for the restaurant meal, 'cos I'm skint.'

'Colm, what's happened? The guards are looking for you. Your wife has reported you missing apparently, but since you've been in contact with me, you're not really missing. Are you OK?'

'Fine Deirdre, fine.'

'This hasn't anything to do with the canning of *Mary Jane*?'

'Nothing whatsoever. I've disappeared on purpose as a mental health strategy.'

'What'll I say to the guards?'

'Tell them the truth. I've been in touch, and you don't know where I am.'

'Colm. Is there anything I can do? I'd like to help if I can.'

'Jut sub me the money for the restaurant review. And to cover the next one.'

'Of course I'll do that. I'll get accounts onto it right away. They've got your bank number?'

'Yeah. Cool. Thanks, I gotta go. Bye.'

Strangely kind. People love pitying others. It makes them feel noble.

'Oh Colm. One last thing. Dan died. Dan the doorman died.'

'Oh, that's terrible. When?'

'It was last Wednesday. He was buried on Friday. I thought you'd like to know.'

'Ah, the poor old codger,' said Colm.

231

Dan finally got his retirement papers.

Colm walked back to the Swan Centre and got himself a coffee and the evening paper. A few people he knew passed by without recognising him. A couple from the Parent Gang. A PR person he knew well. What a relief. If only he could stay like this. If only he could remain this new person forever. And he could exist simply as a voice on the phone. He was beginning to feel safe, and mellow. He decided he'd have two pints, then he'd phone Janet and face the music. Well, not exactly face, you can't do that over the phone. Listen to the music.

He went off down to a large pub he scarcely knew and ordered up his brew, seating himself in a corner with back support. A lone woman in a short skirt smiled at him in a friendly, come-on sort of way. He instinctively pulled in his tummy.

What! Someone looks at me with lust. There must be something wrong with her.

He stared blankly back. The woman was nice-looking. She was in her late thirties and well dressed in a smart red suit and expensive-looking scarf.

There must be something wrong with her to be in a pub on her own at this hour of the day.

'Do you mind if I join you?' she asked.

Like there is something wrong with me.

'Actually, I want to be on my own, I need to think,' yelped Colm.

'Fair enough,' she said, and withdrew her attention. This didn't normally happen to him. Strange women never made approaches to him. It must be the new clothes, they must suggest he's out for some fun. Or maybe failed marriage could be smelt off him. Maybe, like animals, a failed-marriage person sends out some sort of chemical signal which attracts the opposite sex. Shortly after, she finished her drink and left. Red suit looked like a failed-marriage remnant also. He felt a little pang. Maybe he had been unkind not to talk to her. Talk didn't mean anything, and could help a lot. A bit of old jaw-jaw. Perhaps now she'd gone home to slit her wrists. How would he feel then?

Stop imagining things, you eejit.

After his two pints, feeling his courage was raised up, he went off to a quiet street pay phone and dialled home. His old home. It was just after dinner time, and Janet should be at rest, drinking an after dinner coffee. It was a moment of pause in the household. The smallies were allowed to watch a little television, once their homework was done before dinner, and Cordelia generally did her own thing.

The phone rang and rang and Colm prayed that Janet would answer it and not Cordelia or the smallies. The ringing stopped, the phone was lifted and Cordelia's bright and youthful voice uttered the disyllable 'Hello'. Colm tried to speak, to ask for Janet, but his courage failed and he hung up.

Proposal

Colm sat nervously in the corner of the designated café in town. Janet was fifteen minutes late. Unlike her. Colm had phoned the house a few more times and the phone had always been answered by Cordelia, a teenager's prerogative. He had decided he was incapable of talking to Cordelia and had phoned Janet at school, where he got through without any bother. They picked a place in town for their meeting. Janet had taken his call in the staff room, so she couldn't talk freely. Her tone had been as unreadable as usual, so Colm had no idea what he was in for as he sat and waited, chewing coffee and slurping cigarettes, his agitation increasing all the while. Finally, twenty-five minutes late, Janet came in the door, her face flushed from having hurried. He waved at her, and she looked away.

My disguise. Of course. I keep forgetting I'm invisible.

He waved again, and beckoned. She looked over her shoulder thinking the weird guy with the fuzzy hair was gesturing to someone else. Finally he got up and came over to her and put his hand on her arm.

'Janet!'

She turned and stared at him. He raised his sunglasses, and she recognised the eyes. Distinctive dark pools that peered also from the faces of John and June.

'What in God's name have you done to yourself?'

'It's a change of image.'

'It sure is.'

'It's a disguise. I'm in hiding.'

'Are the police after you?'

'No. I'm in hiding from Cordelia and from you.'

'The police have been looking for you. I reported you missing. I was worried about you and they made some enquiries, but you'd apparently been in touch with work, so that meant that you weren't officially missing. No law against dropping out, they told me. Happens every day, men running off on their wives, they told me. It was the same guy, O'Grady, who dealt with Cordelia's disappearance. He was looking at me very suspiciously as I think he held me responsible for the fact that my household has a runaway quotient statistically higher than the national average.'

Now we're onto something.

'And finally, this morning, early, I got a house call from a Detective Smith who said they wanted to talk to you about the demise of James Carter. I nearly dropped on the spot. You didn't have anything to do with that, did you?'

'Is there no end of the depravity you consider me capable of? Child molester. Murderer.'

They returned to Colm's table and sat down. Colm ordered two more coffees, one extra milky for Janet. The specification of Janet's coffee type gave him a horrible shivery intimate feel.

'Why have you disappeared? Why the disguise?'

'I'm in hiding, mainly from Cordelia.'

'Colm, are you well? You're very twitchy. You're giving off a very strange vibe. Why are you hiding from Cordelia? Why haven't you been in touch with the kids? Why haven't you told me where you are? I'm worried half out of my mind.'

Why is she sounding like I'm at fault, like I'm being irresponsible?

'But what about Cordelia? What happened?'

'Oh that's all bullshit. She told me that it was just some story she made up. She's real sorry for it now.'

235

Cordelia's sorry.

'She was furious at me for having believed it. I never really believed it. I'm sorry I ever mentioned it.'

Sorry doesn't quite cover this.

'It's all my fault.'

Janet. So generous she's willing to take on all the blame in the world. It's annoying.

'Janet, you can't take the rap for Cordelia. She needs a damn good giving-out to.'

'Oh God, Colm, I'm just not able for her. All I need now is for her to throw another wobbly. I can't cope. The kids are getting suspicious. I told them that you'd gone to a monastery down the country to write a novel and that you'd be back in a fortnight. They accepted that for a while, but June is beginning to act up about you not being in touch. I told her it was an enclosed order and there were no telephones. But she said she saw a monk with a mobile on TV.'

Colm got a huge pang at the thought of the kids. He was glad that Janet had come up with such a convincing story.

'Where are you staying? I presumed you'd be staying with David, but he says you had a row and he hasn't seen you for ages.'

'I'm in number five.'

'Number five?'

'Candlewick Avenue.'

'You mean you're just down the road?'

'Hence the disguise.'

Janet was unsettled by this, the thought that he had been just under their noses.

'That's that house in flats that always has overflowing rubbish bins in the front garden?'

'Yup.'

'Oh Colm. It must be dreadful.'

'I quite like it, actually.'

Janet paused for a while. She struggled with herself,

236

trying to find the courage to say something inviting, kind and conciliatory. Finally she managed: 'Are you going to come home?'

Colm shook his head. He didn't know what he was going to do but he needed time to be on his own, to think.

'I'm living in the study.'

'What study?'

'It's the same room as my study at home.'

In my old home.

'And that's all? Colm, it's tiny. How do you manage? Where do you cook?'

'I have a two-plate cooker in the corner. I heat up steak and kidney pies on a frying pan.'

Food. Janet's favourite subject of rumination.

'You'll get some sort of food poisoning. Your skin looks awful and the whites of your eyes are dull. Your health will deteriorate. Come on home.'

The food is better.

'Are you seeing her?' Janet asked, looking down at her fingernails.

'Sally? I've seen her once.'

'Did she kill her husband?'

'No.' He winced a tiny bit as he lied. It was good practice, as he was bound to be asked the same question by the police, so he should have his answer nicely practised by then and be able to deliver it unwincingly, convincingly.

'I can't believe you're having an affair,' she said.

Murder, child molesting, but not adultery. Ha!

'I've given the matter a lot of thought since you've been gone, and I think it's all my fault.'

The martyrdom of saint Janet.

'I shouldn't have been so definite about it, you know, us having no more sex, but I just got it into my head, and it was the principle that mattered. It was the principle of it not being fair that I would have to undergo the risk, when you wouldn't consent to a vasectomy.'

Her difficulty finding words led to her voice being a little more urgent than usual. Colm had never heard her talk so explicitly about things between the two of them before. The rattle and hum of coffees and teaspoons ceased momentarily. Colm thought everyone in the café had heard the word 'vasectomy'.

'But now, I realise that there are some things more important than principles. I should have realised it before, of course. But I get stuck in my ways and I can be a bit thick. It's so hard to find time to think, what with the job and the kids and the house. But I took some time off work, and I've been thinking, and I think that I've been terrible to you and that I want you to come back, and I'll try to be better.'

Speaks the doormat.

'Janet, do you remember when I proposed to you? I've been trying to remember it this last while, and I just can't recall it.'

'Of course! Have you forgotten? It wasn't *that* long ago.'

'For some reason, it's slipped my memory.'

'And it was so dramatic. I can't believe you don't remember it.'

'I've been racking my brains, and it's gone.'

Janet sipped her coffee and gave a little sad smile.

'It's as clear to me as if it were yesterday. You called to my flat in Booterstown, early in the morning. It was a Saturday, and I was off work and taking it easy. I opened the door wondering who could possibly be there so early in the morning. I can't remember whether I'd seen you the night before. I'm not sure. But I wasn't expecting you in any case. You rarely appeared before lunch time. But there you were, the rising sun behind you over Booterstown marsh, and you were carrying a huge bunch of yellow roses. The largest I'd ever seen. There must have been sixty flowers in it. I let you in, and once I'd closed the door to the flat, you got down on both knees and proposed. And I was really surprised. You must remember? I hadn't expected it. You hadn't struck me as being a person who was ready for marriage, or even interested in it. And I had no hesitation in saying yes, because I knew you were right for me. I just knew it. Though I hadn't expected it, I must confess that I had fantasised about it. I'd tried it on in the privacy of my own imagination. And I wanted it. You were so good with Cordelia, and I thought we'd make a great family, and we did.'

It was the yellow roses that triggered the memory for Colm. He now recalled all its detail. He remembered being blinded by the rising sun. He remembered staggering under the awkward weight of the bunch of flowers, the flowers occasionally letting him feel their thorns. He remembered falling to his knees and asking Janet to marry him, feeling so unworthy of her goodness, and so needing of her love. He remembered how relieved he was when she said yes. How saved he felt. And he remembered what he'd done the night before.

The night before, he'd gone out to an office party to celebrate the fact that the magazine he was working for was moving to a new premises. He'd invited David along, as Janet couldn't come because she couldn't get a babysitter. The party had been good fun, it was a boozy affair, and Colm had got very drunk. He and David had returned to David's flat in the company of two girls. David's marriage had recently collapsed and he routinely picked up women. The four of them talked and drank champagne from David's fridge for a while. Both girls were interested in David, and making a play for him, their drunkeness robbing the competition of any subtlety. Suki and Sam. Those were their names. They were best friends. At a certain point, it was decided that Suki had won, and she steered David off to his bedroom, leaving Sam with Colm. The two girls worked in the sandwich bar near the old magazine office where they all bought their sandwiches and he had had no previous regard for Sam whatsoever. She started to tell him a story about how the boss had made them cut back on the amount of pickles they were to use on a certain sandwich, repeating herself endlessly, and substantially more exercised than the subject demanded. How the terrible boss had changed the pickles from a quality brand to a much cheaper one and how the sandwiches were deteriorating, and how she hated to preside over this fall off in standards. A lengthy speech on the quality of pickles. 'I may only be a sandwich maker, but I believe in standards, you know.' They kissed, half heartedly and lazily, and Colm led her off to the spare room, where despite their drunkenness and mutual apathy, they had some sort of a stab at sex, and then passed out.

And he didn't once think of Janet. He didn't once think of her sweet open face and her loving nature. He didn't once think he was betraying her. And betraying her for nothing.

The next morning, he woke very early with a terrible hangover. Sam was beside him, sleeping deeply, and there was a horrible smell. It took him a while to figure it out, but the smell was of vomit. One or other of them must have been sick, and the bed was covered in it and so were their bodies. Colm felt so bad. He felt so wretched about having betrayed Janet. And he felt so disgusted with himself for sleeping with a girl he didn't particularly like in a pool of puke. It was the worst thing he'd ever done. He left David's flat, took a cab to his own place, and took a long hot shower and thought. And then the idea came to him. He had to marry Janet. He had no choice. He had to be a better person, and Janet would make him a better person.

And he'd called to a florist in Blackrock, having sat on their doorstep until they opened at eight-thirty, and bought a huge bunch of yellow roses and he called over to her and flung his wretched self at her feet and she'd accepted him and he'd cried not with joy but with gratitude.

And he'd blanked it all from his mind, because he was so ashamed.

Now, in the ambience of this coffee shop, with its stained tables and dirty ashtrays, his mistake was so clear to him. Janet *was* too good for him. He had been morally ambitious in marrying her. Morally upwardly mobile. And it hadn't worked. He needed greater ambiguity in his life. He needed more room to manoeuvre. He had tried to fit into Janet's scheme of things and he had failed. Because it wasn't the right life. It wasn't the right life for his nature.

'The kids will really miss you if you don't come back,' said Janet, her eyes sweetly staring out of her angelic brow, her hair astray. 'They'll just be heartbroken if you stay away at that monastery.'

Confession

Colm tidied up his bedsit, washing the windows and polishing the furniture, dusting his books and sharpening his pencils. He was becoming house-proud. He had never done any housework in the family home, as it was way too vast, but the perimeters of this room accurately described his capability for cleaning. His action had the primary objective of a clean room, but it had the secondary objective of keeping himself mentally occupied as he was expecting a visit from Cordelia, which he was dreading.

His buzzer sounded and he went down the stairs to open the front door. Cordelia stood on the step and looked at him, the face as unreadable as ever. Remorseless, certainly. Slightly cross. The fair hair separated into two neat and defiant braids. He beckoned her to follow him and up they went to his room. Cordelia's big observant eyes took in every detail, the rippled old carpet, the stained wallpaper. The kettle had just boiled, and Colm had fresh milk and chocolate nut digestive biscuits.

'Coffee?' he asked.

Cordelia nodded, and muttered a barely audible thanks.

'Sit down, sit down,' he said, pointing to a newly dusted chair in the corner. Cordelia stared at him with an expression of mild puzzlement. His tight jeans and T-shirt and the shaggy hair had caught her by surprise.

'I've had a bit of a change of image,' burbled Colm as he busied himself with the demands of coffee-making, carefully measuring out spoons of instant as though he were

242

conducting a chemistry experiment.

Colm was totally awkward. His hands were trembling. And he could feel those damn tears, which were now rarely far from the surface, threatening like storm clouds. He flexed the muscles around his ears in an attempt to contain the emotion, gain mastery over himself. He added milk to Cordelia's coffee, and put two biscuits on the side of the saucer, and went over to the girl with the peace offering. She took it, and he could see her hands too were trembling. Colm tried to pull himself together.

It must be difficult for her. She's only a kid. I'm supposed to be an adult and thus experienced at dealing with things. I'm supposed to have life skills. Take charge, you fool!

He tried to say something, but nothing came out, so he went back to the kettle and laboriously made himself a fresh cup, throwing out the remnants of his previous one into a slop bucket, which stagnated brown and teabaggy in the corner.

'So Cordelia – '

'Colm, I – '

They both spoke together, and then there was a series of 'After you,' 'No, after you,' and then Colm sat down. Cordelia got up and turned round and sat down again and then she burst into tears. Great shoulder-racking sobs. She howled with misery, pure passionate teenage desolation. Colm was amazed. Cordelia's normal gamut of emotions ran from cross to angry. Never anything as panoramic as this.

'I am so unhappy,' she managed to get out in between the sobs. Colm got her some tissues.

'Drink your coffee, love,' he said. 'It'll help settle you.'

Finally, after what seemed a very long time, the waves of sobbing stopped, and the emotion was reduced to an occasional snivel and shudder.

'I'm so sorry Colm, I'm so sorry. I've been so wretched

since you left. I never meant anything like this to happen. It's so awful, and it was all a terrible mistake and I am so ashamed.'

'What happened?'

'It's just so terrible.'

'Tell me.'

'I'm so sorry.'

'Tell me. You feel better if you get it out. It's like vomit. When you've a sick stomach, you feel a lot better when you cough it all up.'

Cordelia was distracted by the strangeness of the analogy. She pondered it a moment, took a draught of her coffee and a few deep breaths, and began:

'I think I was upset over my father. Andrew. "Drew. That's what everyone calls me in America." Well, Drew was such a disappointment, he was so weak. I had always thought that he'd be somebody more glamorous. I knew he'd gone off to California, so I had imagined he'd be tall and blond and have a swimming pool. But he was dreadful, such a nothing. I was furious with Mam for having had a relationship with him. And then I thought I'd been misconceived. I was sorry I was born. Not in the angry I wish I'd never been born teenagery outburst sense. But in a deeper way. Mam and *that* man should never have happened. Therefore *I* should never have happened. So, I was just so miserable about that. He was repulsive. His fingernails were filthy and he smelt of BO and he was so thin and unhealthy. I scoured his appearance for any resemblance to me, and I could see one. His nose was like mine, a bit sticky up at the end.

'I met him in McDonald's. You know I hate McDonald's. He thought I'd like it because he thought teenagers like it. Such a schmuck. Eight-year-olds who know no better like McDonald's. He never even asked me a single question about how I was or who I was, he just rambled on and on about how great the United States is, and how

244

backward we are here, about how the priests and the Irish-speaker mafia are running everything here. I mean, what's he talking about? The priests aren't running anything here. I don't think I've ever met a priest. He kept going on about how great the skyscrapers are in America, how tall and ambitious they are, and how all ambition was knocked out of everybody in this country. Talk about bitter, he was a human lemon. I didn't speak during the encounter hardly at all, just sat there listening to his rubbishy talk. I had been so looking forward to it. I had so wanted to meet my father, and I was going to forgive him for running off and leaving me if he had given me even the slightest little thing to be proud of. But he was a nobody and a nothing.'

Still well able to be judgmental, Cordelia. He wasn't great, it had to be said. He'd lost the map somewhere, the poor sap. He had fallen at the first hurdle of adult life.

Colm supped his coffee and listened. So this was the story of Cordelia's meeting with her father. She had kept very quiet about it. Janet hadn't heard anything from her, except that it hadn't been great. Janet had told Colm that Cordelia's father had left Ireland after failing to get a particular teaching job because his Irish wasn't up to scratch. He had obviously never got over this episode, despite its having occurred so long ago.

'And you know Phaedra's father is a mad bastard? Well her mother got a barring order against him a few months ago. He used to beat them both up all the time, Phaedra and her Mam. Well, we just got into this thing that all men are bastards and we decided to re-form SCUM, the society for cutting up men. We found the SCUM manifesto which was written by Valerie Solanis and we got copies of it sent to us on the Internet. We'd have weekly meetings, Phaedra was the president, and me the vice president. We'd meet up, four of us, and we'd swap stories about how terrible men were. I told them all about my no-hoper Dad back from California. But Phaedra got most of the sympathy, because she was getting beaten up by her Dad. Having a loser of a beach-bum Dad wasn't seen as anything much. Carmel's Dad, do you know what he does? He brings home his younger girlfriends to the house, and has sex with them in the spare room, while her mother is in her own room stoked up on Prozac and watching TV. Isn't that terrible? And Veronica's Dad is an alcoholic, and spends all the money on drink, and some days they only have money for porridge for three meals a day. The problem was, once I told everybody about my terrible encounter with my father in McDonald's, that was all there was to tell. We chewed over every soggy chip in the story. But everybody else had new stories of new atrocities. Veronica's Dad was drunk and did a wee-wee in the neighbour's front garden. Carmel's father had a new girlfriend who had actually moved into the spare room and sat down to family meals and her mother had a complete nervous breakdown over it. And Phaedra's father dislocated her shoulderblade. But all I had was the soggy chips and the beach-bum father. So, I did a terrible thing and I am so sorry, but I started to make up things about you. I started to say you were . . . I can't say it. You know what I said, I can't repeat it.'

'Say it,' said Colm. 'You've got to admit what you've done in order to get over it, and be forgiven.'

'Oh, I can't bear myself. I hate myself. I said such terrible things. I said that you were feeling me up. I said I got no peace from you. To begin with, I thought it wasn't too bad a thing to make up, I mean, you're not my real father, it wasn't like incest or anything. But now I realise it was terrible. But I got so much sympathy. They all gave me so much sympathy and understanding and care. And I needed it. I just loved it. In school, Carmel would come over to me and give me a little hug and whisper "I understand that you're suffering" in my ear. And Veronica would leave a little card and a chocolate in my locker

246

which was next to hers. Oh, I felt so cared for, so loved. And then I couldn't stop. Every meeting I'd make up a new story, a bigger and better story. All these stories just came out. It was like I was speaking in tongues. I never pre-planned a story. I just opened my mouth and stories came out. The meetings were confidential, on pain of excommunication and death, so I thought nobody would tell, and I could see no harm in it, but Phaedra blabbed to her mother. And that was that.'

'And what have you said to the other girls?'

'I've told them it was all made up. I told them I have a psychiatric disorder which makes me a compulsive liar. I thought that would sound better than I was simply fibbing. None of them are speaking to me. Now, when I walk into the classroom, they all turn their backs on me. And I've no other friends 'cos we were so thick together, us SCUM members. We looked down on the other girls who had happy lives. They were so immature, so inexperienced. So innocent. Now I'm a pariah. But to be honest, it's a relief, because once I started those lies I was trapped, and this was the only way to bring it all to an end. Only now you've moved out of home. I told Mam she shouldn't have kicked you out. And I feel terrible.'

'Cordelia, tell me this, do any of your friends have awful mothers? Alcoholic, violent mad women? Any mothers bringing home young men to torment their husbands? Any sadistic mothers who make their children bath in ice-cold water? Any mothers who spend all the housekeeping money on designer clothes, while the children go barefoot on the streets?'

'No. For some reason, all the mothers seem to be saints.'

'Just wondering.'

'Colm, I am so sorry. Will you forgive me?'

Colm got up off his seat and came over to Cordelia and ruffled her fringe. He smiled at her.

'Of course I forgive you. You're a teenager. You have

247

the right to do a few daft and inexplicable things. To be honest, Cordelia, I'm relieved.'

'That it's all cleared up now?'

'No. I'm relieved that you're exhibiting some major character flaws. I couldn't bear it when you were a righteous saint. I'm delighted now that you are exhibiting a streak of utter deviousness and compulsive lying.'

'Oh.' Cordelia frowned. 'You're not furious?'

'No. It's not the kind of thing that bothers me.'

'Oh,' said Cordelia. She had prepared herself for a serious dressing-down.

'I know it must've been tough, meeting your father. He was probably a big disappointment. But in life, that happens. He must've been nice when he was younger because Janet wouldn't have loved him otherwise. You must know that.'

'Well, he's gone off like a ripe banana.'

Colm flexed and unflexed his fingers. He wanted to say something more and he was searching round in his psyche for some emotional courage. He found some in a disused corner of his brain.

'Cordelia, when I married your mam, you were only a tot, a little child, and I had always thought that I would be your father, and I know I keep falling down on the job, but I've always intended to be your dad, and I will be again, if you'd like that, and let me.'

'Will you come home today?' she asked brightly.

Ahh!

'I don't think I'm going to go back, Cordy. Me and your mam are having problems.'

'Problems?'

'And I've been having an affair.'

'An affair?'

Cordelia looked shocked.

'Only a little one.'

'You couldn't be having an affair. It doesn't make sense.'

She doesn't think me capable of it either.

'So, I think I'm going to stay here for a while, and get things sorted in my head.'

'So you didn't leave home on account of me?'

'Well, it wasn't the only issue.'

Cordelia drained her coffee. She looked crestfallen. She had thought she would be able to put things to rights by her confession, but now she realised that things were beyond her capacity to interfere. She couldn't fix it.

'Who are you having an affair with?'

'Her name is Sally Carter.'

'Is that the woman who's after killing her husband over in Howth?'

'What makes you say that?'

'I can't remember. Someone said it in school.'

'That's just idle gossip,' said Colm faintly.

'Are you going to leave Mam for her?'

'I don't know, Cordelia, I need time to think. I don't really think so, but your mam and I are in trouble in any case. Sometimes, love doesn't last.'

'What's happened? I always thought you and Mam were mad about each other.'

'What makes you say that, Cordelia?'

'It's the way you look at each other. You watch each other as you move around the room like your eyes are glued in that direction. To be honest, I've always been a bit jealous. When did the problem begin?'

Cordelia looked oddly mature now. She looked like a sociologist, or the relationship counsellor she might one day become. Not a confused silly teenager.

'It's been happening slowly over the years. Withering. I think your mother is too good for me, Cordelia. I think she's too saintly.'

And when I view myself beside her, I am filled with self-disgust.

'So,' Cordelia thought for a moment, 'this other woman isn't a saint?'

'No, a saint she's not,' said Colm. 'That she isn't.'

Fish and Chips

Colm put in a few hours' work at the computer, passing the time in idle accomplishment, until hunger began to rumble. He ignored it for a few hours, and consequently he was absolutely starving by the time he put on his fake leather jacket to head down town and join the other hunter-gatherers in Burdocks fish and chip emporium. He let himself out the front door, and was about to go down the driveway when he walked straight into a gentleman who identified himself as Detective Smith, a member of the Dublin law enforcement community. Smith didn't look like a policeman. He was wearing a suit and tie and a pair of spectacles, and looked like an accounts clerk. He asked Colm if a Colm Cantwell resided in the building.

'Yes,' replied Colm.

'Which bell is his?' asked the policeman.

'Number four,' replied Colm.

The policeman rang the bell. Colm began to panic. He didn't want to identify himself, but didn't want to lie either. He considered making a run for it, but this was ridiculous. He couldn't become a fugitive. He had done nothing wrong, for God's sake. He was an innocent man, and entitled to do as he pleased. He couldn't be arrested for being a friend of a person who's husband died under suspicious circumstances. He was starving.

'He's not inside,' said Colm.

'Any idea where he might be?'

Colm kicked for touch. He was ravenous. He wanted to get down to Burdocks.

'He's just gone out the door to head down to Burdocks for some grub,' said Colm. 'You can come along with me, and meet him there if you want.'

Colm and Detective Smith walked along the street. Smith's stride was much longer than Colm's, who had to hurry himself slightly to keep up.

'What do you want him for?' asked Colm.

'I'm not at liberty to discuss my work. I don't mean to be rude, sorry. But you know regulations are regulations.'

'All right, all right, brother. Didn't mean to ask too many questions,' said Colm, raising his hands in a gesture of laid-back disinterest.

'I'd probably end up in front of a disciplinary tribunal for loose talk. We have to be answerable for everything now. It's all transparency and accountability now. It would give you the right pip.'

'God be with the days when the sergeant took you behind the bicycle shed and leathered you within an inch of your life and that was the beginning and the end of law enforcement,' said Colm.

'Irony. How nice,' said Smith.

'Love a bit of irony,' said Colm.

'How long has Mr Cantwell been living in the building?'

'A few weeks.'

'And what's he like?'

Colm grappled with the challenge of describing himself.

'Hmmmn. He's OK. Quiet. Wouldn't put in or out on you. Likes the few bevs.' He offered his companion a cigarette and they both lit up and smoked as they walked along. 'He seems like a nice enough sort of bloke, eh, but maybe a bit confused and directionless. Looks like he hasn't found himself, you know.' Colm was going to have to say who he was. He decided to wait until they got to the restaurant and had the dinner ordered. If they were going to take him away, at least he'd have a full stomach.

'Do you know him well?' asked the detective.

Colm thought for a minute.

'Fairly well,' he said.

'What does he do all day?'

'He works at his computer. Any time I go in to him, he's sitting there writing. I think it's a novel or something. Maybe poems. I don't know.'

'Has he told you his marriage is busting up?'

'Yeah, I know all about his marriage,' said Colm.

'And does he have lady visitors?'

'Hmmn,' said Colm. 'Naah. Never seen one. Doesn't seem the type.'

'You sound like you know him very well.'

'Ahh. There's Burdocks.'

Colm led Detective Smith into the restaurant and sat into a booth. A waitress came over straight away.

'Do you want anything to eat?' he asked the detective.

'Better not. Just a diet Coke while I'm waiting. How long do you reckon he's going to be?'

'I'll have a cod and chips and a battered sausage and a side dish of fried onions and a glass of milk, thanks darlin'.' Colm's new image had affected his manner. He had now taken to calling waitresses darlin'. He felt it was expected of him. The girl smiled cheekily at him and went off with her order.

'So where is he?' asked Smith.

Colm sighed a deep and weary sigh.

'He's here.'

'Where?'

'I'm him,' said Colm.

Detective Smith looked carefully at Colm.

'You're not him.'

'Yes I am.'

'I've seen videos.'

'What videos?'

'I'm not at liberty to say.'

'Don't be giving me bullshit.'

'OK, OK. A video of Cantwell smoking in the porch of the church at Carter's funeral.'

'Yup. That was me. Your colleague got a light off me. I remember him. Ferrety face. I never saw any video. He must have had it built into his pen or something, like James Bond.'

'Why do you look so different?' asked Smith. 'Are you in hiding?'

'I was in hiding from my wife and children. A spot of domestic bother. So, what do you want to talk to me about?'

'We want to see if you can help us with our enquiries. We know that you are friendly with Mrs Sally Carter. I want to ask you informally where you were on Friday the twenty-second of last month, the day James Carter disappeared. And I want to know if you can shed any light on the matter.'

'Aren't you going to read me my rights, like in *Hawaii-Five-O*?'

'You only get your rights read if you're arrested, which you aren't.'

Yet.

'You may of course refuse to answer any questions without your solicitor present.'

Colm's food arrived, a great steaming mound of fish and chips with a satellite mound of fried onions. Colm liberally doused them with ketchup and vinegar and started to eat ravenously, as though it might be his last meal.

'Help yourself to a chip if you feel like it,' said Colm, pushing the plate an inch or two towards the detective. The vinegar wafted up and Colm could see Smith's nostrils twitch.

'I know exactly where I was on Friday the twenty-second. I went into the office at two-fifteen p.m. to deliver my gossip column, as is, or rather was, my custom. After my dealings with Deirdre Glade, my editor, who fired me, I met my friend David Blake and we drank and ate the rest of the night away in various places in the south inner city. I can't remember exactly where we were, but a glance at David's Visa bill will provide a sad map of our petty debaucheries. I was totally depressed about getting fired, so I drank even more than usual. In the small hours, I went home. I can't entirely recall at what time.'

Smith made a few notes in a small jotter, and as he was doing so, he absent-mindedly ate a chip.

'Had you ever met Carter?'

'No. Well not exactly. I followed him one night out to Blackrock when he was carrying on with the sister, Anita. But they weren't aware I was following them.'

'Why?'

'That's a very good question.'

'It looks rather suspicious. Would it be a normal thing for you to do, to follow strangers home in the middle of the night?'

'I wouldn't quite call it normal, no. Well, I put a story in my column ages ago about Carter and Anita De Brun, not knowing that she was his sister-in-law. Sally Carter contacted me to see was there any truth in it, or was it just gossip. I said I'd try to find out. So one night I got carried away with myself, and I thought I was a private eye and followed them to Blackrock, where indeed it transpired that they were having an affair. Amazingly, there was some truth in the gossip. I reported this to Sally. So that was that.'

'You're her lover, aren't you?'

Lover. That sounds altogether too athletic a description for me.

'Eh, I'm you know, her eh. We've been intimate, all

255

right. We were both in collapsed marriages. The inevitable happened.'

Smith scribbled some more in his jotter. He ate another chip from Colm's plate.

'And what about Mrs Carter? Do you know where she was on that day?'

''Fraid not,' said Colm. 'We're friendly, but I don't really keep tabs on her, if you know what I mean.'

Smith had one more chip before he realised what he was doing and stopped himself. He drank back the end of his Coke. Colm proffered some fried onion rings.

'No thanks. Do you think she might have killed her husband?' He asked.

Here it is. The crucial question.

'No,' said Colm smoothly and clearly.

'You sound very confident of that,' said Smith.

'I am confident. She wouldn't have the strength of character to do that. She's a mouse.'

'How reliable are you on the subject?' asked Smith. 'After all, you are very close to her.'

Colm shrugged and drank his milk. At least now he was fed. He lit up a cigarette and offered one to Smith, who declined. He beckoned the waitress over and ordered a bottle of beer. He then had an idea.

I can write this week's restaurant review about here, Burdocks, my favourite place. I can wax lyrical about chips, ooze about ketchup.

On the strength of this bright idea, he ordered some ice cream. He'd write up the review and e mail it tomorrow. He'd be way ahead of himself.

'Well. That's it for the moment. I'll be back in touch if we've any further questions,' said Smith, and he headed off out the door, leaving Colm with his beer and his ice cream and his cigarette.

Well, that's it. I too am guilty. I couldn't shop her though. She'll have to confess.

Perfume

'Can you believe it?' asked Sally. 'Can you believe it? The skunk. He only left me a small portion of his fortune, half his official possessions, but most of his wealth is tied up in a very complicated patrilineal family trust for young James.'

'Well, half his official possessions is probably plenty, no?'

'It's not the money. It's the fact that it's hurtful.'

'That he didn't trust you?'

'It's not that he didn't trust me. Of course he trusted me. It's that he thought me too thick to be relied on to be sensible with the money, so it's as tied up as possible so I can't do anything with it. James never gave me any credit for having a brain in my head. And the funny thing is, I was much smarter than him. The problem started in the beginning. I lied to him about my leaving cert results, because if he thought I was too clever, he wouldn't have married me. He was insecure that way. Unfortunately, once you start pretending you're as thick as a plank, it's hard to stop. My thickness became so legendary that finally I myself believed in it. So I suppose I can't really blame James.'

'What's the smell?' asked Colm.

Sally sniffed. 'The food? It smells great. I'm starving.'

'No,' said Colm. 'Another smell. Perfume?'

'Oh do you like it? I just bought it today because I needed something to cheer me up. I'm very depressed about James's death, and all the police interviews are doing nothing to help me get over it all. I put the perfume on in the car just before I came up, but I must have put too much on if you can smell it so strongly. It's called "Tarantula". I wanted to get something aggressive, to help me cope.'

Boy, it's strong. It smells like a jungle flower.

Sally gave a wry little laugh and kicked off her shoes to make herself comfortable. The take-away was from a very expensive French restaurant. Sally didn't want to eat inside the restaurant because she was sure she was being followed but had wanted a gourmet meal, so asked them to make her two doggy bags. She wasn't only fearful of a police tail, but she also suspected that James's family were suspicious of her and had possibly hired a private dick to watch her, and she didn't want any photos of her dining out with her playboy floating around at family conferences. Everywhere she went, there were funny-looking guys doing nothing in particular, who looked as though they were up to no good. She was sure they were all surreptitiously photographing her, and made an effort to show them her good side. Colm was starving and ate the chicken dish, which was rich and creamy and delicious.

Sally turned on the radio as background noise. She refused to discuss the 'event' without a screen of noise, in case Colm's room was bugged.

'The detectives have stopped interviewing me, so I think that may be the end of it.'

'A Detective Smith called here and interviewed me.'

'Did he say he thought I'd done it?'

'Not in so many words.'

'I think I may have got away with it. Of course, I can't be sure.'

I hate her talking about it. I can forget about it just so long as it isn't mentioned, but when she brings it up, all I can think of is that poor sod sinking down through the water, air escaping from his fat lips, his wealth and privilege doing nothing for him now.

'You've been a great help, Colm. It's great I've been able to talk to you about it. To be honest, I'd be gone out of my mind otherwise. Here's to you, my darling.'

She raised her glass of white wine and toasted him, and then drank it back. She had bought the bottle of wine in a special gift pack containing two crystal glasses, as she didn't fancy drinking the wine from Colm's tooth mug, which she had done a few nights ago, and been quite put out by the distinctly menthol flavour to the Chardonnay. Colm smiled half-heartedly, and raised his own glass. He felt totally uncomfortable. The rich food and wine and Sally's overpowering perfume was making him feel a bit queasy. Sally reclined on the bed, and languorously stretched her legs. A yawn overtook her whole body, and she writhed luxuriously for a moment.

'You know,' said Sally, 'I'm really going to have to do something with my life, now that I'm starting a fresh chapter. I'm going to have to make something of myself. I feel like I'm just wasting, like dear old Sal isn't making much of a contribution to the planet. Maybe I could work in a soup kitchen for the homeless? That might be fun.'

'That doesn't make sense, Sally. You have a fleet of servants on your payroll looking after your own house, while you're off performing domestic chores in a soup kitchen. Why wouldn't you just send one of your staff down to the soup kitchen, and you could stay home and watch telly?'

'Maybe I could go to university as a mature student or something. Or maybe I could brush up my nursing skills and when the children are big enough I could go and be a nurse in some deprived part of the world where they'd need me.'

'Why this sudden urge to do something?'

'I don't know. I just feel like I have this itch. When

259

James was around, it was as though I was his prisoner. I couldn't just pipe up with "I'm going off to do nursing in South America". He wouldn't have let me. It would be a bit unwifely. But now I'm free of him, the possibilities are endless. I'm only sorry I didn't just say "go ahead" when he wanted the divorce and let him off and marry Anita. Then, I would have had him out of my hair, and everyone would be feeling sorry for me, rather than suspecting me of murder. Instead, I have all the stress of his death and the kids' upset and all. When I heard him say "I want a divorce and I want to marry Anita," I thought the sky was falling in. Now, I don't understand why I flew into such a rage. It seems, retrospectively, like such a little problem.'

Sally refilled the wineglasses.

'So, when all this blows over,' said Sally, 'what'll we do?'

'Do?' asked Colm.

'Do you want to come and live in Longbrook?'

Another cage. Is she out of her mind?

'No. Sally, I like my bedsit.'

'Here? You can't possibly stay here for good. You're nearly forty years of age. You need to live in a proper house. You can't live here with all these scroungers.'

'I like it here. I'm managing to get some work done.'

'Well, you could work anywhere, couldn't you?'

'That's true, up to a point, but I need to sort my life out.'

'But what about us? What about the future for you and me?'

Colm had always been ambiguous about Sally, but now, that she was widowed and free and available for a full-time liaison, and sat there brandishing her tentacles, he was horrified. The circumstances of her husband's death horrified him further. Her behaviour now seemed way out of line. Setting him up to go and live with her. She was totally lacking in remorse.

'Sally, you're going to have to confess what happened.'

'We've been through this before. I can't confess. It's stupid.'

'Sally, I can't see you any more unless you confess. It doesn't feel right.'

'Well you won't see me any more if I do confess, 'cos I'll be in the slammer for twenty years.'

'That may be so.'

'So one way or another, you won't see me.'

'That appears to be the case. I'll visit you in prison, though.'

Sally stared at him, it slowly dawning on her that he was shutting her out. It had never occurred to her that he might abandon her now. She was upset and got to her feet, her face puzzled.

Oh no. I feel so cruel.

'I'll go so,' she said. 'I hadn't thought you would get an attack of righteousness. You may well say that I ought to do this or I ought to do that, but you don't know what it was like to suffer the humiliation of being married to James. I have no remorse, because he doesn't deserve it. I've spared you most of the details of our delightful marriage, because I'm not a whinger, and I never wanted your pity. But I have very little reason to be remorseful.' The temperature of Sally's outburst was rising all the time. 'James crushed me, and I am lucky now to be alive.' She looked at Colm. 'I didn't think I was going to get morality lectures from you.'

She pulled on her jacket and hunted round the room for her shoes and handbag. Tears were streaming down her face.

'Where is my damn scarf?'

She found it in a heap in the corner.

'I thought you were on my side. I thought we had an understanding, you and I. I thought you were a renegade from virtue. Like me. But I find you're not. I think you should go back to your goody two-shoes wife. Goodbye.'

261

She slammed the door behind her and the whole house shook. Colm felt terrible. He got no relief from her exit. Her absence was almost as annoying as her presence. He sighed and turned on his computer.

Better try and do some work.

And her perfume lingered long in the room.

Pyjamas

Colm awoke to the smallies bouncing up and down on his tummy.

'Dad, Dad, how was the monastery? Are you very holy now? Did you bring us back any SWEETS?'

Colm groaned and clutched his forehead. It must be Saturday, otherwise they'd be at school.

'Dad, Dad, why is your hair so funny-looking? You look like a girl,' said June, and she kicked off her rabbit slippers and climbed in beside him. Not to be outdone, John got in the other side.

'Did your mother tell you where to find me?'

'Yeah, and we knocked on the door and a big fella called Brian sent us up here. Hey, isn't this the same room as your study?'

'Yeah.'

'Well, it's a good thing we're allowed in here, 'cos we aren't allowed in the study. Hey, is that a cooker over there?'

'Yeah.'

'Have you any food?'

'Yes, sausages. Do you want sausages?'

'Cool!' said John.

Colm got up and went over to the two-plate, produced his frying pan, and shortly there was the satisfying smell of frying food. The two children sat snugly in his bed.

'Does your mother know you're here?'

'Yes. She tried to stop us and make us put on clothes, but we just ran out the gate and all the way down here, and she was in her dressing gown and couldn't follow us on account of what would the neighbours say.'

Colm cooked the sausages and pulled out a loaf of sliced white bread and made hot dogs for all three of them.

'Cool!' said John, digging his teeth into the roll.

'Why are you down here?' asked June. 'Why haven't you come home to us? Is there something going on that nobody is telling us about 'cos we're only kids? We're always the last to hear about everything.'

'Do you want tea?' asked Colm. He filled the kettle and put it on.

'Yes please,' they both replied.

'Shall I switch on the television?' asked Colm.

'Yeah. Yeah. Yeah.'

Colm switched on the television.

'Where are the 'trolls?' asked June.

'I don't have any. You have to get up and switch the buttons with your hand.'

'Oh. How do you do that?' asked John.

'I'll show you.'

Colm lifted John up onto a chair so he could reach the television, opened the control panel, and showed John all the switches. John put on MTV.

'Why are you living down here? Why haven't you come home?' asked June.

What am I going to say? I can't answer her.

'Here's your tea,' said Colm, bringing over two steaming mugs to the two children.

'What have you done to your hair?' asked John. 'It's gone all bushy.'

'I had a change of image,' said Colm. 'I was tired of the old straight hair. I wanted something different.'

Colm rolled more white bread around sausages and gave the kids a second hot dog.

'I think it's nice,' said John. 'I think it suits you.'

'I preferred it the old way,' said June, her face clouding.

She was smelling a rat. John would proceed innocently along, but June had a suspicious streak. She knew something was up.

What will I say?

'Why are you down here? Tell me. Why aren't you home with us?'

Colm braced himself. 'Kids,' he said, 'I've come down here for a little holiday. I need some time to think about things. And I won't be home for a little while. I wanted to talk to you about it and was going to come and see you in a day or two, but you've come to me. So, eh.'

Words failed him.

'Are you and Mammy getting a separation?' asked June.

'We may well be doing that,' said Colm.

'That's like a divorce, isn't it?' said John.

'Yes.'

June went white. The colour drained from her little face and she looked up at Colm.

'You've run away, like Cordelia ran away. Why does everybody in our house run away?'

'Junie. Things are difficult when you're an adult. Sometimes love doesn't last between mammies and daddies and then they sometimes have to reassess the situation.'

June didn't understand the words he was using, and stared blankly at him.

'Sometimes love stops,' he said.

'And does love stop between daddies and children?'

'No. Never.'

'I don't believe you,' said June. 'Love does stop. If it stops between mammies and daddies it stops between daddies and children. Cordelia's daddy stopped loving her and went to America.'

'I won't stop loving you and John.'

'I don't believe you,' she said, and calmly got out of bed and put on her rabbit slippers.

'This is a cool video!' said John.

She went to go out the door, and Colm grabbed her and gave her a hug. He was horrified by how slender her shoulders were. How little. Those shoulders were too small for any burden.

'I think I'm going to run away as well,' said June. And she darted out the door and down the stairs.

'Stop, June, come back!' called Colm.

Shit. I'll have to go after her.

Colm pulled on his shoes and, still in his pyjamas, ran down the stairs, followed by John. June had dashed out the garden gate, her dressing gown floating behind her like a cape, the rabbit slippers bouncing along the pavement. Colm ran after her huffing and puffing, feeling his bulk lurching from side to side like a heavy suit of armour. John passed him, his young body running easily and expertly.

'I'll catch her,' he said.

Just as she got to the main road, John caught her and arrested her in a big bear hug.

'Let me go!' she cried.

Colm made it to their side, and felt so ill after the exercise he thought he might throw up. They looked incongruous, the three of them in their pyjamas on the side of the main Rathmines Road.

'Let me go,' squealed June. 'I hate you, let me go.'

John kept a tight hold, though she was biting and scratching. Colm took June up in his arms, and John nursed his wounds.

'Ow, she bit me. Ow! Look, it's bleeding.'

'Let me go! You're not my father. Let me go. I hate you,' screeched June, hysterical now. Colm swung her up onto his shoulder. Fit he wasn't, but he was still quite strong.

'Vampire,' said John.

The pyjama'd trio were attracting very strange looks. A passing stranger felt obliged to intervene.

'Excuse me, are you having trouble?' asked a respectable-looking old gent who walked using an umbrella as a stick.

'No, everything's fine,' said Colm brightly.

'He's not my father. I hate him. Put me down,' screamed June.

A car stopped and its occupants got out, a youngish couple dressed for Saturday at the squash courts who had spotted the commotion.

'What's going on? Can we help?' asked the woman.

'He's not my daddy!' screamed June. 'Help, oh help.'

'I think you should put the little girl down, mister,' said the man in the tracksuit.

'She *is* my daughter,' said Colm, trying to be as rational as possible, and not appear as a child abductor or a lunatic.

'It's true,' said John. 'She's my sister, and he's my dad, so he must be her dad also, though my other sister, Cordelia, has a different dad.'

A large crowd had gathered. Saturday morning strollers.

'Help!' called June at the top of her lungs. 'Help. I want my mammy.'

Colm decided to try and explain himself to the tracksuit man.

'You see, we're having a marital break-up, and the child is traumatised because we haven't had time to explain everything to her properly, and I have to stop her from running away. I'm afraid she'll run under a car.'

I don't believe this is happening to me.

'Well, sir, she doesn't seem to think that you're her father. So, we should just stay here until some authorities come.'

'We'll do a citizen's arrest,' said the gent with the umbrella, to a murmur of assent from the crowd. Another man phoned the police on his mobile. 'Yeah, corner of

267

Candlewick Avenue and Upper Rathmines Road, some guy is abducting a little girl. I dunno. Get here fast.'

'He's not my daddy. I want my mammy.'

'Yes he is our daddy,' said John.

'Look,' pleaded Colm with the people nearest him. 'I'm just an ordinary Joe, and these are my kids. Junie is traumatised because her mother and I are having problems. I have to take her back to her mam to calm her down.'

'He's not my daddy.'

'Shame, shame,' muttered an old woman. 'I knew once they introduced divorce the country was finished.'

Now the crowd was so vast the people at the outer perimeters had no idea what was going on at the centre. Word of child molesters had filtered out in Chinese whispers, and people were trying to get a better look. They could see a man and two kids in pyjamas. It looked very suspicious.

The police arrived in a swirl of sirens and parted the crowd like Moses and the Red Sea.

'What appears to be the problem?' asked the first policeman.

For an innocent man, I spend an awful lot of time dealing with policemen.

'Officer,' began Colm. 'My daughter is traumatised. Please can you phone my wife and get her to come here to calm her.'

'And are you the child's father?'

'Yes,' said Colm wearily. 'Yes. Please phone my wife.'

'He's not my daddy. I want my mammy.'

Janet appeared as though summoned. She was dressed and brushed and looked her usual unflappable respectable self. She had called to the flotsam house to make sure the kids were all right, and Brian had pointed her in this direction. She quickly assessed the scene and, unperturbed, made her way to Colm's side. She took June in her arms.

'Mammy,' sobbed June.

'I'm sorry, officer. This is all a terrible mess. This is my husband. If you could get rid of the onlookers, we'll try and calm the child.'

One of the policemen set about dispersing the crowd.

'Bloody gawkers,' muttered Janet under her breath.

Colm was sweating profusely now and near tears.

'Come back with us,' said Janet, and not waiting for an answer she took John by the hand and, still carrying June on her strong hip, she turned with the two children and walked back towards Candlewick Avenue. Colm stood on the pavement for a moment, like a statue in brushed cotton, and then followed Janet and the two children. He followed them all the way home.

A Letter

Colm found a compromise arrangement. He remained in the family home for the evening, and after the smallies went to bed, he went back up to number five Candlewick Avenue for his own bedrest. The ferocity of June's reaction had stopped him in his tracks. It wasn't that he'd disregarded what the kids might say, it was rather that as events unfolded he lurched from crisis to crisis, and didn't get a chance to look at the whole picture. No time had been put into taking care of the kids' responses. John seemed to be taking it all in his stride, but that was his nature. He was eminently practical. But June was much more volatile.

After a couple of weeks little June grew accustomed to the idea, and since it didn't affect the day-to-day reality of her life too much, since Colm was just down the road when he wasn't in the house with them, she calmed down about it. Colm brought the two children down to number five and introduced them to all the inmates, including the Galway girl whose little baby boy had arrived a bit prematurely, but healthy and bouncing. June loved visiting the tiny baby. And John and June both got fond of Brian. On days that Colm didn't eat at number thirty, Cordelia was sent down by Janet with a plate of dinner covered in tinfoil. Colm had at first protested, but when his protests had no effect, he just scoffed the dinners.

Can't let a good dinner go to waste.

It was a lot better for him than the muck he usually

bought. And there was nothing to put him off his beloved fish and chips so much as eating them every night.

David showed up on his doorstep one night, with a six-pack as a peace offering. Colm was delighted to see him, and dragged him inside.

'I'm sorry,' said David.

'I'm sorry,' said Colm.

'I was a prick,' said David.

'No, I was the prick,' said Colm.

'No, I was.'

'OK, we're both pricks.'

'Well. I'm a bigger prick than you.'

'Stop boasting.'

'I'll drink to that,' and they broke open the six-pack and sat up on the bed and tucked in like schoolboys having their first beer. David looked around and inspected the accommodation.

'This reminds me of that grotty bedsit you had in Sandymount when you were a student,' said David.

Colm had forgotten about that particular dive, but yes, it was like here.

I have to go back to then, and try to grow up again, and second time round, hopefully have more success.

'You're so free, Colm. I envy you that. Because you're so uninvested in material things. Whereas, I'm a prisoner. Allegedly, I own all my shops and clubs, but in reality, they own me.'

'I'm glad to see you pal,' said Colm, and gently punched his friend in the arm. 'I missed you a lot.'

David blushed and looked away. Nothing would drag a recriprocating testimonial from him but Colm knew that deep inside the lump of macho flesh that was David, beat a loyal heart.

'I'm really sorry,' said Colm, 'for not listening to your problems. It was wrong of me.'

271

David wanted to quieten Colm fast, avoid mucky personal chat at all cost.

'Don't mention it, don't mention it. Sylvia and me are getting on great. Wow! What a woman. She has a legal brain, but a criminal body. Two nights ago, she called me from New York . . .'

He's off. David and his women. It's so easy for him. Why is life so easy for David?

Colm worked away happily on his computer, doing page after page of writing. He wondered why he'd never been able to work at this pace and with this concentration before.

Because I was living the wrong life, that's why. You can't find the mental space to work when you're dealing with the static of living the wrong life.

Cordelia called in to him a lot. He was her major confidant now that they'd had everything out. He was the only person who understood her weirdness. She wanted to move to a new school, away from her SCUM-mates. She was in transition year, and next year she'd be starting the Leaving Cert programme and she wanted to go to a mixed senior college. Janet had agreed.

'I think I have a boyfriend,' said Cordelia one day, her face turning bright crimson, splendid and glowing against the roots of her blonde hair.

'What do you mean you *think* you have a boyfriend?'

'Well, he hasn't asked me to be his girlfriend, but he asked me to go for a walk, and he asked me back to his house to meet his mum and sisters and he asked me to play pool with him. So that's three dates, kind of, but he hasn't kissed me.'

'And do you like him?'

'I think so, but it's hard to know. How do you know when you like someone? What are the signs?'

You're asking me? Relationship disaster incarnate.

'I can't say Cordelia, except that you'll know when you feel them. At least you'll think you know, which is the closest anybody gets.'

'I get flutters in my tummy when I see him.'

'Well, that's a sign.'

'I want you to give me away when I get married,' said Cordelia.

'Steady on, girl. You haven't kissed him yet.'

'I didn't mean this guy. I meant generally. I want you to be my proper dad, because I think you're great.'

'Get out of here.'

I love that girl. It's funny, but now I love her dearly. She's growing up lovely.

The silence from Sally was alarming. Every day Colm expected to come back to number five and find her sitting on the doorstep clutching a bottle of antique champagne and exercising the outer fringes of her personality. He felt the odd twinge of guilt. Though he knew it wasn't the case, he couldn't help feeling that he was somehow responsible for Sally's perdition. If he hadn't followed Carter and Anita out to Blackrock, maybe Sally'd never have known for definite that they were having an affair and then maybe Sally and her husband wouldn't have had the argument and she wouldn't have pushed him over the cliff and he wouldn't be dead.

Colm passed silver Audis with alarm and suspicion, expecting her to jump out at him. He had heard no more from the police. Possibly their investigations had run into a dead end. Or maybe they were just biding their time. He didn't feel it would be appropriate to enquire.

The front page of the evening paper brought him news.

Thank God for the print media. I'd know nothing otherwise.

Sprawled across the top of the page was MRS CAR-TER MISSING. Colm bought the newspaper, fumbling about in his pocket for the 65p. There was another photo of Sally, poised and coiffed and immaculate. Very recently taken, a black polo neck denoting a frisky widow vibe. The story ran:

> Sally Carter, wife of recently drowned millionaire lager magnate the late James Carter, was reported missing by the family nanny who is minding the two bereaved children in their home. Sally Carter was last seen in a distressed condition walking along the hill of Howth, and lamenting. Family friends fear she took the death of her husband very badly, and had ceased to be able to cope. Security sources say that she was in fact being investigated for the murder of her husband, but this is denied by the family.

This made Colm feel really bad. Colm surfed the airwaves and found a news bulletin on one of the more sensationalist radio stations which informed him that a pile of Sally's clothes had been found down beside a disused warehouse in the harbour. A pink suit and pink suede high-heel shoes. The newsreader reported speculation that she had drowned herself, followed her husband to his watery grave.

The next day Colm flicked through the household post at number five and immediately recognised the loopy handwriting. It had been posted two days previously from Howth. He ran back up the stairs to his room and sat on the bed, his heart thumping. He opened the envelope and out wafted Sally's recently chosen Tarantula perfume.

Longbrook
Howth Hill Rise
Co Dublin.

Dear Colm,

I entered your life in a letter, and think it appropriate to leave it in a similar manner. I have had enough. I can no longer cope. I think the best thing for everybody is if I do away with myself. I have had a useless life, and prolonging my presence on this earth would only compound it. My children will be better off. I just wanted to say goodbye and thank you for the good times. I hope you go back to your wife, and be happy with her. You probably don't rate my opinion, but I know I am correct when I say that you are a better person than you think you are.

Goodbye,

Sally.

P.S. See you in the next life.

Why did the PS sound like a threat? Colm started to hyperventilate. He read the letter again and again. He lay down on the bed and buried his head in the pillow. He was so shocked. Sally dead? This was a terrible outcome. He lay there for a while, and then he came round. He didn't believe it. She wouldn't have the guts to kill herself. She'd been rumbled and had skipped the country. He was sure of it.

A day later, his suspicions were confirmed by a visit from Detective Smith. They had found a witness. Sally had been spotted with Carter on the hill that rainy day. A neighbour had seen them both go up and was sure it was Sally despite the wax mac, as she recognised the particular shoes. Sally had been asked to produce the shoes for forensic inspection, and had claimed she'd lost them. The net had been tightening but the fish had slipped through and swum off. Anita had also received a suicide letter. Smith inspected Colm's correspondence from Sally suspiciously.

'And have you had no other contact?'

'Not in weeks. To be honest, we had a row, and I haven't seen her in ages.'

'Do you think she killed herself?'

'No. Not in her character. Too decisive a thing for her to do.'

'Has she ever mentioned any foreign destinations to you?'

'No.'

'And where would you think she might go?'

Colm shrugged. 'No idea.'

'And have you any further comments that might be of help?'

'None.'

'You still say you think she didn't murder her husband.'

'That's my opinion. It's not in her character.'

'Can I take this letter away?' asked Smith.

Colm wanted to hold on to it, but shrugged. 'OK.'

'Goodbye, Mr Cantwell.'

'Goodbye, Detective Smith.'

Sally will find some corner of the earth where the sun will shine and people will be kind to her.

Colm couldn't help but feel relieved.

A Hot Date

Colm went down to number thirty to meet Janet. She had asked him to allow her to bring him out on a date for her birthday, as they hadn't been out for dinner in years. They had never done it because Janet had always felt breaking in a babysitter would be too much of a bother. But now Cordelia was big enough to leave with the smallies for an evening.

'She has a boyfriend who's going to stay with her to keep her company,' whispered Janet to Colm as he came in the door, widening her eyes in a gesture of impressed wonder. 'They're in the TV room.'

Colm went into the room, and there was Cordy, and sitting beside her was a handsome black youth, about sixteen or seventeen, but self-contained for his age. Confident and comfortable in himself. None of the gawkiness of adolescence. The young man stood up to shake hands.

'Colm, this is Othello.'

'You're kidding,' said Colm.

'Well my real name is Seamus O'Neill, but my friends all call me Othello. After the play.'

'Cordelia and Othello. I need a drink.'

Janet came into the room with two gin and tonics, put one in Colm's hand and raised the other in the air.

'Sláinte,' she said.

Janet was dressed in a frock, and her hair was loose and she looked quite quite beautiful. She was unusually skittish. Perhaps it was the birthday date, but Colm thought that it was because Cordelia had a young man. Janet had been so sad about Cordelia's adolescent unhappiness that the obvious pleasure of the teenager with the beautiful boy was gladdening her mother's heart.

'Have you ever thought that you might be tempting fate, Cordelia and Othello, by drawing together the energies of two such major Shakespearean tragedies?'

'I think,' said Othello, 'that Othello would have been better off with Cordelia. Desdemona is such a wimp, don't you think?'

'And certainly, Cordelia might have spent a little less time mooning about her father if she had a handsome Othello to take her mind off things,' laughed Cordelia.

'I see you've thought this through,' said Colm.

John and June were bouncing around in their pyjamas. June was particularly thrilled as she knew her Mummy and Daddy were going out on a date. And she thought this was splendid.

'Okay, kids,' said Janet. 'We're off. You're to be good.'

'Happy birthday Mummy,' said June and they all broke into a raucous rendition of 'Happy birthday to you', and they opened the front door and the voices followed Janet and Colm into the night.

They drove to a glamorous and opulently decorated restaurant in Ballsbridge. It was a strange choice for Janet. Expensive. Reckless. She seemed to be thoroughly enjoying herself, quite inexplicably happy. They ordered their meals, and settled in for the night. It was to be one of those long, many-course meals that'd go on for hours and cost the earth.

I know it's her birthday, but I hope she's paying.

'I'm just so relieved about Cordelia,' said Janet. 'She's transformed. And I think it's great she has a boyfriend. It's just what she needs. And he seems like such a nice boy. Didn't you think?'

'Yes, a grand young fella.'

278

'I never liked that Phaedra girl. She was ghoulish. And a bad influence.'

'I think they were a bad influence on each other.'

'Cordelia looks different now. Her whole face is transformed. She looks pretty.'

'She's happy. Happiness makes you beautiful. Did you ever see anyone who wasn't beautiful on their wedding day? It's the happiness that shines out of them. We'd all be beautiful if only we were happy enough.'

Janet smiled at Colm.

'You've changed, Colm.'

'In what way?'

'You've changed so much. You're cleverer than you used to be. Well, you were clever in the beginning when we first met, then you stopped being clever for a few years, but you're clever again now.'

Colm preened himself a little. He hadn't been admired by Janet in so long. It was gratifying. Janet reached down to her voluminous handbag and pulled out a brown paper envelope with Colm's manuscript inside.

'It's fabulous,' she said.

She's read it already?

'I sat up all night reading it. I couldn't put it down, and I'm dying to read the rest of it. Hurry up and write it. I'm dying to know what happens. It's so good, you've got to finish it.'

'Well, at this stage to give up would be as tedious as to go on, as the man said.'

Colm glowed with pride. Janet's admiration didn't come easily. She would say if the work was utter shit. And he was proud of it. Proud of the fact that he'd reached chapter two. And chapter three. And four, five, six. He was about halfway through the work which would eventually be a novel. Whether it was publishable or not, whether it would ever see the light of day, was immaterial to him at that moment. The most important thing was he had got past chapter one. He had *achieved*. Well, he had half-achieved. He felt so well. It was as though weights were dropping off him, and he was becoming younger. He had needed to change his life. That was all. A big change was all he needed.

And Janet now looked at him with pride. She looked at him with interest and with pride. And he was glad of that, after the years of being looked at like as though he were an insect. They ate their meal in good humour, swapping stories about school and the residents of the flotsam house. They were both enjoying themselves immensely, chatting like old friends. Or brothers.

'Will you come back to us?' asked Janet, smiling over the cherry pie.

Colm thought for a long while. He looked at Janet, whom he did love and whose particular angelic beauty never failed to tug at him. He thought about June, and the love which he felt for that little girl which alone had the power to make him do almost anything.

'I have to finish what I'm working on first. I have to stay where I am to finish it. It is the one thing that I have to do before I do anything else. Because the most important thing I need to nurture right now is my self-respect.'

Janet played with her ice cream, which was melting, and she made swirls with the cherries in it and looked very sad.

'Cheer up Jan. We'll see what happens.'

Janet sniffed. 'I just feel sad,' she said, 'because I think we've lost our marriage through neglect. I think we got bogged down with the smallies, and with Cordelia, and with the daily grind of work and housekeeping. We never kept any time for ourselves. And I think we didn't spot the problems until it was too late. And now, it's too late.'

It was all so civilised. Colm should have known that marriage break-up with Janet would have the gentle smooth quality that was characteristic of all her actions.

He was numb. He didn't feel anything certain, just a series of vague proddings.

It would be easiest to go home. Life would be easier.

Janet drove them back from the restaurant and they went in to number thirty for a nightcap and to see how the babysitters were.

Cordelia and Othello looked fine. They looked like they'd been having a very nice time. After a cordial twenty minutes, Othello said his goodbyes and Colm decided to accompany him down the avenue as far as number five.

It was a beautiful warm summer night. The sky was clear and star-laden, and a bright full moon was rising and casting deep shadows. The well-tended gardens of the well-to-do offered up their sweet summer-night smells to the passer-by. Candlewick Avenue looked lovely in the moonlight.

'So how are you and Cordy getting on?' asked Colm as they strode along together.

'She's a really nice girl,' said Othello with enthusiasm. 'She's not like other girls, she's kind and funny and wonderful. And she is so pretty, she looks like an angel. When I compare her to other girls, I think Cordelia is way ahead of them in every way. And my mum likes her. And I've never been as happy as I am with her and I'm so glad I've no exams this year because I just want to see her every day and I'm looking forward to the summer when we'll do lots of things and go to the sea and . . .'

The delights of Cordelia were wonderful to hear. Her good humour and her generosity. Her sense of fun. Perfection was Cordelia. Colm walked alongside, matching his step to the pace of the youth, and happily listened to the gentle and passionate delusions of love.

Newport Library and
Information Service

Z347690